The
Age of the
Conglomerates

The
Age of the
Conglomerates

A Novel of the Future

Thomas Nevins

BALLANTINE BOOKS NEW YORK

A Ballantine Books Trade Paperbacks Original

Copyright © 2008 by Thomas Nevins

Published in the United States by Ballantine Books,
an imprint of The Random House Publishing Group,
a division of Random House, Inc., New York.

BALLANTINE and colophon are registered trademarks of Random House, Inc.

LIBRARY OF CONGRESS CATALOGING-IN-PUBLICATION DATA

Nevins, Thomas.
The age of the conglomerates : a novel of the future / Thomas Nevins.
p.   cm.
ISBN 978-0-375-50391-7
1. Depressions—United States—Fiction. 2. Political parties—Corrupt
practices—Fiction. 3. Social problems—United States—Fiction. 4. Social
control—United States—Fiction. 5. Old age—Economic aspects—Fiction.
6. Older people—Social conditions—Fiction. 7. Women geneticists—Fiction.
8. Grandparent and child—Fiction. 9. Political fiction. I. Title.
PS3614.E558A7 2008   813'.6—dc22   2008021003

Printed in the United States of America

www.ballantinebooks.com

9 8 7 6 5 4 3 2 1

Book design by Debbie Glasserman

Me: "Hey, Dad, how are ya doin'?"

Dad: "Not bad, for an old coot!"

For my mother and father,
Pat and Pete Nevins,
thank you for everything.

The
Age of the
Conglomerates

Prologue

The Social Security Administration failed. So did the massive bailout waged by the government to save it. Medicaid and Medicare fell next, and then the insurance companies and the health care industry soon followed. As investments evaporated, the stock markets collapsed. Company after company went bankrupt, as did the pension plans promised to employees.

This economic implosion coincided with another shock: the early retirement packages offered to control costs and reduce corporate vulnerability came due just as a generation of workers reached retirement age, provoking a mass maturation of 401(k)'s and IRAs. This confluence of economic disasters overran the courts, the banks, and the national and global markets. And thus was ushered in the age of the Conglomerates.

The Conglomerates, a political party that emerged from the private sector, quickly assumed control of the republic. The party consisted of a group of chief executive officers who were united in greed and who had, through the first half of the twenty-first century, embezzled their way into personal security and mutual protection. They were the only ones to have money, and, in fact, they had been pulling the strings that controlled everyone else: the president, members of Congress, and the businesses of banking, industry, and commerce.

Now that they were in power, there were no checks and balances; the Conglomerates had taken over everything and everyone.

Manhattan was the capital of the Conglomerates, as it was home to the financial markets, to business, and to the executive board running the party. Washington, D.C., was where the president of the United States lived and served as a talking head for the party and its policies. Since D.C. played well to the media and the masses, it diverted attention from the real business of running the country. All that took place in New York City, from the office of the party's chairman.

The Conglomerates instituted their platform and enforced their will of an economic martial law to insure that budgetary surplus and cost control were matters of constitutional amendments rather than of company policy.

They had seized control of the economy by eliminating

paper and coin and transferring all moneys to a digital standard of currency under the auspices of the Federal Reserve. Not only was a monetary system of paper and alloy obsolete, but it was also said to contribute to the overall health risk of communicable diseases as the germ-laden agent changed hands. At least, that was how the Conglomerates marketed their currency innovation to the public. In addition, this new means of money eliminated the vulnerability to individual identity theft, as all identity was controlled by the state. There was no need to mention that this new policy was a mask of the government for control of personal and public finance, and the Conglomerates didn't; nor did they bring up the IRS accountants, who loved this means of tracking and taxing.

The Coots, as the elderly were called, were those born during the baby boom of the twentieth century, and it seemed they would live forever: the ranks of the elderly had swelled, depleting not only the country's economic resources, but its emotional and psychological resources as well. The elderly came to be seen as a constituency that was robbing the population of what was new and productive. The boomers had borrowed from their tomorrows and couldn't pay them back. This produced a perceived cultural divide: those who had abused the economy and those who had to pay the price; the aged against the young. The deficit mentality of the me generation produced disastrous results. It was felt that the past had sucked the lifeblood out of the future. This resentment toward the elderly evolved into a force of hatred toward an entire generation, an emotion that spread through ethnic groups, sexual identities and persuasions, race, religion, place of origin; all were becoming united in a hatred of the Coots. The Coots were a constant reminder of why the economy had gone bad and why the society was in such a deplorable condition. Besides, these people were living too long, and there wasn't a place to put them.

To ease the burden that the nation's families had to bear for the sins of their fathers, the Conglomerates created the Family Relief Act, through which the government assumed control of the octogenarian generation. Families were relieved of the expense of their elderly, financial as well as emotional, in exchange for the elderly's assets and properties. It was a mandatory retirement program that removed the burden and the decision from the family, and it removed the elderly from sight, as well as home. The Coots were removed to retirement communities in the desert Southwest.

The properties they had owned were seized in an act of eminent domain, and the elderly were removed to "more suitable housing," which was defined by the Conglomerates as any place they wanted these people to be. Besides, the economic collapse had produced a mass migration of youth to the major urban areas—Chicago, Houston, Los Angeles, and Seattle—while the New York metropolitan area now sprawled all along the eastern coast.

The elder care policy proved a popular success and became a precedent that the Conglomerates exploited and expanded to include a way of dealing with another burden on the populace: troublesome children and adolescents. And so the Dyscards were born. A legal option was created whereby families could discard a progeny that had become a social, family, or genetic problem. The nuisance was removed from the home; the child was transferred to the so-called custody of the state. In fact, these young people were discarded and lived in the city's subways, an underground world.

At first the Dyscards were a pilot program for the New York City area, and then the program expanded to the rest of the nation, providing the means to get rid of what people no longer wanted: the problem child. The Conglomerates replicated the Coots program and shipped these kids into New York. The city's system soon swelled beyond control, and the Conglomerates authorized new discard dumping grounds in Orlando, Detroit, L.A., and San Antonio.

The participating parents of the discarded child were eligible for a new child selected from a program of personally designed reproduction, whereby troublesome and inferior traits in one's future offspring could be eliminated from the family unit through individually chosen genetic manipulation before conception.

And this was how life was at the start of this story about a man, a woman, and a family, in the age of the Conglomerates.

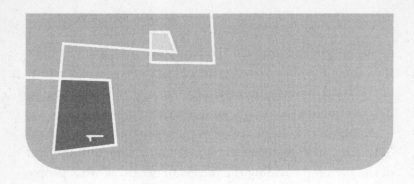

Christine's World

I t was New Year's Eve and, for once, Christine Salter had the dress and the plans. True, you would expect the director of genetic development at the New York Medical Center, a position of professional power in the age of the Conglomerates, to be a popular woman and a woman with a full schedule. The director had the year end to wrap up; she had to reel in the budget; she had a lot of product to process, rank, categorize, and deliver to their expecting mothers. And Christine had a number of adults to process besides.

Under Dr. Christine Salter's direction, Genetic Development had changed from being a cost sieve to become the division that led all others in the medical center in productivity, fame, and profit. People wanted to go there to create, or re-create, the infant they wanted, or to enroll in a newly developing program that would enable a person to re-create him- or herself through genetic manipulation. Which traits of theirs would they like to develop, which eliminate? Soon it would be possible to act on this personal improvement initiative. There was a waiting list of patients for the medical center's programs, and these lists represented future growth and revenues. Dr. Salter was determined to retain the premier position for her division, even though lately she had begun to feel uncomfortable about some of the decisions she was being forced to make.

As soon as Christine thought about that, she thought about Gabriel, and that led to thoughts of her dress and what might happen between them during the evening ahead.

She looked down at the year-end report she was compiling on the "the Pool." The division of genetic development was nicknamed the Pool by those who worked at the center, a term that referred to the department's work in improving the gene pool of their clients. Through the procedure of genetic contouring, a process at which Christine and her team excelled, those who could afford the expense, and who came from the correct demographic groups, could now design, or redesign, their basic genetic structure and adjust their offspring's appearance and behavior before birth. It was possible to select the characteristics of one's children. The Pool worked to provide the child you had always dreamed of and one who could contribute to the state, but Christine's own special initiative had been the division's new process whereby genetic manipulation would be extended to adults.

In the interest of self-improvement, less desirable existing genes could be replaced with more desirable ones. "Why not be skinny and bright?" was the line they were working on to market the campaign. These were trickier, more complicated operations, with so far untested results, but that hadn't stopped the Conglomerates from enrolling. At the moment, the procedure was available to only an elite few, but Christine believed it would soon roll out to a large segment of the party. This new initiative would increase profits, the Conglomerate way.

Babies were still the Pool's core business, however, and the source of the revenue stream at year's end. Not only were babies from the Pool marketed to be smarter, healthier, and more productive members of the economy. They were designed to be individuals who would add to the nation's resources through their efficient, productive use of the resources left—a generation that would develop innovative alternatives and not further deplete those resources, as their fathers and their fathers' fathers had done before them. Contouring babies was just the beginning, the higher end of this cleansing policy. The Coots and the Dyscards were at the other end of the scale, people who only sucked the system dry. But they were an entirely different matter and one that was not part of Christine's life or responsibilities, and so she preferred not to think about them at the moment. And, anyway, it was New Year's Eve, and Christine had the dress and the plans; she had a date with Gabriel Cruz.

She looked back at her year-end report. The Pool had improved productivity by introducing a standardized, automated approach to genetic manipulation. What their clients wanted was a more intelligent, more attractive, more resilient child—in short, a better offspring than they thought they could produce on their own. Though the clients might think they wanted a choice, when it came down to it, they all wanted pretty much the same things in their children. Dr. Salter's department had designed a genetic template whereby a gene was split, altered, and fused with a preprogrammed outcome that implanted the genetic adjustment into the product. And while all designs were in effect standardized, the doctor was in control of the process and could offer exclusivity of design for an appropriate price, thereby increasing the program's profit. Genetic Development had implemented these changes, along with a reduction in workforce, in a streamlined approach to the process.

Christine turned back to the performance reviews. She printed them out and began to study them further. Some of the findings were unsettling, no doubt about it. She didn't want to draw attention to them, or to the information she had uncovered. This year the department of genetic development had conceived and processed 11,753 babies for their customers, a pretty good number. It was higher than last year—it had to be—but this number exceeded their goal by a double-digit percentage.

Christine opened the folder she had placed beneath the stack of reviews. She frowned. She had noticed something in the numbers before and she hadn't been able to brush it aside. She looked again carefully at the center's overall statistics. Gross volume was up, that was true. They had produced an increase of 17 percent above the previous year. Still, while they had delivered more perfect babies, their overall success rate was dropping. With the increase in patient volume, there was also an increase in fees associated with settlements paid to disgruntled consumers.

She looked down at her folder, and her frown deepened. Statistics on the number of babies born with defects—or, more precisely, where for some reason the contouring process had not taken effect, babies that had been born not to the parents' specifications but with deficiencies ranging from crooked teeth to a lack of interest in competitive skills—those numbers had increased in the past year to a disproportionate percentage.

Christine ran her fingers down the spreadsheet, studied the overall statistics, and made notes. She uncovered the sheet with the statistical breakdown by employee. And there it was, all in the numbers—what she had been vaguely aware of and had feared. Gabriel Cruz, her best employee, a man she was half in love with, and one with whom she had a date this evening, was responsible for a significant number of the flawed products. Too great a number, in fact.

Christine shut the folder, tapped her fingers on the desk. It was late in the afternoon; even at this prestigious medical center, many people had already gone home to get ready for New Year's Eve, or had gone away for the holidays. The silence in the center felt strange. Christine thought about her dress, Gabriel, her plans, and she decided to go home herself. She locked the papers in her desk and hoped she could lock her concerns away along with the incriminating news.

For the last few New Year's Eves, Christine had worked, covering the overnight shift for the Pool. She had never really minded. She liked her work, and it kept her distracted from the fact that she wasn't seeing anyone and her family wasn't close. But this year Gabriel had invited her to a party. She had been so surprised that he had had to ask her twice. The second time he had given Christine a chance to catch her breath, and then she had accepted. The attraction between them had become more and more obvious. She liked him, and she liked the way he made her feel. He was funny, and unlike a lot of people, he looked into her eyes when she spoke. Sometimes he even made her forget that she was director of genetic development at the New York Medical Center, as he had when she had accepted his invitation. Christine knew it was highly inappropriate, and she had never dated a coworker before, never mind someone who reported to her, but she had found herself saying yes anyway.

As a doctor, Gabriel Cruz had made a name for himself before he had come to the med center. He was smart, clearly, but Christine also recognized that, at times, he was even smarter than she was. She hadn't often found that to be true with men. Cruz was Latin and lean, he moved like a cat, and Christine hadn't found that in many other men either. He had become indispensable to her, even though some of the things that he said to her seemed close to being politically incorrect.

But when Gabriel worked, he focused, no matter the distraction. He was a master technician, with faultless hand-eye coordination and a statistician's interest in breaking down data. But it was his talent with people that had especially impressed Christine. He seemed to be a natural administrator who could get his peers as well as the support staff behind him, supporting his decisions, following his direction and goals. The productivity that had resulted with Gabriel's addition to her staff couldn't be denied.

Christine stood by the elevator bank and stared at the elevator button. What was taking so long? She tapped her feet, folded and unfolded her arms. She wanted to get to the lobby and away from the center.

When Christine had joined the New York Medical Center, she had agreed to work to achieve the standards and contributions required by the Conglomerates. Christine had never been concerned about either before. The elevator came and she got in.

As the old elevator began its descent, Christine ran over the numbers again in her head, trying to determine what needed to be implemented to improve the performance of her group. She thought of the political seas she would have to navigate in order to sail out of the Pool and into open waters. If Christine thought about it, she could not recall a time when at least part of her mind and most of her energy had not been occupied with getting ahead and with being the boss.

Christine blew the hair out of her face as she looked up at the camera in the corner of the elevator. That brought her back to just where she was.

You would think that by now she would have been used to it. The Conglomerates were everywhere; they were always watching everything—or you should assume they were. But today the constant security eye made Christine feel on edge. Everything live all the time, live transmissions, live feeds, live action, live reads. Christine hadn't voiced her objections because to some degree she had been aware that she was working for the Conglomerates and benefiting from the association. She had joined them and had experienced first-hand just how deep the Conglomerate desire for control went. It had been Christine who had come up with the idea to upgrade the existing surveillance system, equipping the cameras with scanners and adding a corresponding chip to the employees' I.D. badges. An employee's location and movement were monitored using that I.D. badge, allowing the system to match an employee's actual location to where the employee was supposed to be. Christine saw it as an efficient use of the security system and a means of controlling movement within the facility, minimizing the risk of corporate espionage and internal theft. But med center employees resented it and claimed it was an invasion of privacy; management deemed it the right of the facility, adopting the monitoring technology at all buildings throughout the government system.

When Christine told Gabriel of the innovation, Gabriel made a comment about "1984" that Christine didn't understand. She asked him what he was talking about.

"It's a book," Gabriel said, and Christine was immediately transported back to her grandparents' house in Staten Island.

That house had been filled with books. Both her grandparents had loved to read. Now people only read from a screen, and a small one at that. Her grandmother Patsy had been reading all the time, "steamy stories" she had called them. Books, another reason Christine liked Gabriel Cruz.

She recognized, just then, a change in her attitude. She found herself resenting the fact that she was on view now, was always on view, and subject to scrutiny. Did this discomfort have to do with those unsettling statistics about her department, with Gabriel, and with her instincts to hide the statistics? She was almost afraid to wonder.

DR. CHRISTINE SALTER had not been the only one to read and research the disturbing figures on Gabriel Cruz. When Christine had printed out the spreadsheets, to avoid drawing attention to the discrepancy by viewing it online, the printer had stored, read, and—as the machine was programmed to red-flag specific words or patterns—forwarded the file to security. The security officers were even now researching Christine's findings, and had alerted the authorities to these alarming trends.

The administration of the Health and Human Services Corporation found the statistics unsettling as well. Equally unsettling was that they had not heard about them from their star, Christine Salter. They wondered why. Was she involved in Gabriel's activities, as well as with the man? If Salter was complicit, how deep did this insurrection go? Something had to be done. Insubordination would not be tolerated; it threatened the core of the system. Also, the Conglomerates could not afford to have this revenue stream compromised. Dr. Salter was important, for now. Cruz, on the other hand, could be replaced, after he answered some questions. The office of the chairman of the Conglomerate party was brought into the loop. They wanted Cruz in custody.

.   .   .

AS THE ELEVATOR descended, two agents on loan from the National Security Council were driving a Con Ed utility van up First Avenue. They stopped at Thirtieth Street and set up shop across from the New York Medical Center. The agents were dressed like Con Ed workers in coveralls and hard hats. The white utility van's overhead caution light spun around while the four-way lights flashed. The agents put up the orange protective gate and put reflective cones around the manhole. One agent remained in the van while the other removed the manhole cover, took out an orange caution flag, slapped it out twice, and tied it to the protective gate.

"It's too cold to go down into that hole," the agent said to his partner. "I'm waiting in the van too."

The other agent, at his station inside the van, activated the surveillance system in silence, ignoring his partner. He'd only been with this guy a day and already he'd had enough. Luckily, before his partner could get back into the van, he saw Christine Salter's image pop up on the monitor.

"She's going down in the elevator now," he said as he watched the figure on the screen. "It's a go."

Christine was looking directly into the lens. Even with the lousy camera and the grainy image on the screen, the agent saw a good-looking woman, the green of her eyes, her red hair, and that got his pulse pumping. "Nice," he said.

The other agent started down the ladder into the manhole opening, and as he descended below the street level, he saw a fire engine speeding through the intersection of First Avenue and Thirty-fourth Street. The fire truck did not have its siren on or its emergency lights going, but it was going fast.

There were no other FDNY vehicles accompanying the huge hook and ladder. The truck made a wide turn below FDR Drive, where a half dozen orange Con Ed cones had been set up to restrict parking. A firefighter jumped out of the hook and ladder and gathered up the cones while the huge rig pulled in behind and parked in the rear of the medical center. A half dozen firefighters got off the truck and walked to the fire exit, where two agents dressed as medical center maintenance workers waited for them at the door. These agents had set up a stanchion along the sidewalk around the open fire exit doors. While it was out of the ordinary to see a fire truck parked here, neither the firefighters nor those working with the center seemed to be alarmed.

THE ELEVATOR DOORS opened and Christine stepped out. She looked up at the clock on the lobby wall and wished that Gabriel had come on for his shift before she'd decided to leave. She couldn't wait to see him, and that was a strange sensation. She was going to go home and get dressed and meet Gabriel at the party. He would be in charge of the Pool until eleven, and then he was going to meet her at the party before the ball fell in Times Square at midnight. Her heart jumped in spite of herself.

She was not sure how her current management would react if they knew just how important Gabriel was to her, so getting this relationship under control had become a goal for her, a New Year's resolution. She wouldn't be getting off to a great start on that resolution, not if she could help it.

At the thought of a New Year's resolution, Christine was

transported back to thinking again about her grandmother. She hadn't seen her grandmother in fifteen years, since Christine was twelve or thirteen years old. Her grandmother Patsy must have been sixty-five or so then, and she had still looked terrific; trim, taut, and with a wit that was quick, and that—when aimed at her grandfather George—could be lovingly delivered as well. Christine's grandparents had clearly been crazy about each other, but her grandmother's barbs in the give-and-take had usually gotten the best of her grandpa.

But the New Year's Eve that Christine thought back to had been before that. Christine could see her grandmother's image in her mind and hear her voice still. Christine couldn't have been more than six or seven and had been in her grandparents' home in Staten Island for the holidays. She had just heard about New Year's resolutions, and she had asked her grandmother what her resolutions would be. Her grandmother had looked at her with that light in her eye that she got when she had something up her sleeve.

"Sweetheart, I hope to have the resolve to hold off any resolutions until another day," Christine's grandmother had said. And then she had winked, which had added a twinkle to the light in her eye.

It had taken Christine some time to understand what her grandmother had meant, but when, years later, the meaning behind her grandmother's message had become clear, she had had to admire her grandmother's response. Christine hoped now that she would have the strength to hold off anything that might restrict her own spontaneity. Try as she might to emulate her grandmother, Christine couldn't help but make a mental list of the many things she had resolved to do, especially tonight.

She pushed her way through the revolving door and left the med center. She shivered when she thought about what might have become of her grandmother. Or was it the brisk wind that was blowing off the water that made her feel so cold? Christine couldn't see any bus turning up Thirty-fourth Street, and whether it was New Year's Eve or not, Christine didn't expect to find any cabs down here. Nor was she about to wait for one.

She noticed the back of the fire truck at the rear of the medical center. What was that about, she thought, but she didn't have time to consider it; the wind was at her back, and she hurried on.

She went down into the subway entrance, and as luck would have it, she didn't have to wait long for a train. The car wasn't crowded and she got a seat. She'd caught the express so it would be only one stop to West Fourth Street. Subway Safe Zone or not, Christine was not a big fan of riding the trains. It was too easy to get lost and wind up where you didn't want to be. And then there were the rumors and stories about kids living down in the subway tunnels during the last few years, and that made Christine nervous. All Christine would need would be to get caught up by a bunch of Dyscards and have them find out that she was director of the department of genetic development at the New York Medical Center.

About a dozen people got off with Christine at the West Fourth Street stop, and though none of them acknowledged one another, they all stuck together as they walked along the platform and up the stairs to the exit. Once they reached the street, they split up and went their separate ways. No one exchanged a "Happy New Year." Christine shivered and hunched her shoulders against the cold. It took only a few minutes to reach her building and open the door of her apartment.

Christine hadn't been sure exactly what to wear to the party, and Gabriel had convinced her not to worry about it. People dressed up a lot, or didn't, it didn't seem to matter. But Christine had heard her grandmother's voice in her head and had seen again the twinkle in her eye; and she had thought of the dress she kept in her closet. She felt it had been her grandmother's idea to buy that kind of dress in the first place.

It had probably been around the same time when Christine had heard her grandmother's feelings on New Year's resolutions that her grandmother had told Christine her opinion about a great dress. She had said that when it came to fashion, or just plain what to wear, some women would tell you that you couldn't go wrong with a little black dress. And while that might be true, that common opinion had led to a lot of women wearing little black dresses all at the same time. What Christine's grandmother had said was, "Wear a red dress, the littler the better," and if the dress was tight and you were too, then you couldn't get much better than that.

As soon as Christine had made some money, she'd gone looking along West Broadway until she'd found a place on Hudson Street that had this vintage red dress. Christine had seen it on the manikin and known that it was the one. She would not have been surprised if she had found her grandmother's name written on the inside.

Now Christine hoped the dress would still fit. She checked the lock, put the chain across the door, and headed straight for the bedroom closet. She shoved aside the hangers that held her work clothes and looked for the covering in which she had stored the dress. It would be easy to find; the bag was bright pink. As silly as it was, Christine had been thrilled when she'd seen that bag, and she was proud of the dress. She still drew confidence from the fact that she had this great dress tucked away in the corner of her closet and her life. She pulled the pink bag out and held her breath, glad she was alone.

Christine unzipped the bag; the red dress sparkled. She pulled the zipper of the pink garment bag all the way down, and her heart quickened. There it was. Now all she needed was the nerve to wear it.

Inside the bag was the camisole and panties. She couldn't imagine wearing them without the dress, and she wasn't sure she could imagine wearing them with the dress either. She wondered if Gabriel was going to get to see her in them. Christine put her face toward the fabric and smelled the lavender she had placed in the bottom of the bag.

GABRIEL CRUZ WAS having a hard time focusing on the screen of his phone. He had a sense that something was up. He was walking down Thirty-fourth Street toward the med center directly into a sharp wind that blew up from the river. He had already left two messages on Christine's office voice mail, and she hadn't returned either one. He text-messaged her.

"At least I know she's not at work," Gabriel said out loud. He was pretty sure Christine would have called him back if she were still at the center. Since he had begun working for her, he'd been feeling a little uncomfortable about some of the things he was doing, or not doing; but he had also made a commitment and he believed he was right. What he hadn't anticipated was that he would feel another kind of commitment, a competing one, to a woman he admired, one who, he thought, could be on his side, by his side.

Gabriel liked working with Christine. She was smart, she was pretty, and she liked to laugh. Underneath her drive, he found a sense of humanity and a warmth that he did not think many had seen. Gabriel thought that if Christine were aware of his true mission at the med center, she might even be a little sympathetic to his activity. And then there was the fact that he could feel a heat coming from her, and it equaled his own.

Gabriel checked the time, put his cell into his pocket, took it out again, and tried Christine one more time.

"Me again," he said after the beep. "I was hoping you weren't there but I wouldn't have minded if you were. . . ." Gabriel paused. "I am almost at the center, so maybe I'll see you soon." Gabriel closed his phone and quickened his pace in order to get there faster. Maybe he could catch her; maybe she was walking up the street right now.

IT WOULD HAVE been difficult for the two agents from the National Security Council to work any faster. The agent in the hole had located, isolated, and secured the cables that controlled the electric current that ran this part of the med center. The agent in the van was busy at the computer, editing images that he had recorded from the security monitor. He was putting together the overlay that they would send to the security cameras during the short phase of the operation.

The agents disguised as firefighters moved into the medical center, secured the fire exit, and began to move up the emergency stairs. It was their job to lock all of the fire exit doors, prohibiting entry into, or exit from, the stairwell.

"I sure hope we don't have a real fire," one of the agents said. "We'll have some explaining to do."

"There won't be a fire. There won't be any explaining."

Two of the agents dressed in firefighter gear had commandeered the freight elevator at the med center and brought it up to the floor of the department of genetic development. They flashed their fake I.D.'s and announced a drop-in inspection of the facilities. No one questioned the firefighters—and as the FDNY inspections were unscheduled, it was not unusual for these men to show up at the med center. The other agents stayed behind to cover the door and guard the truck.

National Security Council or not, this team wasn't about to have their vehicle stolen, especially this vehicle. There were any number of abandoned piers nearby from which the Dyscards were known to operate. The agents didn't want to be responsible for the loss of a fire truck to the Dyscards, or any piece of apparatus, for that matter. That would not only be fatally embarrassing, but would also be a loss of what could become a strategic weapon in the Dyscards' hands.

.   .   .

CHRISTINE STOOD IN the shower and massaged conditioner into her hair. The warm water helped her relax; she thought of Gabriel. She had to admit to herself that Gabriel was responsible for her going out at all, let alone to this party.

His manner and his consideration of others had improved the quality of work at the center. Since such consideration was in short supply in the age of the Conglomerates, any effort shown was appreciated by people and could produce subliminal results. And of course when business was better, Christine was better, and that had a way of improving things at the Pool. Gabriel's demeanor was inclusive; the team had responded to that. Christine had noticed that wherever Gabriel happened to be, people were in better moods.

Christine had first spotted Gabriel Cruz some months ago, when his work from the operative group that supported Christine's team at the Pool had been consistently superior. Christine had kept track of him, and it hadn't been that difficult to do. She had noticed that the time listed on Gabriel's work calendar varied. He handed in work in the early hours, prior to the first shift, of which he was part; or he handed things in on the first shift and on the second shift. Christine had never liked keeping regular hours either, although as director now she did. Finally, she went to meet him. She used her authority at the center to find out when and where Gabriel Cruz would be in the building, and then she approached his station a half hour before he was to be on duty. She found him there, hunched over his keyboard, appearing as if he were focused on the data on his screen, except that his eyes were closed. When Christine saw that his eyes were shut, she had a sudden sense of misgiving. She knocked on the molding that framed Gabriel's cube, and Gabriel was so startled that he sent his remote mouse into orbit.

"Did I wake you?" Christine asked. "Excuse me. I'm Dr. Salter and I'm looking for a Dr. Gabriel Cruz." Christine had a file tucked underneath her arm and Gabriel noticed the r-u-z peeking out. He looked at her and said, "I'm Gabriel Cruz."

He stood and shook her hand. "But I see," he said as he lowered his gaze to the file under her arm, "you've already met me."

"Yes, I guess I have," Christine acknowledged, finding she liked her hand in his grip. When had she noticed that? She left her hand in his for an instant before she pulled it away and said, "I admire your work. But do you often sleep on the job?" Suddenly, she was aware of how aggressive this might have sounded.

Instead of becoming aggressive himself, Gabriel Cruz smiled and said, "Some of my best ideas were produced in such conditions. Sometimes I have to close my eyes to see the big picture," he said. "I'm less distracted and better able to see the details that way," he said. "Anyway, how can I help you, Dr. Salter?"

And it had started from there. Cruz's résumé was impressive, as was his work, and Christine soon offered him a position on the genetic manipulation research team, which he accepted with the proviso that he would still be able to work in Prenatal. As Prenatal was the business producing revenue, Christine saw this as an additional advantage.

Neither of them had expected what had followed. And, as Christine thought about it now, it was because neither of them had been prepared for the attraction between them that it had been able to happen. It was part of their lives before they knew it. Christine hadn't come across too many people who could keep up with her, and at times she found Gabriel a step ahead. She enjoyed that and it had turned into an intellectual competition between them that she anticipated with pleasure. Then, one morning, Christine woke up thinking about Gabriel before she had even opened her eyes. She was looking forward to seeing him at the center later that day, and she wasn't sure if she was looking forward to the rapport they shared, or to sharing a space with such a handsome man. Christine made a mental note that she would have to keep that feeling in check, but she took extra time getting dressed that day anyway.

That had been a few months ago, and Christine was still working on keeping her feelings under wraps. Nevertheless she was really looking forward to tonight, and even more to what might happen after.

"THE SECOND SUBJECT is in the facility," the agent said, his eyes on the monitor. "The first has exited. Repeat. Male subject is in the facility. We are at go." And that was all that he said, because that was all his teammates needed to know to go into action. The grumbling agent in the cold hole clamped into the power source, ready to incite the surge into the system that would allow their planned cover to commence.

All but two of the firefighter agents left their posts at the truck, got onto the freight elevator, and rode up to the Pool. It wouldn't be long now.

The agents dressed as the New York Medical Center maintenance staff closed off University Street between the park and Kips Bay Plaza, restricting traffic below. Meanwhile the agent in the back of the van set in motion the program that would override the security cameras by providing the cameras with images previously recorded. As long as the team didn't have to take too long and force the computer to repeat prerecorded images too many times, no one should be able to tell the difference. By the time anyone would be able to tell the difference, this team would be gone.

THE LIGHTS FLICKERED as Gabriel stepped onto the elevator. He was startled; he thought of the Con Ed van he'd seen outside. Then there had been a fire truck parked on the corner, he now recalled. If it had been an emergency, like a fire, there would have been more than one fire truck and he would have seen firefighters. Something in him went on alert. But Gabriel had a lot to think about, and getting onto the floor and through his shift as acting director for the evening was paramount. And then there was the rest of the evening ahead.

THE NEW YORK Medical Center security officer at his post in the basement scanned the bank of monitors; nothing appeared out of the ordinary. The elevator car that carried Gabriel upstairs appeared to be empty, so the security officer's eye traveled right by that monitor. The operation had indeed begun.

The men dressed as firefighters abandoned their mock inspection and fanned out across the floor of the Pool. The employees were alarmed. The security officer at his station in the basement of the building checked in on the Pool as he scanned the floors, and saw nothing but the staff at work.

The office manager for the Pool looked in Christine's empty office. She knew it was empty, but that didn't stop her from hoping Christine would be there. The elevator doors opened just then and Gabriel walked out.

"Thank God you're here," the woman said.

Gabriel knew he wasn't receiving a blessing from the woman. He thought about Christine and watched the firefighters approaching him. What was going on? Suddenly he realized that if there were a real fire, he would be smelling smoke, he would be hearing the alarm. Wouldn't you know it? Christine wasn't going to believe this, he thought. An inspection—tonight, of all nights.

"What's going on?" Gabriel asked the office manager, who just pointed at the firefighters. Then Gabriel noticed that one of the firefighters was carrying a stretcher.

"Can I help you?" Gabriel asked.

"Cruz, Gabriel Cruz," the lead firefighter said, and he wasn't asking Gabriel for confirmation. "Come with us." Then Gabriel realized he was surrounded. And that this was no inspection.

"Why would I want to do that?" Gabriel said. Was this

even the fire department? The police, or something worse? He thought of his subversive work, the kids he had saved. Then he knew why they were here.

Gabriel back-kicked the knees of the firefighter carrying the stretcher, which went flying out of his hands. Gabriel grabbed the stretcher in the air and brought it across the jaw of the firefighter standing adjacent to the one who had just gone down. He used his leverage and jabbed the stretcher into the crotch of the man standing opposite. *Only a couple to go,* Gabriel thought.

The office manager was screaming. The rest of the staff was too, but Gabriel didn't hear them. He looked to the fire exit before he brought the handle of the stretcher up into the throat of the man directly in front of him. *I may just get out of here,* Gabriel thought, and just then a fire extinguisher that had been ripped from the wall bounced off Gabriel's head.

CHRISTINE DIDN'T NEED to pass through the foyer of the party host's home to feel out of place. The color scheme throughout the apartment was beige, brown, and cream. The room had walnut woodwork and terra-cotta tiles. Christine hadn't noticed her hostess right away, as the woman was dressed in a pantsuit to match her décor. Christine had felt the woman's eyes taking her in as Christine turned toward her.

"What a lovely room," Christine said in hopes of establishing some kind of social footing.

"But look at you," the hostess said, eyeing Christine up and down. "That dress is very . . . red," she said, and then she waved Christine into the room. "C'mon in. Everyone is here. Almost," she said, "Though no sign of Gabriel yet." She winked.

There was a gathering of about a dozen people mingling in a corner. They too were dressed in a variety of browns. As far as she could see, no one had a skirt on and most of the women seemed covered up from neck to toe. Conversation stopped as most of the men and all of the women looked at Christine, her legs and her neckline.

"Where did you get that dress?" a woman asked, leaning her head back in order to look down her nose at Christine. Christine had the feeling the woman wanted to know where Christine had bought it so that she would never shop there. But it didn't matter, as the woman did not wait for Christine to respond.

"Where's Gabriel?" the woman asked, as Christine began to wish her pager would go off and she could tell Gabriel to meet her at her apartment.

EVEN AFTER GABRIEL had been hit on the head with the fire extinguisher, he still kept his ground. They held him up and punched him. The squad leader had lost control over his men, and his men had lost control over themselves.

"The fire exit's locked," the office manager yelled.

"I can't get a signal," someone else shouted, holding up a phone, while another worker motioned at the security cameras to indicate what was going on.

The security officer at his post in the basement continued to scan the screens of the bank of monitors before him. He kind of liked working these holiday shifts; nothing going down, or up. It was as quiet as church.

The firefighters punched at Gabriel until one of them pointed to their boss, who had caught his breath, and the squad leader said, "Inject him, you idiots. Stop beating him." But Gabriel was out cold.

They injected him anyway, and the squad leader said, "Help me up. We've got to get him out of here. Get him onto the stretcher. And then give me his cell."

One of the agents turned Gabriel's pockets inside out and handed the contents to the leader, who dumped everything into a plastic bag. He retrieved Gabriel's phone, flipped it open, and punched a pattern into the screen before he typed a brief message, snapped the phone closed, and dropped it back into the plastic bag.

"Let's go," the squad leader said as he pointed to the freight elevator. Two of the agents took either end of the stretcher, with Gabriel strapped onto it; one agent assisted his commanding officer as they all hustled into the waiting freight car.

CHRISTINE'S PAGER WENT off—her wish answered!—and she jumped. Her hostess raised an eyebrow, but when Christine saw that the message coming was from Gabriel, she was more than relieved. She saw it was a text message. "Return at once," it said. No greeting, no affectionate sign-off. It was a little odd.

But she responded in the affirmative. "At once," she typed on her phone. She apologized to her hostess, said she had to return to the medical center, got her coat, and left. Once on the street, she decided not to go home to change into her work clothes. She'd go straight to the med center. Getting a cab on New Year's Eve in midtown Manhattan was going to be impossible. Indeed, almost all of the cabs Christine saw were either occupied or out of service, and the normally dense traffic was made more so by the rerouting of traffic around a closed-off Times Square.

The med center was about thirty blocks from where she was. She estimated that with the traffic, the distance, and the sparse availability of cabs, she could be halfway back to the facility before she saw a free taxi, and so she started to walk. As she started to walk, she wondered; there was something odd about that message from Gabriel.

BETWEEN THE BEATING Gabriel had taken and the amount of muscle relaxant that had been administered to him, Gabriel might as well have been dead. He was hardly breathing and his pulse was faint. The squad leader from the NSC assigned to bring Cruz in thought he was dead, and panicked. He had not done a good job of it, to say the least. They couldn't bring Cruz in like this. The squad leader's mind was racing. No matter how he spun the situation, it wasn't good. He would have to make a decision as to which scenario would have the fewest negative ramifications, or the squad leader might be thrown to the Dyscards. That gave him an idea. Judgment can be faulty when arrived at in fear.

"Get him on the truck and wrap him up," the squad leader ordered. He looked up at the security camera in the hallway and thought of the Con Ed van. They would have seen everything about this screwed-up job! He walked out the fire exit door and saw the Con Ed van idling behind the fire truck. "Wait!" he barked, and his men froze. The squad leader looked down at Gabriel, reached into the pouch underneath the stretcher, and pulled out the blanket that was stored there. He covered Gabriel with the blanket, and once he had the body covered, he pulled up the edge to cover Gabriel's face and head.

"Put the stretcher into the Con Ed van," he said, and pointed in that direction. They would have to get rid of the body, and that was how he was going to do it. Get them to share in the need for a cover-up.

As he approached, the squad leader motioned for the guy on the street side of the van to open his window, but before the squad leader could say anything, the driver said, "What the hell happened up there?"

The eyes of the squad leader instinctively scanned the van for indications of a recording device.

"Don't worry. We're not recording you," the driver said— as if the squad leader might ever believe that.

"You saw, correct?" the squad leader said, and the man in the passenger seat who had been monitoring the security system nodded.

"Well, no one told us he was Mr. Martial Arts," the squad leader said. "Frankly, I will have to write up these men," he said, motioning toward the unit behind him.

"Will you mention how you beat the crap out of him?" the man in the passenger seat asked.

"It was self-defense. He was armed. You couldn't see on

camera," the squad leader said. "In any case, you've got to take him." The squad leader had rank.

"Why us? What're we going to do with him?"

"We're compromised," the squad leader said, pointing back at his team. "The chairman's office called. They want you to dump him. Nobody knows you're here. You just came from down there, didn't you? He's just another Dyscard."

"How come the party office didn't contact us?" the van's driver asked.

"We're already corrupted. They wanted to leave you pure to finish the job," the National Security Council squad leader answered.

"I don't like this," the agent in the passenger seat said. He pointed at the squad leader. "Remember," he said, and motioned toward the screen of the monitor that held the history of the event on the hard drive.

CHRISTINE HESITATED A moment and looked over at Central Park, a dark field in the valley of neon light. It looked inviting and dangerous at the same time, but Christine didn't have time for either so she turned and headed down Broadway. There was a contrast of light as Christine headed toward Times Square and the New Year's celebration.

At first Christine was too distracted to be cold, but by the time she reached Fifty-fifth Street, the temperature was low enough to take her from her distractions. She wasn't wearing much of a coat, and when she thought about it, she wasn't wearing much of anything. She took a deep breath and felt a wave of disappointment. She was angry with her grandmother for recommending a dress like this, and then Christine was angry with herself for being so ridiculous as to blame anyone other than herself, especially her grandmother. She looked down at the dress and herself in it. She had put too much hope into a dress, and into an evening.

By the time Christine reached Fifty-third Street, she was at the edge of the crowd that had assembled at Times Square. Christine walked across a closed Broadway and took Fiftieth Street across town. She walked through Rockefeller Plaza and it was as bright as a movie set. She turned right on Fifth Avenue. She thought a minute and looked toward Saint Patrick's Cathedral behind her. The old granite building was so well lit it did not cast any shadow. A Conglomerate Ranger stood guard on each corner and at each of the cathedral's huge bronze doors. The soldiers carried automatic rifles and wore camouflage flak jackets over their black uniforms.

In Manhattan, Christine thought, it seems that no matter which way you walk, you walk into the wind. The height of the buildings and the layout of the streets created a maze that the wind chased through, feeding on itself along the way. Christine pulled her satin jacket around her shoulders and shivered. She looked down at her pumps with the three-inch heels.

"No wonder it's taking me so long to get anywhere," Christine said. "Nothing about this has been a good idea."

But the wind took away her words even before she had time to hear them.

That was when she saw someone getting out of a cab. She raised her hand like they do in the movies; she got into the taxi. The driver took advantage of the interior light being on to take a look at Christine as she fell into the backseat and the warmth of the interior of the cab.

"Where to?" he said.

"The New York Medical Center."

"Well, I'll take you as close as I can get. Then I'm going to have to drop you off," the cabbie said. "Police activity over there. They got the whole place sealed off. Still want to go there?"

"Yes," Christine said as she looked through her purse. "I'm a doctor," she said. "They'll have to let us through." She waved her I.D.

The cabbie made a left and headed away from the Times Square area. He made a right on Second Avenue and they encountered police cars screaming downtown. The cab couldn't go any farther than the intersection at Forty-second Street; a uniformed officer was pulling all but emergency vehicles to the side, and traffic was building behind them.

"Looks like this is the end of the line, Doc," the cabbie said.

"I'll pay you what I owe you and I'll walk from here," Christine said as she handed him her currency card and then opened the door. She walked across Forty-second Street and stopped at the yellow caution tape. She lifted the tape to go underneath. Two armed Rangers in flak jackets and boots came toward her.

"Where d'you think you're going?" one of them asked.

Christine reached into her purse and found her credentials. One of the cops took the I.D. and held it to the light before taking a good look at Christine.

"I guess that's you," he said, handing Christine back her I.D. He held the tape up for her to go underneath. Although, she realized, he didn't hold it up too high, in order to get a better look at her as she bent to get under it.

There was an obstacle course of squad cars scattered along Forty-second Street as Christine walked toward First Avenue. Most of them were occupied with cops staying out of the cold. Some took notice of her, while others seemed to be writing reports. Christine made a right on First and weaved her way toward Thirty-fourth Street. There was a blockade set up there. Christine had to show her I.D. and answer questions and explain why they should let her through. Even though the officer at the wooden horses didn't want to, he let her through anyway.

She passed a police car with the door open. The overhead light was on and Christine could hear the radio bark from inside the car. Christine walked so she could hear what sounded like a crowd roar from the radio. She thought it was static until she heard the sound in the air traveling down from the festivities at Times Square. Then Christine heard the countdown start. "Ten, nine, eight . . ." She leaned her head toward the car and heard the countdown coming from the radio, along with the soft, plaintive notes of the New Year's Eve song "Auld Lange Syne." When the crowd reached "one" and yelled "Happy New Year," laser lights lit the sky with the year, 2–0–4–8 . . . 2–0–4–8.

Where was Gabriel? She wanted to be with him now. He hadn't called her back to fill her in on what had happened. Could he have something special in mind for tonight? It would be just like him to do the unexpected. One more thing that Gabriel did for Christine that pleased her so much—he got her not only to expect the unexpected, but to look forward to it.

The man had gotten under her skin, and she liked the way it felt—and that had been unexpected too. There were other aspects that she would have to resolve—mainly that their increased attraction to each other was interrelated with their work.

In any case, she still had tonight. She looked at the police activity around the center, and then it hit her: What if all of this was for Gabriel? Had something happened to him? The heat she had felt at the thought of the night ahead turned cold at the idea. Had something gone wrong?

She straightened up and took her phone out of her purse. She flipped it open. Then she closed the phone and started to walk as fast as she could, the refrain from the New Year's Eve song repeating in her head. She didn't know all the words, but the sound of the words along with the melody filled her with regret.

"Whoa," someone said as he grabbed Christine by the arm and pulled her back. An NYPD officer was holding Christine by the elbow, his grip tight. She couldn't reach into her purse to produce her I.D. She was starting to explain when the officer interrupted her.

"We're waiting for you," he said. Then she found herself being taken by the elbow and escorted across Thirty-fourth Street toward the medical center.

There was a black town car with black tinted windows blocking the intersection. No one tried to move it, or approach it either. In fact, everyone moved around the car as if it were supposed to be there. The beams of the town car's headlights lit Christine as she went across the street.

The med center was illuminated by floodlights around the periphery and also from above by lighting attached to the roofline. Christine had walked in and out of this entrance hundreds of times, but tonight, as emergency vehicles surrounded it, it looked completely different.

The agent holding Christine Salter's elbow squeezed with her into the same section of the revolving door as they stutter-stepped around the half circle and into the building. Fluorescent light assaulted her senses and she lost all detail in a glare of white. The hair on her arms and the back of her neck stood up as she realized just how cold she was. A blast of steam-heated air hit her skin and filled her nose, which started to run. She wanted to reach for a tissue, she wanted to change out of this ridiculous outfit, and she wanted a cup of coffee.

"Dr. Christine Salter?" Christine's eyes had not yet had time to adjust; all she could see was a silhouette shape appear in front of her. "Please come with us."

"We'll take her from here," another voice said. "Thanks for your help. And Happy New Year to you and your family." The officer let go of the grip he had on Christine's arm and backed off.

Christine had sometimes felt more comfortable at work than she did at home, but now she felt disoriented, as if she had been caught breaking and entering. The two men at either side of her were now guiding her into the elevator. As the elevator doors closed behind them, the elevator was also flooded in fluorescent light so that she couldn't see for a second. It wasn't until he spoke that Christine knew there was someone else on the elevator.

"Dr. Christine Salter," the voice said.

It was directly after Christine heard this voice and understood that there was an additional person on the elevator that Christine realized the elevator wasn't moving.

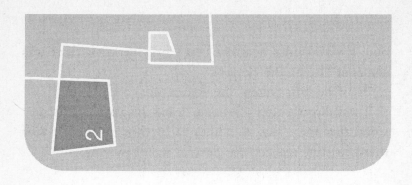

Patsy and George Meet
the Captain of the Galaxy

The gangplank leading from the terminal gate to the entrance of the transport plane, a C-5 Galaxy, was thick with people. Patsy and George Salter were among them, and from the looks of it, George thought, they were among the younger ones too, or they were at least lively in comparison. They were to enter the C-5 Galaxy through the open nose of the aircraft, which tilted upward on a hinge on top of the mammoth plane to become a gaping mouth directly ahead. *We are marching straight into the belly of the beast,* George thought.

He looked to his left and his right; old people everywhere. It was an old plane with two engines, each bigger than the van that had brought them to the airport.

The gangplank, makeshift at best, permitted them to

walk two to three abreast. It ran on a steep incline from the open terminal gate to the ramp of the transport. There was a backup of people trying to board the plane.

Patsy and George were with the first group, and they were being pressed by the people behind them. There were recorded announcements that urged everyone to keep moving, but the gangplank was too narrow, too steep, too full of old people who were stepping on themselves and one another.

George could feel a sense of panic rising around him, and then he realized he would have been in that state himself had it not been for Patsy. He was too worried that he might be separated from his wife to panic. He walked behind Patsy, with his arms around her, his fingers locked around her stomach, and he used his knees to push her forward, shuffling his feet without picking them up off the surface of the ramp. He could tell there was no panic in Patsy; she was so relaxed that she just kept gliding. Pretty soon she and George had reached the carpeted floor of the C-5 Galaxy. Other passengers around them were stumbling, and Patsy reached down and hoisted a woman up.

There were Conglomerate Rangers in full gear everywhere, camouflage flak jackets atop black jumpsuits, automatic weapons slung across their backs. They guarded either side of the entrance to the plane. A voice came over the PA system: "Keep moving."

"Help that woman there," a male voice behind them said; it seemed to be the voice of someone about Patsy and George's age. One of the Rangers reached over and took the fallen woman's arm. George was surprised that these guards would be taking orders from a Coot. He was of medium build, and on the thin side. He wore black pants, boots, and a brown leather bomber jacket, with a white silk scarf wrapped around his throat. He had on dark sunglasses. George didn't like him right off the bat, nor did George know what to make of him. Then the man spoke again to the guards. "Please show this lady to her seat," he said, gesturing to a guard who started to lead Patsy away. Patsy stuck her thumb out in George's direction and said, "Him too!"

"Of course," the man with the glasses and the scarf said, and off they went. So, George thought, *this guy's in charge.*

The attendants didn't seem too pleased to be ordered around by an old guy, but they had Patsy and George by the elbows and were leading them into the plane. George was surprised once more by the inside of the plane and decided he had better get used to being surprised and try to just take things as they came.

The interior of the plane resembled a warehouse more than an aircraft. Rows of red tape were laid across the floor in a graph that ran the length and width of the plane, and the plane seemed as long as a football field. There were about sixty people on board, scattered about the cabin. One woman, who seemed to have a cut above her left eye, was being led off the plane. George wondered if she was indeed the lucky one, to be left behind. For this was a Coot roundup, and they didn't know exactly where they were going. Like everyone else, George had heard rumors about what was at the other end of these flights. It seemed everyone knew of someone who had been transported to the camps out West. That in and of itself was scary enough, but neither George nor anyone he knew directly had ever spoken to someone who had made the trip, and that fact had always put a knot in his gut. But now all George knew was that he wanted to stay with Patsy, no matter what.

So when the man with the sunglasses came up behind them and spoke, they both jumped. "I wanted to come back here and make sure you two were okay." He seemed to bow in Patsy's direction. George opened his mouth to say something, but Patsy looked at the man and said, "Him too!" The man laughed and said, "I am sorry. Of course, him too." George had been getting Patsy settled, tucking a blanket between her and the window, fastening her seat belt, and primping her in a fashion that Patsy was unaccustomed to and clearly didn't like.

"Excuse me," the man said, "I am the captain of the Galaxy." And he extended his hand toward George, who shook it.

George didn't want to call attention to themselves; he was afraid of being found out. He went back to what he was doing, bending down to fix Patsy in her seat. But the captain seemed interested in them anyway.

The captain looked at Patsy, and his delight in her made him feel guilty. "Hope to be back soon," he said, and he walked back down the aisle.

George half collapsed into his seat, realizing that if the guy had really talked to Patsy, he might have found out what was wrong, and that would have meant trouble. Coots with debilitating illness were . . . Well, he didn't want to think.

He looked down and felt Patsy's hand on his leg, giving his knee a little squeeze. He turned to face her so they could look each other in the eye. Then Patsy turned back to the window.

George was aware that Patsy wasn't really looking out the window. She was living someplace else, and with some other person, which is how George had come to think of her disease. Try as he might, it made him a little mad. Here he was giving her all his care, and he was being replaced by a vision, a delusion. George could get angry about this, his wife choosing to communicate with a hallucination instead of with him, and then George's anger would be redirected at himself for being in competition with a disease. The disease was kidnapping Patsy's personality, and her past, and his frustration came from the fact that there was nothing he could do to bring her back. He had tried mental exercises and memory tests. He would review their family tree for her, with their daughter, Judy, and their granddaughters, Christine and Ximena. And even Patsy's beloved Christine, who was the apple of her grandmother's eye, brought no recognition now. *Damn this disease,* he thought, and then he looked at Patsy, right there next to him. He was responsible for her, and their love had gotten them as far as they could get together. It was as simple as that, and George knew that Patsy would have done the same thing for him—had done the same thing, and would still do the same thing.

He leaned back; he didn't have time to be depressed. Circumstances just wouldn't allow it. *Christ, just look at us,* he thought. *We look as batty as everyone else on this plane.*

. . .

THE CAPTAIN OF the Galaxy walked back up the long aisle toward the flight deck, but he really wasn't looking where he was going. His eyes were lowered. He wasn't sure if the hum inside himself came from the engines beneath him or from the buzz he felt inside. There was something about that woman. It was highly unusual in circumstances such as this transport for anyone to exhibit an independent act of initiative. If their spirit hadn't been broken by age, or infirmity, or by the loss of the tangible—and in most cases the intangible as well—the Conglomerates saw to it that they brought the Coots past the precipice and pushed them into the abyss of defeat.

But now he was at the flight deck door, and it was open, and standing in the open doorway was the flight's navigator, and in his hand was the flight's final plans, with the latest weather, the route, the expected traffic. The captain was annoyed at himself for allowing this particular navigator to catch him being distracted. He was a report-happy fellow, and the captain was sure he would report the captain to his superiors. The navigator could file a complaint with the Conglomerates, and depending on how the administration received and reviewed the complaint, the captain might be forced to go through neurological testing. It was all a scam. They had no one else who could fly this old plane. A flight simulator was one thing, but actually sitting atop this monster took balls. The captain looked at the navigator. *Good luck,* he thought.

This C-5 Galaxy was built in 1968, conceived from the funds for the Vietnam War. It cut its teeth in the Middle East and proved itself a warrior during Operation Desert Storm in 1991; that is when the plane and the captain met. The Galaxy had a wide berth in the air and on the ground. There were only a couple of people capable of piloting her. It didn't matter that the captain was old. He was the cheapest way to transport the most old people from here to the Southwest, and he was one of the few who could do it. Also, the Conglomerates couldn't care less if a plane full of old people should crash. The C-5 Galaxy had rescued the captain from retirement and had brought him back into service, but it was hardly a rescue. Though the captain sometimes felt it was. He hadn't had much choice.

Coming back to the present, he thanked the navigator for the flight plan, which was not what the navigator had expected. The man raised his right eyebrow and studied the captain as the captain made his way to his seat. "Let's have a good flight, shall we?" the captain said, and he meant it. His navigator took it as sarcasm and made a mental note to add attitude to his report.

The captain logged on to the Galaxy system and saluted the camera housed in the panel among the dials of the cockpit. He recited the litany of his equipment checks. He looked at the levels on the control panels and checked his communications. It was then that he made up his mind that he should do some communicating on his own.

He thought of a way that he could get to go back to see that woman one more time. While Patsy's husband had flitted around her, the captain had known that the man had

had every right to be nervous, and he felt sorry for the guy, if not a little jealous. He decided that to help that woman, he really had to communicate with her husband. He wasn't sure if this was a rationalization or the right thing to do, but finally he decided either reason would work.

He concentrated on what to say to let the man know that he'd better be more vigilant. He didn't want to raise the suspicions of the navigator, or provide drama for the cameras. But, then again, the captain liked a challenge.

He lowered the zipper of his brown leather jacket and pulled out the white scarf. With the edge of the scarf he reached down and wiped the lens of the security camera, gave it a wink, and finished up the rest of his routine while he contemplated his options. Then he tucked the scarf back into his leather jacket and took the flight plan from his inside pocket. What the hell did he need a flight plan for? he thought. Out where they were going was probably where they would assign him later, like some ferryman to the afterlife, schlepping souls from here to there. The captain felt he knew this route and this Galaxy as well as he knew anything; even the air currents were in his muscle memory. Besides, anyone who picked up this monster on their radar kept their distance, especially the helicopters and small planes of the Conglomerate executives. In a real way this bird owned the sky, and so the captain did too.

After the Gulf War, the captain had piloted this baby through a half dozen corporate consolidations prior to the Conglomerates coming to power. He had more hours refueling this plane in the air than most active pilots had flight hours. Even if the Conglomerates were to find the captain "neurologically unsound," they weren't about to find anyone else who could pilot the Galaxy, and until they found a less expensive way of getting the Coots to their place in the sun, they were going to need the Galaxy, and by extension, him.

As for the Conglomerates, they were overextended, and thus they needed the captain, even though he caused a quandary for them. The captain was a Coot, a senior, the enemy. Still, they needed his talents and service. They had tracked him down—not that it had been that difficult, since they could find anybody—and they had assigned him to a community in Arizona and conscripted his talents. The captain hadn't taken that much convincing. Bereft of his life partner and the enthusiasm one needs to live life, the captain, like so many others, had been glad for the chance to report back to work. He had made no demands on the Conglomerates; in fact, he was pretty much willing to do what was asked of him. But no matter how agreeable the captain was, and how powerless he was within their system, the Conglomerates kept a close eye on him. The captain had to believe that was the role of the navigator, because the captain couldn't find any other reason, or talent, that would explain why the man kept his job.

The captain nodded at the camera and unfolded the flight plan, positioning the plan so that it obscured the camera's view. The captain knew it probably was a computer that was monitoring the camera, but you never could be sure. His heart sank as he started to realize this was a hopeless cause. Because really, what could he do for this woman and her husband?

Once, the captain had been willing to do anything to protect his wife from the eventual, willing to do anything to hold on to his prize, his life. But the captain had been unable to do that. He could imagine how that woman's husband felt. He had to find something to write on.

His pen was clipped inside his jacket pocket. As an old-timer, the captain did not feel complete without a pen, though he hardly ever used it. No one did. Probably no one had even seen his handwriting for years—maybe his signature, and that was a scrawl anyway. If the captain were careful, and he'd have to be, there would be no tracing the note back to him.

He tapped his breast pocket to make sure the pen was still there and at the same time noticed the stack of napkins in the ship's galley. A napkin wouldn't necessarily be traced or look out of place.

He refolded the flight plan, tapped the pen again, rose, stretched, and squeezed his way into the galley. He grabbed a handful of napkins, wiped at his nose a couple of times, and went to the crew's lavatory, saying "Right back" as he closed the bathroom door.

He hung his cap in front of the surveillance camera lens, a common practice among veterans of the crew, and an act that, he hoped, would draw little suspicion. *I mean, you have to draw the line somewhere,* the captain thought.

He covered the seat, unfastened his belt, dropped his pants, reached down, and removed the napkins from his hip pocket and started to write:

Look, there are cameras all around you. If you want to help your wife, you'll have to stop drawing attention to yourself. There are hundreds of passengers and only six crew members. The crew won't catch you; the cameras will. Let your wife be herself, and you watch. Be normal. Good luck.

He folded the napkin and slid it under the band of his watch; now all he had to do was get it to that woman's husband without the cameras seeing him and without the navigator seeing him. *What am I thinking?* the captain asked himself, and the answer was in the line of that woman's face.

When he came out of the lavatory, the navigator was staring at the lavatory door; they were ten minutes from takeoff.

"I'm going to make one last check of the passengers," he said. "Then we can be on our way."

As the captain walked down the aisle, he realized that he couldn't just go to the couple directly—too obvious. Instead, he nodded at them and continued on down the aisle. In the crew's galley he saw a bucket with water bottles and it gave him an idea. He grabbed a bunch of water bottles and headed toward that couple's seats. When he was close to them, he started to hand out bottles of water. When he got to them, he handed the woman the last bottle of water, and handed the note to the husband in the same movement. "Wait a minute, and then read this," he said. Then he headed back to the flight deck.

George wasn't sure what the captain had just said. *It must've been something about needing this,* he thought, as he rubbed the napkin between his fingers. But it had sounded as if the man had said "Read this." George looked down at the napkin. Read what? And then he saw what looked like writing.

George read the note. It started off with "Look" and concluded with "be normal," and he thought, *What the . . . ? Be normal! Is he kidding?* Then George looked around him. *First he tells me there are cameras all around me, and then he tells me to be normal!* All George saw around him were people whose will had been broken.

But not the woman next to him. Patsy's will clearly wasn't broken, and George's expression lifted into a smile.

George had to admit that the captain's note had a point. He had acted too nervous over Patsy, like she was an invalid. *Jeez, some invalid,* George thought. "Let your wife be herself." He knew he couldn't stop her if he tried.

Despite her will, however, Patsy was losing parts of herself every day. George could see the deterioration of her personality, but at times Patsy was no less for the loss. She was still his wife, and George was a patsy when it came to her, and that's just the way it was, and always had been, and always would be.

He lowered the napkin into his lap, and suddenly Patsy grabbed it from him, brought it to her lips to wipe her mouth, and then squeezed it into a small ball inside her fist. George looked from Patsy's fist to her face and didn't notice the navigator walking by them, though the navigator wouldn't have mattered much to George. But what mattered to the navigator was that these old fools were drinking his water, and he'd bet there was another old fool that had something to do with that.

No one saw the napkin balled up in Patsy's fist, but everybody saw George bump his head on the seat ahead of him as he quickly bent down to look for the napkin he thought he'd lost.

When the navigator reached the flight deck, the plane had just begun to be led away from the makeshift gateway.

You gave it to them, the look on the navigator's face said, and combined with the navigator's dramatic entry and what the captain had just done, it made the captain believe he had been busted.

Then the navigator said, "You gave them the bottles of water, didn't you?" And the captain looked up and said, "Sit down. You're holding up my flight time." He shifted the throttle, causing the plane to buck slightly, which sent the navigator flying into his seat.

The navigator had to admit that they had to get this cargo of Coots out of New York and settled in Arizona. The Coots' property had been seized and sold. Their possessions had been processed and moved along. There was no room for these old people anymore, and there were only more Coots coming along behind them. Besides, he had his little stash of contraband to consider.

THE GALAXY HAD achieved thirty thousand feet and the captain had made the necessary adjustments for them to lock into a cruising speed of about five hundred forty miles per hour. The plane was nearly over the Ohio Valley when the captain noticed that the Galaxy had sensed the storm before its instruments had anything to report. But the captain always derived some satisfaction from feeling the plane change before anything registered on the gauges. The captain could feel the body of the plane hunker down into the accelerating wind. It was during this moment that the captain felt the plane drag for a bit, and then he heard the first raindrop smack against the windshield like a gunshot.

The captain didn't look at the navigator but said, "Whatta ya got?" and for an instant the navigator thought the captain knew what he had been writing. Then the captain said, "Whatta ya reading?" and the navigator said, "My report." Now the captain looked away from what he was doing to face the navigator. "What is the forecast?" he said. The navigator caught on; he'd have to improvise. "The system just went down," he said, inching his fingers toward the off button. "But looks like we'll be in this for a while."

The captain had been pulling the wheel toward him to give the plane some altitude. Even though they were nearly at the maximum altitude for the Galaxy, the captain was hoping he'd be able to fly over this storm. He felt the plane lifting. He hoped to get the nose of the plane up to let air pressure get to the undercarriage and beneath the 223-foot wingspan, and maybe then he could get them above this frontal system. Just as the captain pulled as hard as he could, and hoped a little harder, he felt the plane begin to lift. He could hear the Galaxy straining against the wind until there was another change in direction, and then the captain heard nothing at all.

It felt as if the C-5 had hit something, as if the plane had stopped. And it had. The navigator wasn't sure if he could hear the engines, or the storm, but the captain was sure.

They didn't hear the engines because the gale winds of the new frontal system were blowing straight at them with such intensity that the opposing force had stalled the engines. That was the bad news, the captain thought; the good news was that the wind was also holding them up. The captain knew it would be only a couple of seconds before the Galaxy's 400,000-plus pounds started to plummet. He started to shut down all systems as quickly as he could. His hands flew from switch to knob. The navigator watched the captain with his mouth gaping and his grip tightening. They felt the nose of the Galaxy drop.

The captain had a plan that went back years. The plan was to jump-start the engine, just like his father had always started that red Volkswagen that stalled out in the middle of shifting gears. His father would keep that baby rolling, and then if he could get a little momentum, he'd started that engine already in gear, give it gas, and hope the whole thing caught. It usually did for his daddy, and usually with a loud bang.

What the hell, the captain thought. The silver Galaxy was only about a couple thousand times larger than that red Volkswagen.

The few seconds it took for the captain to have all of this run through his mind, and through his hands, was enough time for the Galaxy to begin its plunge. He had also been busy readjusting the instruments with the engines in the off position, and as soon as the captain had everything the way he wanted, he opened the throttle and flipped the electric ignition switch.

The Galaxy had an emergency generator with enough reserve to provide the basic electric function. It didn't seem to have enough for the ignition system, and nothing happened when the captain flipped the switch. He quickly returned the switch to the off position, thought of his late wife, and tried the switch again. This time the captain heard the engine cough, then pop. Then there was a small explosion and the engine began to purr and the plane's descent to slow. The thrust caused by the explosive start of the engines added enough momentum for the airplane to regain its climb.

"Hold on," the captain heard himself saying, and the Galaxy kept climbing. Now the captain could pray, and he did, even with several thousand feet to go.

He looked over at the navigator, whose head was bowed, and the smell of vomit began to fill the cabin.

"Are you okay?" he asked, and the navigator said, "I think so."

They had almost achieved enough altitude to clear this weather system, or so the captain hoped, and after a couple of agonizingly long moments, they saw a rod of sunlight pierce the dark. He stared straight ahead as he flew the Galaxy through the rainbow of color that followed the storm, and wished that he had the energy to enjoy it.

The passengers, for the most part, had been too subdued by the events of the past few hours to know what was happening. The entire episode of the storm lasted about ten minutes, but sometimes the duration of time is irrelevant, especially if your life has just flashed before you.

George looked out the window while the plane broke

through the gray cloud bank and emerged into a beautiful day. He thought he'd better assess the situation and force his mind to review where he and Patsy were, what had brought them here. When George thought about it, their life together, it had always been just that, the two of them, together. Back in Staten Island before they had a house, before they had their daughter, and their granddaughters, it had all started with them, and here they were, on their way to who knew where, but they would, still, have each other, still be together.

George had considered tracking down their granddaughter, who was doing pretty well for herself in the Conglomerate world, to see if Christine could help. But he couldn't think of anything she could do for them. They had reached that age and were on their way West. There was nothing anyone could do for them now; time had taken care of that. Even though he didn't know where they were going, or what their options were, George felt compelled to think about it, as if, if he just kept at it, everything would fall into place.

He was suddenly exhausted, and he wondered how he could possibly maintain the stamina it would require to take care of both of them.

Within the last few months, Patsy's deterioration had been pronounced. It seemed she had simply forgotten some of the things that had been inherent to her life. Then George had seen what she had been able to accomplish today. He wondered if Patsy's fuzziness on the details was due to a deeper understanding of the human situation. Had Patsy's intuitive nature been left undisturbed by her disease? Does the seat where the soul resides have nothing to do with the

brain? Could a disorder that debilitated motor functions, coordination, memory, calculation, and apparently all of the
intellectual functions, leave the deeper understanding un-
touched? *It must,* George thought, as he remembered Patsy's
performance on the gangplank and as he looked at her now.
Patsy probably did not know she was on a plane, or remember that she'd left her cat and her home behind, or know
that they didn't know where they were going to spend the
night, or get their next meal. But Patsy knew how to take
care of others, and how to take care of a life that had been
bruised along the way.

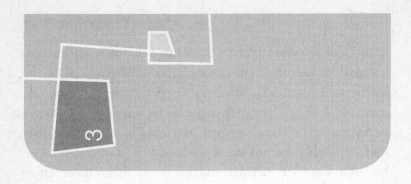

Ximena in the Underworld

Ximena Salter, known as X, was lying with her eyes shut, but she could still see the strobe as the light hit her shut eyelids and changed from black to red to black again. She opened her eyes, but it was too dark to see much of anything. She knew enough to realize that she was underground; she was in the world of the Dyscards.

She raised herself up on her elbows, and another flare of light blinded her. She covered her eyes with her forearm and let her head fall back down. Her ears were ringing like a tuning fork; her pulse pounded behind her temples; her tongue felt thick. She could taste a residue in the back of her throat of the drug they had used to take her down. She felt a vibration beneath the small of her back, and she knew what that meant. She bolted up and crawled forward on her hands and knees, thinking that fear overcomes pain. Then she hit her head, and everything stopped while she folded up inside. She took a breath and tried to scream, but nothing came out. She balled herself up as tight as she could against the wall. She put her hand to her throat; she still wore her pendant.

The vibration and then the sound X heard was a subway train. When X looked up, she saw a pair of headlights coming straight toward her. The train roared passed her, inches from her feet, and with the passing lights she realized that what she had thought was a wall that she was leaning against was actually a steel girder. There were dozens of these girders, creating arches and trestles in layers of underground tracks stacked one on another. X seemed to be on a platform between the girders and the tracks. There was a wall across a series of tracks and there was a pattern of shapes on the wall, a word, and the word was "Welcome."

"Welcome?" X said aloud. "What the . . . ?"

X REMEMBERED YELLING at her mother and her mother yelling back, and there was nothing new in that scenario. That could have been any time, though this time it was different. When X thought about it, the memory hurt. X's head was pounding and she wondered if she had taken a pounding too. At first she couldn't remember much else, and then she did: Two guys had been waiting outside the door of their apartment in Queens. It could have been a movie, when X thought about it; they'd even had on trench coats. X had no-

ticed them because she'd found it strange to see these characters waiting in the hall. X hadn't known they were waiting
for her, or that her mother had called them.

When her mother had started to explain, the yelling had
started.

"Ximena," her mother had said. X hated it when her
mother called her that. She hated her name. It bothered
her that her mother had thought it was a good idea to give
her daughter such a name. She had never heard of anyone
else who had this name. She had started calling herself X
as soon as she'd figured out that she could, even though
people looked at her funny when she introduced herself.
Sometimes they would ask her what X meant, and she
would reply, "Ten," or "Multiply," or whatever struck her,
anything instead of her name. Even those lines produced
less of a reaction than when she had used her full name.
But mostly X hated it when her mother said Ximena, because of her tone of voice when she said it.

"Ximena," X's mother said again, "these people are here
to ask you a few questions. To help you. In fact," X's mother
said, "they're here to help our family."

What family? X wanted to shout. *Your husband left you to find
a younger version, and Christine couldn't wait to leave home.* But X
didn't say anything. It occurred to her that her mother must
have a new man in mind, so it was time for her mother to
clean house and start over. X realized she was about to be exchanged for a new baby and a new life. That was the family
that her mother was talking about. And that was why her
mother had been so interested in X's grandparents' transfer
to the West. X realized her mother would have gotten a cut

of her grandparents' assets that had been assumed by the Conglomerates. Her mother would have used that money to get X off her hands and buy herself another chance.

X knew that she was about to become a Dyscard.

Though no one would admit that the Dyscard community existed—certainly not the mass media, nor the state—everyone knew about them. There was talk, no matter what methods the Conglomerates used to try to airbrush the Dyscards out of the collective culture. X didn't like it at home, but she wasn't about to volunteer to be discarded.

But before X could offer up too much of a protest, the two men in the trench coats were sitting in the living room. X noticed that one of the men wasn't a man at all, and that made sense when X thought about it. They would want a woman involved if they were going to be dealing with a young female client. X wouldn't be able to contact anyone; they had canceled her phone. She wouldn't be able to get in touch with her sister, Christine. Even though they had never really gotten along, and had been competing against each other all their lives, the designer daughter versus the deter- mined one. And, when X thought about it, the sisters had never given it a chance. They had been set up against each other and had never really had the opportunity to be sisters. As a result, they hadn't spoken in a while, but Christine knew what their mother was like and might understand what X was going through. She might be willing to help. But there wouldn't be time for that now.

X was surprised that she felt betrayed by her mother when these two were invited to sit down. But here they were, sitting in the living room. It shouldn't have been news to her that her mother had had it with her. In a lot of ways X had made sure that she had. But still, X felt like throwing up when she thought about it.

"This is all for the best, Ximena," her mother kept repeating. Who was she trying to convince? Herself? It was all going on in their own living room, except it wasn't her living room anymore. It wasn't her home anymore, and X had to wonder if it ever had been her home. Then the two trench coats intervened and it really hit home just how much it wasn't her home anymore.

A sense of calm prevailed over the household when X heard the woman in the trench coat say to her mother that they'd be taking over. That was pretty much the last thing X recalled.

X HAD OTHER things to think about now. She was dehydrated and drugged, and it was difficult to move without pain. Sweat was rolling into her eyes. Her clothes were dirty and damp, and her shirt was sticking to her back.

"It's got to be a hundred degrees down here," X said, and she wiped at her forehead with the back of her hand.

"Well," she said, "that sign, it must mean that somebody else has got to be here, and they'll have water." She wanted to get moving before the next train went by. The only problem was, where was she going to go?

The only thing X could see were tracks and rails and girders and beams, and everything else was black, even in the light. She could taste the dark. The air contained a smaller

ratio of oxygen content to the levels of carbon dioxide, nitro-
gen, and countless other impurities that trickled down into
the underworld, and all of that was collecting in X's throat.
She was going to have to move. She was going to have to find
something to drink and someplace to go where the air was
better. Whoever had dumped her here had chosen this spot
for a reason.

"So that's settled," X said. "I'm staying put."

"PLEASE, DO NOT be alarmed," a voice announced from within
the darkness. "How can we help you?"

After X gasped, she said, "Water?" If they were going to
kill her, why bother to be polite?

"Yes," another voice answered, and X accepted the bottle
of water from a hand that stretched out of the shadows.

With that, two men stepped into X's space. They were
older then she was, but not by much.

"We're not as scary as we look," the first voice said.

"I wouldn't be so sure of that," the other one said.

"Where am I?" X asked. Even though it seemed obvious,
confirmation might be a good thing.

"The New York City subway system. A convenient means
of transportation, and . . . ," said the one that X associated
with the second voice. He raised a finger, pointed toward the
tunnel, and said, "Our home."

"Yours too," the first voice said. "Welcome to the land of
the Dyscards."

X had always thought of herself as a tough girl who could

take whatever came her way, but this was more than she could have imagined and was sure more than she had ever dealt with before, including being kidnapped by the trench coat duo. She was glad she was in the dark. She took another sip of water in hopes that it would help her get ahold of her emotions. She felt like she was going to cry.

She cupped her hand, poured water into her palm, and splashed the water into her face, just in case. She took a long pull from the bottle and swallowed hard. She had heard about the Dyscards, and some of her friends had dropped out of sight. She didn't know much about it; nobody did. This wasn't something the Conglomerates wanted in the media, or that families wanted to admit.

Since these two were assigned to pick up the new arrivals, they had expected X's dismay at waking up a Dyscard, and they were silent as they waited for her to catch her breath. The second man reached over and handed her a small towel. X wiped her face and started to tear up again. She felt as if these two had saved her, and maybe they had, but in truth they really hadn't done much at all but hand her a towel and give her a bottle of water.

She noticed the taste of what she was drinking. While it felt like water in consistency and texture, there was a sweet aftertaste that felt like it was giving X a lift. She held the bottle up to her face and said, "What is in this stuff?"

"Good old tap water," the first voice said. "That plus some tea and a few other tea-like ingredients."

"Where did you get tea?" X asked.

"Does it matter?" the second voice wanted to know.

X had to agree, but at least she wasn't crying anymore.

She was coming around, and her eyes were adjusting to her surroundings. She noticed that there was a dotted line of small blue lights that went in different directions until they veered off into the dark. There were red lights and yellow lights strategically placed. There was reflective tape over handrails along the walls and on the edges of steps. There were small boxes and alcoves that lined the walls. And there was writing on the walls, graffiti of all scripts and shapes, faded and fresh. Years of it, from the way it looked. The ringing in X's ears had subsided, and she noticed the sound of water running and a steady drip. She could hear the hum of electricity.

She pulled the towel away from her and saw that her head was bleeding.

"Well, we'd better clean you up a bit before we go anywhere," the second voice said, and grabbed at the strap across his shoulder. X flinched and pressed harder against the steel girder at her back.

"Sorry," both men said in unison. "Just a first aid kit."

One looked down the line of X's chin as X watched his eyes come upon the pendant around her neck.

"It's funny that they let you down here with that," the second voice said.

"I probably wouldn't let them near it," X said, staring straight at the man. "Or anybody."

The first voice said, "It's just unusual, that's all."

The second man said, "You must've put up a good fight, though it looks like you paid the price."

X remembered what had happened, and there hadn't been anything funny about it.

. . .

THE TRENCH COAT pair had gotten on either side of X and were badgering her with questions. The male half was pecking the info into his phone as the woman asked X questions. She spoke in a clipped and measured manner, it seemed to X, as if the woman never took a breath. *That explains it,* X thought, *she isn't human.* But X knew this couldn't be true because it took a human to get a kick out of cruelty. The lady trench coat was clearly enjoying this.

Since X couldn't make out what the trench coat terror twins were saying, she decided to change her tack and appear as if she would cooperate, not really providing any answers but to see if she could determine what to do next. She was trying to detect if there was a way out that they might not have covered, when the woman reached into her hip pocket and came out with a spray that streamed into the air in front of X's face. X immediately held her breath, but it was too late. X could see the fright in her mother's eyes, but she wasn't sure she saw regret.

Then the arm of the trench-coated woman reached up toward X's throat and the chain around her neck. X wasn't thinking about her mother now. She wasn't going to let them take her pendant. That was her mark, her identity, her X— safe, protected within a band of gold, guarding her heart. She had found it in an old shop downtown and had thought it must have been designed for her. She had worn it ever since. It was her validation, her name, X. This bitch wasn't going to take it away from her. X didn't hear her mother scream "No," but it wouldn't have mattered if she had.

X was going down but she wasn't out. She focused her will into her leg and pumped her knee at the female officer, catching her in the crotch. The female agent bent over as if she had been shot; the male agent intervened. X transferred her will to her hands as her nails lashed out at the approaching officer, at the soft spot below his chin. He grabbed X by the wrists.

"I thought you said no violent tendencies," the male agent screamed at X's mother as the cell phone skipped across the floor.

"She's never been like this before," her mother said.

"Let her keep the thing," the female officer said, her hand between her legs. To X's mother, the agent said, "We were just making sure she didn't choke on it." Her mother was crying now, but still she did nothing to help her daughter.

The female agent in the trench coat straightened herself up; the male agent had retrieved the phone and was punching something onto the pad. The female agent gave X's mother the transfer code and receipt. Her mother was still crying. But X didn't see that now as her eyes rolled back into her head.

"We're on our way," the female agent said into her phone. "We had to put her out." That was the last thing that X heard before she came to in the land of the Dyscards. And that was the last image of Ximena her mother had, and that picture stayed with her a long, long time.

X PULLED HERSELF together. The two men with her waited; they had been through this many times before. They also would never forget their first time coming to this place. There had been no welcoming for them, as there was now. They knew to wait, as the kids who had come here had been drugged, gassed, sprayed, or worse, to get them to come in the first place. Some were dealing with chemical dependency and some had been beaten. It looked to these two like this girl had gotten the full bloody treatment.

They often told the new Dyscards that they may not have wanted to come here but soon they wouldn't want to leave. Kids never believed them because some things about human nature never change, no matter what they did to genetic makeup. There were certain traits people shared, skepticism being among them.

Unpredictability was another. No matter how many comparison studies were conducted, profiles offered, roles and scenarios figured out, there was always the variable of human emotion that was impossible to forecast. So these two whose job it was to gather the newly discarded had found it best to wait for the kids to adjust. They hadn't done so well by this one, and they were beginning to become concerned that she wasn't coming round. This wasn't abnormal, however, since most of the new arrivals felt scared and resentful at what had brought them here in the first place. It wasn't as if they had something to miss. It appeared this girl had gotten the full realization of what was happening to her pretty late in the picture, and she saw the totality of her predicament all at once.

"If you like, X, we might be able to help you," the first voice finally said.

"How did you know my name?" X asked.

"Just a guess. And then there's your necklace," the second voice said.

"If X is your name, you'll fit in fine down here," the first one said.

"You'll learn more later," the other said, "but down here you get to pick your own name. Seeing as how it was your parents who named you and those same parents who threw you out, one of the things you can do is give yourself your own new name. But in your case, I don't know. Your parents named you X?"

"Not really."

This was a lot for X to take in, but the part that X was stuck on was the "parents who threw you out" part. She really hadn't thought of it that way. She had thought it was more complicated than that. But, when you came down to it, that pretty much summed it up.

The welcome guys felt they had at least brought X out of her brooding, and they determined a little bit about her state of mind.

"Well, I guess I gave myself that name—X, I mean. My mother gave me a name I shortened to X."

"Couldn't get much shorter," one said.

X replied, "I guess not," as if she hadn't thought of that before either.

"So, you're ahead of the game," the other said.

"Either that, or behind," X said.

"Ha," was their simultaneous response.

"Let's clean you up a bit," one of them suggested. He was feeling X's time of panic had passed and that she might let them assist her.

"Or perhaps you would like to clean yourself up a bit instead," the other said, and that sounded good to her. For his part he had felt the possession and the protection she gave her pendant as well as her name, and he thought that quality showed a strong sense of independence and that X would probably prefer to do things for herself.

"Thanks," X said.

He reached back and brought the satchel that he had behind him around. He opened the bag and took out a foil envelope, tore it open, and took out a moist sterile disposable towel. "Here, clean your hands with this one first," he said. That was when X noticed he was wearing gloves that were barely perceptible. "It has an antibacterial that will clean you up, and then you can use this antiseptic spray that will form a temporary bandage that will dissolve on its own."

X flinched, remembering the spray from the female agent, and the second guy said, "Look, you don't have to."

"Well, we've no time for that now, 'cause here comes a train."

X didn't hear or see a thing, and she didn't feel anything either, but she followed the two as they pressed themselves against a girder, one on either side of her. They wrapped their arms around her as another stainless steel express roared past them like a storm. X could feel the transfer of the train's vibration into her cheek, all the way into the roots of her teeth. The ringing in her ears returned. The side of the girder was warm, and the sensation of the vibration became like a dentist's drill in X's head.

And just like that, the train was gone, leaving a wake of dust and debris swirling behind it.

Once the rumble had passed, X said, "Now, with a little luck, I'll be fine."

"You do have us," one said.

"The Lucky Brothers, I'll call you," X said, and she added, "And I'm lucky to have you, really. Thanks. I'm sorry for how I reacted. It's all kind of unexpected, you know?"

"Well, maybe it is time we introduced ourselves."

"You don't have to," X said. "You're Lucky Brother Number One and he's Lucky Brother Number Two. If I can name myself, why can't I name you?"

"Well, we are brothers," Lucky Brother Number Two finally said. "But I don't know how lucky I am for that privilege."

"You two are real brothers?" X asked.

"It's worse than that," Lucky Brother Number Two said. "We're twins."

"Enough," his brother added. "We've got to get out of here. Why don't you take my arm?" Lucky Brother Number One put his hand on his hip, making a hoop of his arm as a target. X put her arm through the opening, and Lucky Brother Number One did feel lucky, although X was a little too young for him. He never thought of the kids they picked up that way. In this case the sensation that passed through him was the current of privilege.

"Look," X said, "I was set up by my own mother. Set upon by a Conglomerate version of you guys." Now it was the brothers' turn to be offended, and they wondered what a Conglomerate version of them would be like. "I get gassed and then beaten in a true demonstration of Conglomerate rage. I wake up. I'm disoriented in a dark strange place that smells like piss and carbon monoxide. I'm bleeding. I've got a concussion, I'm sure. And then I am almost hit by a train!" X couldn't help it; she stopped to absorb it all. "And then I meet you guys. Believe me, I am grateful, but now I am going to have to navigate tunnels, avoid more trains, meet new people who look funny and name themselves."

Then the ground started to shake. X had never heard of an earthquake in Manhattan, but she was sure that the world had cracked open, and then another train went by, and then another in the opposite direction.

The grip of the brothers tightened around X. The wind whooshed violently enough to knock them over.

"The best thing about that is?" Lucky Brother Number One asked.

"It's over," the other replied.

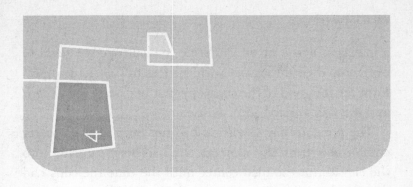

The Next Day

In the capital city of the Conglomerate nation, Manhattan, Christine Salter's alarm sounded, "Good Morning, Christine." And what followed were selected recommendations from her personal profile for her own New Year / New You opportunities: news from her financial portfolio, her daily diet tip. Christine reached over to turn it off. She didn't feel like starting her day with a sales pitch. She got dressed and started the second day of the New Year.

"What a year already," she said, "and it's only been one night." The dark had dissolved into ascending angles of light. She knew that she would have to go back to work at the Pool and carry on with med center business as usual. As a manager, it was up to Christine to challenge the team to overcome their difficulties with the loss of Gabriel and perform for the good of the company. But her heart wasn't in it and she was worried and confused.

The previous day Christine had not been allowed to get comfortable from the moment she had been escorted into the elevator at the med center until the time the cops had dropped her off at her apartment. Once she'd gotten home, Christine had climbed out of her dress and gone directly into the shower and scrubbed everything, including her memory, beneath the redeeming steam. She'd then wrapped herself in a terry cloth robe and positioned herself between the hissing radiator and the cold night air and fallen asleep in the chair.

When she had arrived at the med center earlier on New Year's morning, she'd thought she would assume control of the situation. Instead she was surprised that all they wanted was her cooperation. She hadn't even made it out of the elevator before the investigator sent from the office of the Conglomerates had advised her to answer honestly what she had uncovered about Gabriel Cruz's subversive activities and to explain why she had not reported these allegations to the Health and Human Services Corporation management committee. While they had lost their lead suspect, the investigation into the breach of security at the med center would continue. They repeated questions as to what she knew of Gabriel's involvement with others at the facility and the real nature of their relationship.

That's what got Christine the most. She really didn't know anything about her relationship to Gabriel or about his activities, and that hurt. She didn't want to admit it. Had he used her? That hurt even more. Christine had differences with her parents and had distanced herself from them even before she had moved away. She really hadn't had many relationships—until Gabriel, the first person she had come to trust, and now he had betrayed her, but she didn't want to believe that. She loved him. That was real, she believed it still. He had to care for her. She couldn't have been that wrong about what was happening between them. Could she?

The investigator alleged that Gabriel was with the radicals and had undermined the genetic reengineering process with impunity, all within the department of genetic development at the center, Salter's department. Christine had countered that her ignorance hardly amounted to collaboration. But ignorance was not a defense on which Christine had ever relied. She said that she had not reported her findings to management because she had been sure there was an explanation. After all, Cruz had been a model employee and Conglomerate. She'd wanted to confirm the numbers, and if there had been a problem, of course she would have reported it, corrected it, and assured the Conglomerate management of her commitment to the team and the team's commitment to profit.

Then the Conglomerate party interrogator let it fly. The bastard asked, "So, who do you think would want Cruz dead?"

Christine's knees buckled. The Conglomerate interrogator took Christine by the arm and looked up at the security camera and shrugged. This was not the reaction he had expected. The investigator put his fingers to Christine's wrist; her pulse was racing and her skin was cold, a condition one could not easily fake. After the questioning, the investigator didn't think Christine knew about Cruz's role in the rebellion, and he thought this reaction proved that. And if Salter had been honestly ignorant of Cruz's activities, then what would the chairman make of this response?

The light was intense. Christine couldn't see anything. But she felt the investigator's eyes on her and she could feel his fingertips on her wrist. She would process the information about Gabriel later; now it was time to try to regain her composure.

"Excuse me; it has been a long day. Would you repeat that, please?" Christine asked.

"We were hoping that you might be able to help us determine what happened to Gabriel Cruz," a different voice asked, more nasal than the first.

"I thought you just said he was dead," Christine said.

"Missing, for now. But when you see the crime scene . . . ," the Conglomerate investigator added.

Christine didn't want to, but she was able to straighten herself up and pull her arm away. The elevator stopped, the doors opened, and they stepped out into the Pool. Christine flipped open her phone and called her boss at home. She couldn't contain this any longer, and she wanted to speak with her boss before she saw what had gone on in her department. Christine wasn't sure she would be able to manage that. Besides, her boss would agree that Christine should not have called until she was on the premises. And after all, it was New Year's Day.

.   .   .

CHRISTINE SAT IN her apartment now, in front of her open window. The red dress danced on the hanger. She looked out at the city, trying to summon the confidence to walk out into the day and go back to work. And then it hit her; what if her boss had acted as if she were unaware of the break-in at the Pool because she'd been in on it all along? She had to have been. Nothing happened at the New York Medical Center without her boss knowing it, even on New Year's Day. Of course the management committee would be cooperating with the Conglomerates, they'd have to be.

"First my colleague," Christine said, "and now my boss."

It was time for her to go to work.

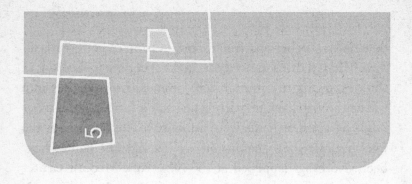

The Chairman

The chairman of the Conglomerate party descended from his Brooklyn office atop the Clock Tower Building; a converted factory in the DUMBO section of Brooklyn that faced the water and the New York City skyline. He stepped out onto Main Street and entered the waiting black town car; the chairman's driver closed the door behind him.

The red message light was blinking. A *ding* announced a new e-mail. Live feeds from international markets streamed across the screen; chatter in different languages came through the back speaker. The chairman ignored it all. He reached up and tapped his driver, who nodded and raised his hand in reply. He knew how to proceed as planned, without the chairman saying anything or being compromised, at least by the driver. He had done nothing but prove himself loyal to the chairman.

The precaution was to avoid providing any more detail than was already available to anyone who might be listening. It wasn't as if the driver were going to talk. He had never developed the ability to speak. The chairman had selected him from the service pool, when he himself had been a young political adviser. He knew fresh talent when he saw it, and the driver had been with the chairman ever since.

The driver navigated the town car along Adams Street to Tillary around Flatbush Avenue and onto the Manhattan Bridge. The black town car belonging to the chairman of the Conglomerate party was authorized to go wherever necessary, but such access did not presume freedom.

The chairman of the Conglomerate party had rotated a number of figureheads through the White House. He had more than planned their campaigns and written their speeches; he had manipulated them and their administrations. Every congressional committee head was in his employ, he had the majority vote of the Supreme Court at his disposal, he controlled the funding to every major program and pork barrel in both houses, and he had the media that covered it all in his pocket as well. But now the calendar had caught up with the chairman, as it did with everyone. He had reached his mid-fifties, the end of his terms as the party chair. It was time to pass the torch. He had introduced these requirements himself some fifteen years ago, to dispose of his predecessor. But he would not be removed if he could help it. The chairman had an idea, and it involved a positive outcome from the Cruz debacle.

He avoided the nagging message light, the streaming numbers, and turned toward the window. He could still see the flashing in the reflection of the tinted glass.

The chairman said, "The party needs me." There were many problems to be resolved before he left office, the Coots and the Dyscards among them. *They're like vermin,* the chairman thought, but he wasn't about to say that, as his driver had been a Dyscard himself, until fate had brought him into the chairman's life.

The driver's hand went up and then he turned his palm toward the chairman and looked in the rearview mirror, awaiting direction.

"I am sorry," the chairman said, knowing the driver was reading his lips. "Nothing for you. I was only talking to myself." The chairman looked up and saw the driver's eyes linger before returning to the road ahead. He didn't need to speak for the chairman to know what was on his mind.

The town car turned north on the Bowery and headed for the East Side. The chairman stared down at the flashing light, the streaming numbers, and the e-mails, one on top of the other. He watched the news images of the day as he listened to the shouting from the market floor. He was sure that his staff as well as his enemies would find out where he was, but if he could get there before they really knew, he might just stay one step ahead of this.

. . .

THERE WAS NO way that Gabriel Cruz could have known what had happened to Christine on New Year's Eve, because Gabriel wasn't sure what had happened to himself. The last thing he remembered was putting up a fight. He had been drugged, that much he knew, because it had taken him a while before he'd known how bad a beating he had taken. Even with the drugs, he had ached all over. He was beginning to feel more like himself now, and, with his eyelids closed, he listened to his surroundings. He tried not to guess at a sound's identification but waited for the source to come to him. It was difficult to listen to his instincts, because his pulse was pounding in his ears. He guessed he was in a medical facility, from the antiseptic smell and the tension in the air. He was bandaged and his wrists and ankles were restrained. He was in custody, clearly, but by whom, he did not know. He decided his best option was to wait.

There was a girl, X they called her, who shared the ER with him. That's when Gabriel realized he must be among the Dyscards. The girl was a new arrival too, admitted for medical attention, although she wasn't being treated as Gabriel had been. While the staff all wore masks around her—he could tell this from the muffled speech, and they wore masks around Gabriel too—they weren't as tense as they were around him. She had been brought in while he was unconscious. She said she was eighteen years old—at least she had been that morning. She said she felt a lot older now.

. . .

THE MUFFLED VOICES told X that through coincidence she and this Conglomerate Gabriel Cruz had been brought to the ICU simultaneously, and as a result it had been decided that it was best for everyone, including X, that she be quarantined for forty-eight hours to determine any effects from the interaction. Once Gabriel had been identified as other than a Dyscard, the Dyscard leaders had quickly moved to isolate the Conglomerate and decide what exactly they were going to do with him.

They did a complete physical on Gabriel. Other than being pretty beaten-up and drugged, he appeared to be healthy. If he were a bomb sent down from above, set to explode infection in the underground, he didn't appear sick. What testing the Dyscard medics could do found him sound. As a Conglomerate, he might be useful.

The girl had made her way to the cot next to Gabriel's gurney and gone to sleep. At first she had used the blanket as a pillow, but somewhere along the way she had pulled it out from beneath her head and covered herself with it.

He watched her sleep, and there was something about her face that reminded him of Christine. He guessed he missed Christine more then he knew, he was seeing her face in the face of others. He wondered what she would make of this place.

Gabriel listened to the sounds around him, tone, memory, memory, tone, sounds that hummed like a chord. He half expected to hear the groan as patients turned over on metal bed frames that moaned no matter what institution

Gabriel had slept in, no matter where they had schlepped him to, or from, as a kid. Gabriel saw again the endless hallways all painted the same industrial green. He heard the muffled sound of shuffling shifts and remembered the "wah-wah" of the court-appointed therapists who always talked but never listened. It seemed to Gabriel that a lot of people trained in the skill of listening were taught to ignore what they heard.

Adoption had not been an option when Gabriel was a child. In a consumer society where parental choice came complete with purchase of an offspring, a product of designer genes with cut-and-paste behavioral applications specified to individual taste, one wasn't expected to take in the castoffs of others, the kids who had been left behind. Gabriel had been a Dyscard, maybe even the first one.

Proxy-Care, the Conglomerates had called it, and it was a forerunner of the Family Relief Act, a state home system created to assume control of minors who were not being cared for through reasons of death, disability, divorce, or dollars—or more specifically, lack of dollars.

Gabriel was among the first group. His parents were dead. At least that's what he'd been told growing up. This made Gabriel learn to have a goal, and that was to make it to be old enough to leave his state-run home and come out from under the Proxy-Care system.

Now Gabriel listened to the sounds around him, and when he sensed it was safe, he opened his eyes and raised his head.

He had to admit that the equipment in this Dyscard medical unit was first-rate. The cabinets were stocked, and the doctor was a few years younger than Gabriel but more than capable. From what Gabriel heard, there was a social organization and a hierarchy within the system. It seemed to be a societal structure that resembled the order that had just kicked these kids out. It only made sense, when Gabriel thought about it. For what social order could there be other than one that mirrored what had preceded it?

"Excuse me, please," Gabriel called out to the girl. "Can I ask you a question?" X slowly rolled over and looked at him. Was he calling her?

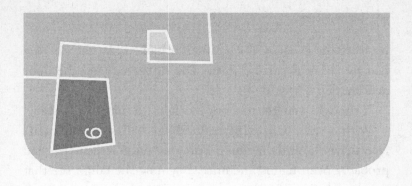

Conglomerate Manipulation

Christine was walking toward the med center, having avoided being hit by a car, then a bus. She pulled her collar up and put her head down, and so she didn't see the man step in front of her, until she walked right into him. She stepped back. Was he a cop? A mugger? Worse? He put his hand out, and Christine took out her I.D., realizing in the age of the Conglomerates that anywhere was an opportunity for a checkpoint.

He entered a short text message into his cell phone before he stepped aside and ushered Christine toward a black town car parked outside the entrance of the New York Medical Center. The motor was running and a cloud of steam puffed up from the exhaust. She realized it looked like the car that had just almost run her over. The driver opened the door and handed Christine in.

"I thought you got to work by eight," a man's voice said.

With a start, Christine realized she had seen this man's face maybe a million times, but only on a screen. He had probably been handsome once, but now she could see that despite surgery his skin was veined, and there were dark lines beneath his puffy eyes that the makeup couldn't hide. His pupils were dilated behind contact lenses. His hair was colored, a good job, but nevertheless Christine could see it was more than a style choice.

What would the chairman of the Conglomerate party want with me, Christine thought, and almost flinched when she realized what.

In the dark of the backseat of the black town car, behind the tinted windows, the lights blinked on the phone console, the monitor installed in the rear streamed numbers and images, and the chairman ignored it all. He looked at Christine; she tried to smile back at him.

"Please sit back," the chairman said, and he motioned to the driver, who had been watching in the rearview mirror. The town car began to move, headed along Thirty-fourth Street.

"While you can't always believe everything you hear," the chairman said, "I have heard that you have had your difficulties lately, professionally and personally." The town car made a quick right and entered the Queens-Midtown Tunnel as Christine sank lower in the seat.

How do I answer this man? Christine thought. It was clear

that he was waiting to see what she would do and how she would react. Her gut was telling her to keep her mouth shut, while her brain was sending other impulses. She decided to say nothing.

"I can help you out of this . . . problem," the chairman said. "But I'll expect something in return."

Of course, Christine thought, but kept her silence.

The party leader went on. "At this moment, as far as I know, you and my driver are the only people who know we are here together. My driver and I have gone to great lengths to keep this vehicle secure, and we are in the tunnel, so I believe our conversation here is just between us. There is an element of risk in what I am about to ask. I did not inform your supervisors of this interview as it does not directly concern them." The party leader took a breath. "However, I understand that you may have to answer to them. If they do contact you, you are to call me directly."

Then the party leader handed Christine an envelope.

"What is this?" Christine asked.

"You can open it now if you like, but I'd preferred we speak while we are in the tunnel."

Christine ran her hands along the envelope. It felt like it was filled with cash.

Black market, she thought. *The chairman of the Conglomerate party is providing me with the means to deal with the black market?* This couldn't be about anything good. It also added to the evidence mounting against her. She looked at the interior of the car for the camera as a bead of sweat began to run along the ridge of her lip.

"Are you all right?" the chairman asked.

"I guess I get a little nervous whenever I'm given money by a man I've never met," Christine said.

The chairman of the Conglomerate laughed. Christine could see in the mirror that even the driver was smiling.

"What am I supposed to do with this?" she said, and held up the envelope.

"That is a little something for your trouble that can't be traced to me," he said.

"This isn't necessary," Christine said, handing the envelope back to the party leader. "I am at your service." *He probably doesn't see this very often,* Christine thought, and she wondered why the car didn't ram into the tunnel wall, the driver was so intent on watching everything in the rearview mirror.

"I insist," the chairman said, dropping the envelope into her lap as they burst from the dark of the tunnel into the daylight of Queens. The chairman of the Conglomerate party put one finger over his lips and his other hand on Christine's leg. The sudden light disoriented Christine, and so did the chairman's hand on her thigh.

Is this what he wants? Christine thought. *Is this what the money is for? Why me?* Cash could buy anything. The car swung into a sharp U-turn, causing Christine to lean into the chairman's side as the town car went through a toll plaza and back into the dark of the Queens-Midtown Tunnel.

"I need a surgical procedure," the chairman finally said, removing his hand from her leg. Christine let out a breath in relief. "Of course," she said. "How can I help you?" Then she thought, *He has the greatest minds in medicine at his disposal. Why me?*

"I'd rather this be between you and me," he said.

"I am an administrator of genetic research and development," Christine said, "as I am sure you know. I am not a surgeon per se. I can refer you to a physician."

"We don't have much time," he said. "I am interested in you for your expertise in genetics. Like many, it seems I was born with a faulty gene. I would like it repaired," he said. "For the good of the state."

"You want a gene graft?" Christine asked.

"Precisely," the chairman said.

"What would we be genetically reprogramming?" Christine knew he was asking about the experimental genetic cleansing in which a graft of enhanced genes was put into the person's original DNA and then the DNA was reintroduced back into the patient's biology as it replicated itself, creating a real new you.

"What I need is to be my former self, but better," the chairman said. "And that's where I need your service. I've done extensive research. What I would like for you to do is swipe a strand of my DNA, wipe the sample clean of all genetic defects, and set back the body's aging process. Then implant it back to override and reproduce itself throughout my system."

While they had had success with overriding behavioral problems linked to heredity, reversing aging with a genetic graft was difficult. But was she in a position to disagree?

"In addition to my small gift," the chairman said, gesturing to the envelope in her lap, "maybe there's something else I can give you."

"And what might that be?" Christine asked.

"Information on your friend Gabriel Cruz," he said.

. . .

THERE IS AN edge along the borders of nations, a point where one's territory begins and another one's ends. But sometimes the boundary is unclear. There are times when there is no line along the latitude or longitude, and so the borders of one world blend into the borders of the next. That interrelated region can be a land of conflict. To the Dyscards belonged the night, or so it was believed and so it was justified. For it was the Conglomerates who had left their children to the dark, and thus what the dark bore belonged to the Dyscards. The night was their natural resource. Necessity had forced the citizenry to claim shadows, shade, cracks, crevices, and the underground as their own. If a Conglomerate was to trespass into the neighborhood of the night, such an individual would have wandered from their rights.

Working within the free zone, as the Dyscards called it, was a group of Dyscards that was considered criminal by the Conglomerates and held in the highest regard by the Dyscards. This group possessed a formidable physical presence, and as in any society, this was a characteristic that people admired and feared. While the Conglomerates would consider them thugs, the Dyscards thought of them as justice.

These protectors, known as the Border Patrol, were made up of those who had been among the first to fall victim to the discard option of the Family Relief Act. They had been among the first group of young people who had been "selected" to be sent away, or in effect deleted from the family unit. They hadn't done anything to threaten their parents, or teachers, or the community. It was their differences that had determined their selection. Some were felt to be too big to control and too opinionated to be that big. That begot the Border Patrol.

As outsize physicality and power always had the potential for abuse, all who shared these muscular attributes had been encouraged to work in the Border Patrol and funnel their rage and brawn toward those who might threaten the Dyscard community or trespass against it. The Border Patrol had made a commitment to protect all in the Dyscard world; they were enlisted in the defense of the night. As a shadow moves unnoticed in and out of the darkness, the Border Patrol penetrated the spaces in between.

They sometimes extended justice without question, which was usually not questioned by the rest of the Dyscards either. Most times there wasn't anyone left to ask questions. The network of the night belonged under their jurisdiction. They could feel the intentions of intruders, by instinct. They saw themselves as white blood cells attacking a virus for the health of the underground nation. They operated with impunity. Their method of defense was quick, quiet, and clean. The Conglomerates didn't respond to the Border Patrol's justice, as a trespasser was in violation of the unwritten law against congress with those whom society had discarded.

The idea of Dyscards was born in a state of panic in an age of disposability. The Conglomerate culture was self-centered; there was no room for the mention of Dyscards within the Conglomerates' marketing campaign espousing contentment within the Conglomerate nuclear family structure. Hence, there was no official recognition of the existence of the Dyscards.

Still, the number of Dyscards was alarming. The reproductive management program, launched at the New York Medical Center, was lauded as the paradigm of genetic engineering and personal responsibility. The Conglomerate populations believed with sincere conviction that those who participated in the genetic engineering program were using their roles as parents to control, improve, and hopefully eliminate the weak and self-destructive personality traits that had caused problems in the past.

The reduction in the number of children resulted in a reduced demand on resources. Wouldn't everyone benefit? Or so was the Conglomerates' marketing theme. Mistakes happened when the unknown was involved, and those mistakes could be eliminated. While the unknown might have been all right in mathematics, in genetics the unknown often resulted in something one had to live with, which might be unpleasant, or worse. Hence the Conglomerates' administered discard option. Also, there was no formal or informal acknowledgment that the new genetic engineering system could ever produce a problem. Consequently, there was no formal or informal acknowledgment of the Dyscards.

For making public—on the Web, in the media, or among friends—any genetic faults, such as behavioral or physical problems—everything from autism to addiction—the penalties were social as well as legal. Peer pressure on parenting was such that the disclosure of a problem child was tantamount to an admission of parental failure. The Conglomerates would contend that the problem was in the family or the environment and not at the med center or in the government's interaction in people's lives. The legal ramifications of disclosure of a problem allegedly caused by the Conglomerates were economic, and charged against your compensation account. In addition, the reporting couple forfeited any right to participate in any state-run prenatal program in the future.

A family could be eligible for the discard option for an offspring that was diagnosed to be a problem child. The criteria for diagnosis could change according to the amount the family was willing to charge against their account and their future income. All professional and personal accounts were controlled by the Federal Reserve bank's department of digital management. After payment was completed, the official family record was wiped clean of the problem child and the couple's eligibility to become parents was reinstated. For an additional fee, the couple could be referred to a state-run genetic development center, with New York Medical being the best. As for the bad kids, it wasn't as if they would be missed. Parents had been convinced that a problem child would be brought to a better place that was more suited to his or her personality.

The presence of the Dyscards was categorically denied. After all, some of the Dyscards might be considered proof that the Conglomerate technological intervention had gone wrong. Not all children were born through manipulated means, to be sure—only parents who could afford that option were allowed to participate—but any family could have a troubled teen. There was no immunity to that. Not everything worked out as planned. The Conglomerates didn't want to be reminded of that.

What about the neighbors? They chose not to ask, if they even noticed that a child had disappeared. While people loved to gossip, no one wanted to turn anyone's attention on themselves, their children, or their own homes.

THERE WERE TWO young people who had been among the first to arrive in the underworld and who had eventually begun to try to get things there organized. They were precocious kids, among other discard optional criteria, and they called themselves At No, for atomic number, with brave hopes to hold the center, and Descartes de Kant, a wish for a wise and philosophical perspective that ran the gambit. They soon went by A and Dee, and together they had implemented a social structure and given strength and a unified will to this band of irregulars joined by need, trust, and a belief in the unthinkable. Together, A and Dee set about organizing and socializing the forsaken, unifying the isolated. As with the Border Patrol, soon no one argued with them. This provided order, wisdom.

At first the Dyscards had laid claim to abandoned subway stations, tunnels, and lengths of inactive track. But as the population grew, so too did the demands for space, yet they had established an immigration policy that accepted anyone that the state rejected. A and Dee sent some of the best members of the Border Patrol to the more recent communities established in Detroit's abandoned auto plants and overgrown industrial parks, in the houseboats that lined the river walk in San Antonio, Texas, in downtown Seattle. They were determined to organize the Dyscards into a power that was greater than the Conglomerates' plans.

After a couple of years of the discard option, and as the revenue streams grew—money flowing to the Conglomerates from the personal accounts of families involved in genetic manipulation—the subterranean population also grew. Space became the Dyscard nation's greatest problem. The territory was in flux; the community was a commuting culture of tunnel nomads. They took whatever transportation they could steal, though Dee preferred to call it appropriation. While there were Dyscard hubs around New York City, buried beneath the subway intersections at Grand Central, Columbus Circle, and Union Square, as the population grew, the Dyscards were forced to establish outposts aboveground, stretching from Van Cortlandt Park in the Bronx to Far Rockaway in Queens, with a beachhead on the sands of Coney Island. And so, the Dyscards moved from place to place. It seemed that in no time there was no room and the Dyscards were forced to annex the night. They moved onto the old piers along the boat basin on Seventy-ninth Street up to the old pollution control plant on One Hundred Thirty-fifth. They had to relieve the pressure pent up from a day in the crowded underground, staying out of sight and off of the streets in daylight. Whenever the sun went down, the kids came out wherever they could. This was mostly on piers and in parks. And if while the kids were out and about something of value should present itself, they were to consider it an opportunity for all and to remember that, as Dee said, "the hunting and gathering instinct is genetic." This provided quick results for food, medicine, and equipment and inspired Dee's theory of appropriation, the application of which was that if the group had a need and the solution to that need should be close at hand, the relation of the solution to the hand was a gift and should be accepted accordingly.

The Dyscards who had been badly beaten, or who were among the seriously defective, were moved beneath the Triborough Bridge to Ward's Island Park. As Dee said, "It seems kind of fitting, an island with a name like that." Ward's Island became a place that would house the wards of this alternative state. The Border Patrol guarded the footbridge to the island from Manhattan. It was an easier location from which to protect and defend those Dyscards who were most vulnerable. Ward's Island Park was next to the state hospital and was connected to Randall's Island. That proximity to the hospital, field, stadium, and pool provided the Dyscards with space for services and supplies. The field became the staging area.

The seat of the Dyscard government, such as it was, was wherever A and Dee sat down. As Dee said, "What good is a government if it can't pack up and run?" But A and Dee wanted to stay close to the enemy and were determined to base their counterculture within Manhattan and near the Conglomerate home.

ABOVE AND AROUND the Dyscards, the Conglomerate city had grown in one long urban sprawl along the East Coast. Even though the whole world was encased within a wireless web of access and connectability, the majority of the citizens of the world insisted on living on top of one another. That was pretty much how it was from Boston to Atlanta, one long line of multiple housing, a super-urban stretch dense with people.

As the edges of the Dyscard nation expanded and the Conglomerate nation contracted around them, the Border Patrols were forced to go farther afield in defense of the Dyscard populace, and this brought them closer to the day-to-day life of the city. And so the interaction between peoples grew in frequency and tension.

THE SOUND OF the tent door flapping woke Gabriel up, coming into his sleep as the image of a gold-fringed flag slapping in the wind. The design of the flag wasn't clear but the sharp smack accompanied by the heavy scent of the air made the dream feel even more realistic. Gabriel opened his eyes, expecting to see that flag, and instead saw the spires of the Triborough Bridge.

Even though he had been on Ward's Island for what felt like a lifetime, he still woke up with a start, not sure where he was. Today he felt as if he should be in a military camp, and then he remembered that in fact he was. The bridge looked like a Roman aqueduct joining Manhattan, Queens, and the Bronx.

Gabriel got up, walked to the flapping tent door, and tied it back. It was still dark and the air was thick with fog. The ground beneath his feet was wet.

The camp was still asleep, but that wouldn't last long.

Soon the newcomers who needed medical attention would be coming across the footbridge from Manhattan. Some would come unescorted while others would come on stretchers. All would pass through the Border Patrol. As the Conglomerates needed more revenue, more and more Dyscards were arriving daily. Almost all of the newcomers needed help.

When Gabriel had made that first crossing, they had had to clear the way for his arrival. He still thought of it whenever he saw the footbridge from Manhattan. Gabriel's reputation had preceded him; word that a Conglomerate from inside the New York Medical Center had been dropped among them had produced a fear that had spread like contagion. The Conglomerates hadn't disposed of one of their own in this way before. Would there be a flood of Conglomerates coming? Was he sick, or worse?

And when this was followed by the news that he was from Genetic Development, the panic had peaked. Some Dyscards wanted this enemy thrown back to the Conglomerates, while others said why bother, just dispose of him. Others pointed out that he was a Dyscard too. After what Cruz had told them, A hadn't known what to do with Gabriel. Dee had suggested that Cruz be moved to Ward's Island: this would remove him from the general population and control him as a subject at the same time. A had agreed and it had been done, which was usually how things worked in the Dyscard nation. Gabriel had been transported from the underground to Ward's Island in restraints to reassure the Dyscard populace, and he had to still have been feeling the effects of the Thorazine administered when he was attacked at the med center, because the journey to Ward's Island didn't hurt, or scare him, as much as it should have. He remembered being passed from guard to guard with a snarling crowd just out of range. When Gabriel got to the bridge, he had been more impressed by the New York City skyline in the soft morning light than he had been concerned about what might lie ahead for him.

He had been brought to a tent; two prime Border Patrols had been posted outside. He had been left alone. He'd heard muffled voices from beyond the tent, and it had been hard to make out any words through the January wind, but the cadence and tone had sounded familiar. The tent door had finally separated and A and Dee had entered the space.

"Welcome to Ward's Island," A said, "and to our primary health-care facility."

"Your new home. For now," Dee added.

"Thank you," Gabriel said. He wasn't sure if he was being sarcastic or not.

"You pose a dilemma for us," A said right away. "While you are, or may be, one of us now, your origin as a Conglomerate is too close to the source of our problems for the comfort of some. To be honest with you, there is even greater concern that you are, or were, a Conglomerate employee at the New York Medical Center, the department of genetic development. It has many on edge."

Gabriel told them of his work, from the inside, against the system. He didn't think they believed him.

"I didn't just go along with the people who abducted me either," Gabriel reminded them.

"Another thing in your favor," Dee agreed.

A continued, "It has been decided that you will be given an undetermined probation period during which you will be housed here on Ward's Island, where you will be assigned to the community service area. You will be expected to assist and help in the medical emergency unit. Your movements will be monitored. Your cooperation is advised." Gabriel was about to point out that his cooperation would be impaired by his confinement on Ward's Island, when two guards entered the tent. They approached Gabriel and started to undo the restraints he had been in since he had regained consciousness. It seemed to hurt more as the blood rushed back into his arms and hands than it had when he had first been confined. Gabriel shook himself and stood up; a security guard pushed him back into the chair.

At this point there were plenty of things that Gabriel wanted to ask; just what kind of justice was this? Hadn't they said monitor his movements, not forbid them? Wasn't he really on their side? Hadn't he convinced them of his sympathies, with the risk he had taken and the price he had paid for his actions at the med center? He thought of Christine and winced.

"Thank you," Gabriel said again, while he rubbed his wrists. This time there was no hint of sarcasm in his tone.

"You'll start performing community service immediately," Dee said. Then A and Dee walked out of the tent, the guards following behind.

And so Gabriel had begun. He had barely been able to drag his bruised body around, but he hadn't thought that calling in sick on his first day was an option. He couldn't imagine that he would come across people who would be in as bad a shape as he was.

A lone Border Patrol guard led Gabriel to a tent that looked very much like the underground emergency facilities back in the subways. Inside, the tent was divided into two sections. In the first there were sleeping bags on top of cots, from one wall to the other, arranged to allow for narrow aisles. At various points chrome poles held clear bags connected to IV tubes. As Gabriel scanned the space, he saw one attendant sitting on a stool tending to a patient. There was an antiseptic smell in the air, punctuated by the groans and moans of those too sick to care how they sounded. Gabriel flinched as a guard grabbed him by the shoulder and pointed to the woman. She was younger than Gabriel, and she was hunched over the cot.

"How can I help you?" Gabriel asked her.

"Get me six trained people and come back immediately," the woman said, never looking up from her patient. "More if you find 'em."

Gabriel looked confused; but the woman was too busy to notice.

"Don't worry," the woman said, and she looked up at Gabriel. "They told me who you are and where you come from, and you may be better trained than most to help us out here. Still, we need help. Although, working in a lab is no training for this place."

As she turned her attention back to her patient, she said, "Until such time that you can do things on your own— which I hope will be soon—I will not hesitate to hand you back over to the guards, should you give me the slightest provocation. There are those here who would be happy to see you gone, or worse. Go wash your hands and put on some gloves." She pointed to a portable hot water heater and sink. This was the first chance Gabriel had to get at soap and water, and he used some paper towels to dry off. The woman was peeling back the edge of a sleeping bag.

Fruits of your labor, the woman was about to say, looking at the new arrival. When she looked up and saw Gabriel's expression, she didn't say anything. She hadn't expected that look on the face of a Conglomerate, especially someone from the gene shop.

Gabriel leaned over and looked into the patient's eyes. He took hold of the edge of the sleeping bag as carefully as he could, to make sure he didn't disturb the girl any more than he had to. He looked at the rows of patients, some of whom were the results of genetic manipulation gone horribly wrong. This was the case of the girl before him. Some had been beaten so badly by their parents or the Conglomerate handlers that they required emergency help. Some were coming out of the grip of addictions. Others were dealing with the extreme shock of their young lives.

Gabriel looked at the woman next to him and shuddered; she looked at Gabriel, trying to determine just what his reaction meant.

"My name is Dr. Walters," she finally said with a slight nod, surprised by her feelings. "It's my real name, by the way, though I did add the 'doctor' part. Might as well. I do the work of one, and studied it too. But they wouldn't let me into their medical schools, and, besides, who'd want a problem doctor. Or so they thought. Shows you just how much they know."

"I suspect from how this place looks that you're more of a doctor than many I've met," Gabriel said, thinking of his past life. He looked down at the girl. "Besides, I have heard of you, Dr. Walters," Gabriel said.

Now it was the woman's turn to blush.

"What's over there?" Gabriel asked, pointing to the canvas wall that divided the room.

"Pediatrics," Walters said. "We'll get to that." She had planned on bringing him in there right away, to maximize the impact of what he had done, but she had changed her mind when she'd witnessed how Gabriel took to this girl. When Dr. Walters did take Gabriel behind the wall and he saw the infants swaddled in rows of makeshift incubators, Gabriel became a true Dyscards recruit.

GABRIEL WAS STILL on Ward's Island under house arrest, but the terms had gradually been relaxed. By now he looked like just another Dyscard, and there was plenty here to keep him busy. Gabriel liked the work and he applied himself as if he had something to prove. Besides, it kept his mind off Christine. He learned as much as he could from Walters, even though she had to be ten years younger than he.

Now Gabriel had earned enough of Walters's respect and trust to be assigned a task away from the island. Two Border Patrol guards accompanied Gabriel on that short trip to Columbus Circle and back to deliver medicine to a clinic beneath the station. Everything went well. Gabriel did as he was told and hoped more missions would follow. They did. Gabriel started to travel the underworld to Dyscard outposts. He dropped in on the ER he had come to on the day he had arrived; they didn't seem too comfortable with seeing him. Gabriel wanted to ask them about the girl X, but he knew it was better for her if he didn't show any interest.

Gabriel took notes wherever he went. Even if Gabriel didn't have much time, he took out a folded-up paper and lead pencil and scribbled his impressions, captured images and ideas, sometimes the faster the better. In time Gabriel's missions for Walters became more sensitive or dangerous, and the Border Patrol continued to escort him. They were never comfortable with outsiders, especially someone with Gabriel's past, but Gabriel's training lent itself to the task of relaxing the guards' behavior, and he learned quickly how to move in and out of situations without jeopardizing the team. It wasn't too long before he had earned respect from the guards as well.

All of these experiences gave Gabriel the confidence to try to contact Christine. He couldn't stop thinking about her. He wanted to see if he could contact her without getting caught.

He planned his visit to Christine, and he worked on his note to her. He wrote her a poem. He wanted Christine to recognize it was from him, but he didn't want it to be too obvious a message, or a threat to anyone, and he wanted to give her a sense of what was going on below her and around her.

One night Gabriel made his move. He made it into her hallway, left the note beneath her door, and vanished again.

Gabriel hadn't heard anything back. He knew that it would be impossible for Christine to respond to him, but that hadn't stopped him from hoping she would find a way. He knew he was crazy for trying, but there were so many things he wanted to know. What had happened to her at work and with the police? He also wanted to explain things. He wanted to ask her if she had found the note, if she had not changed her mind about him. He wanted to ask her to join him here, which was the craziest thought yet. Christine probably wanted to have him arrested, if not shot. Even if he could convince her to see him, it was foolish to think this was a viable plan. Just imagine how the Dyscards would feel about the director of genetic development being among them. Still, Gabriel wanted Christine to see just what was going on, and he felt confident that if she did, she would want to help.

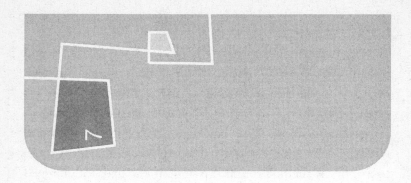

When Patsy and George Arrived Out West

The Scottsdale Municipal Airport was not equipped to deal with a plane the size of the C-5 Galaxy. The captain made it work. He could see the buses here to transport the Coots to the registration and processing area.

The airport looked like any airport, but this one functioned differently from most. One entire terminal was devoted to processing the Coots and relocating them to their new communities. There was no welcoming committee. It was strictly administrative. The small size of the crew on the Galaxy was evident now as they each took an aisle, making sure that the arriving retirees were all in their seats. Those who objected were medicated, and others were given additional restraints.

"Stay calm," George said to Patsy, and he put his arm around her shoulder. Patsy seemed normal, her muscles were relaxed, but George's pulse was racing and he knew that his message was in fact directed at himself.

"Let's stay together," George said, and he realized he was saying this for the thousandth time, and that this too was self-directed. Still, he hoped the repetition would make an impression on Patsy, who responded by putting a hand on George's knee.

The Galaxy stopped thirty feet from the end of the runway and the waiting buses. The captain shut down the engines. The temperature aboard the plane rose quickly as it sat beneath the blazing Arizona sun. George heard a hydraulic hum and the nose of the plane started to separate from the rest of the fuselage. The desert sun poured in. George heard metal scraping against metal as the nose continued to go up. Patsy and George watched the plane split open before them.

A team in hazmat suits carried out the processing of the new arrivals. They swept through the plane as if it were a hot zone, and in most instances they didn't say anything to the arrivals. Rather, they would scan each I.D. card and produce an identification bracelet. They'd slap the bracelet around the wrist of the new arrival with as little contact as possible. The arrivals who were violent or abusive were transferred to wheelchairs, strapped in, and removed from the plane. This kind of treatment served as a quick incentive to get cooperation from the newcomers. But the biohazard-suited agents didn't really need to provide much more incentive.

A white-suited visor-faced agent stepped up from the seats behind Patsy and George. "We'll need to ask you a few questions," he said. "We need to get you set up in the system."

George wanted to respond, *That's okay. Don't bother.* But instead he said, "Fire away."

The agent asked a series of questions—their identification, place of origin, personal health—and George answered the questions as quickly as he could. He did not want to detain the agent or allow any further detection of Patsy. The agent seemed eager to move on as well. He scanned their registration cards and snapped I.D. bracelets onto their wrists.

As the white-suited agents worked their way to the back of the plane, one of the buses that had been parked at the end of the runway moved toward the Galaxy. The bus was black with tinted windows and "FBI" stenciled on the side. This didn't make George feel any better. The bus door opened and a team of agents disembarked. They had Plexiglas shields and automatic rifles, and they had video cameras too. They had the same biohazard suits worn by those who had just administered the bracelets, except theirs were black with black tinted visors and "FBI" emblazoned on the back.

The agents advanced toward the plane with the shields in front of them. The captain and another man stood at the edge of the open front of the plane. The captain started to move, and all of a sudden the agents stopped, dropped their Plexiglas shields into upright positions, put one knee to the ground, and brought the butts of their automatic rifles up to their shoulders. They were pointing their guns at the captain and whoever was at his side.

Everything stopped, including George's breath. It lasted only a couple of seconds but it still gave George a pain in the chest. Then the captain moved toward the ramp and jumped off the edge to the runway below.

At first George thought the captain must have fallen and gotten hurt as he went down, but then George watched as the person with the captain went down the ramp and fell to the runway as well. After the two men were down, the agents moved toward them. When they reached the men, their weapons pointed at the captain and his companion, they leaned over and searched them, one at a time. The agents must have found what they were looking for, because they led the men away. Two agents, the one who had searched them and the one with rifle at the ready, pointed at the man who had been with the captain. Then the captain followed them, and a lone agent closed up the rear.

George could see that the captain was looking back over his shoulder as they led him away, and George could've sworn that the captain was looking for Patsy.

IT HAD BEEN hard, even for the navigator, not to notice the FBI bus parked in front of them. He had looked from the bus to the captain and thought they'd finally come to take this old Coot away. It wasn't until the captain looked over toward him with a quizzical expression that the navigator thought about the container of jeans in the cargo bay.

The cargo was to be unloaded by the ground crew, who would come aboard and make the exchange: a container full of jeans for an envelope full of cash left in its place. Through an elaborate network of distribution, the jeans would wind up gracing the legs, calves, thighs, and the better sides of people who had to work in this forsaken place. They needed something to help them get by, and for the privilege of covering themselves in someone else's pants, they were ready to pay a handsome sum. You couldn't get jeans like these anymore, except on the black market: you had to have cash to shop in that store.

The incriminating envelope of cash was on its way and there was nothing the navigator could do now to stop it.

The kind of deal the navigator was involved in brought the cash back East and into circulation on the black market. It was a good business. One of the results of the U.S. currency transition to digital was a rapidly escalating rate of inflation as prices soared and income stagnated. The base of the digital standard seemed in perpetual flux, and this affected the rate of exchange for goods and services, or the rate for obtaining raw materials, which in turn negatively affected the quality of the goods and services. There was a big demand for hard cash. People still had faith in money, and they wanted to have and to hold their cash in their hands. People were hoarding it or spending it in the black market economy. Nobody knew how long cash would last, or how long the goods and good times the cash bought would last on the black market. At least with the illegal black market, the value of the goods and services could be determined. This wasn't the case in the Conglomerate marketplace, where you paid an exorbitant amount from a government-controlled personal bank account of questionable value for a product of questionable value.

But the workers found a resource in the camps, as the elderly smuggled whatever they could bring with them out West: phones, laptops, portfolios, artwork, and bonds, in addition to gold, cash, and jewelry. Cash was everyone's top priority. The Coots traveled with money taped to them, stuffed into the bottoms of their shoes, with diamond rings hidden away. And, in almost all cases, the valuables were intercepted. That was how the personnel who worked in retirement services obtained cash to buy the jeans and whatever else they wanted that they couldn't get through the usual Conglomerate channels.

Some of the workers stole from the Coots outright, in shakedowns or through more subtle means. It was a case of "Let me take good care of this for you, honey." Or, "What the hell do these Coots need cash for anyway!" This often summarized the prevailing attitude toward the elderly and their so-called personal property.

The supplemental income was in bootleg cash, and the FBI had a supreme interest in that. The black market was growing geometrically, and the cash was flowing back into the economy. The Conglomerates had to do something about all this. To be effective, the digital currency depended on the illegitimacy of the old standard, and if cash was thriving on the black market, supporting the commerce of illegal suppliers of goods and services, it threatened the people's dependency on the new economic system. The Conglomerates were leaning on the FBI to get a handle on this and to shut it off, and the FBI needed to have something to show fast. They'd been following the navigator for a while and thought of him as a sure thing, if small time. They knew he'd have contraband to swap for the cash and be a clean media opportunity to make an example of what happens to those who engage in illicit activity.

IN A FEW minutes the black bus stopped within a few feet of the Galaxy. George felt sorry for that captain, and for Patsy and for himself, but he didn't have time to feel sorry for long. The black bus with the tinted windows and the letters "FBI" stenciled in white across the side left in a blur, and the engines of the silver buses started up, one by one, like the sound of an orchestra tuning up. They climbed up onto the runway and made their way toward the plane in a single file of steel and chrome.

George wondered what had happened to their luggage. He saw carts parked underneath the plane and he saw men coming and going from the cargo bay, unloading boxes, bags, and suitcases, and placing them on the carts. However, it didn't appear to George that these men were going anywhere near the buses with the cargo they had removed. The cargo, and the carts, headed toward the terminal.

The bus that Patsy and George boarded filled quickly and pulled away from the open nose of the Galaxy with a jerk. The bureaucrats obviously didn't want the Coots anywhere near them, which was probably why they wore the biohazard zoot suits. George looked at the bus driver. He wasn't wearing a suit, but the driver was one of them, a Coot. What did they care about a Coot? George wondered if the driver's job, like the job of the captain of the Galaxy, was a perk or a punishment.

SIX TV SCREENS hung along the length of the ceiling of the bus, and they blinked to life and the logo of the Conglomerates filled the screen. Two stylized hands of indiscriminate race and gender engaged in a handshake, an icon meant to evoke an image of mutual success through cooperation. To George the symbol seemed to serve as just one more reminder that the current state of affairs was a done deal. Their fates had been signed, sealed, delivered. The logo dissolved and the black screen lit with a desert sunset above a golden landscape filled with cactus and boulders and rolling foothills bathed in twilight. Then the focus fell upon what appeared to be a neat little town of cul-de-sac town houses thriving in the middle of the desert Southwest.

"Welcome to Cootsland," the narrator's voice began.

"Can you believe they call it that?" George said to Patsy, but Patsy wasn't watching the screen; she was looking out the window. Why watch it on TV when you've got the real thing out the window?

In this commercial about the Conglomerate town, there weren't any cars or buses in the streets, but that didn't seem to limit anyone's activity.

"Our residents are active. There's so much to do," the narrator continued. Sidewalks were bustling with folks of every stripe, walking and rolling along in shiny wheelchairs, all in an orderly fashion. They were all old.

What's the purpose of this commercial? George wondered. It wasn't as if the Coots had to be encouraged to buy into all this; they didn't have a choice. Under the Family Relief Act, once you reached eighty years old, you were automatically registered for the program and the rest was just administration. If you were married, or partnered, you got to wait until you were both eligible. If you were lucky, you got to wait. *And that's what passes for luck, in the age of the Conglomerates,* George thought.

"And you can too!" the voice exclaimed, accent on inclusion.

As the cameras scanned the crowds of people, four faces repeatedly reappeared. There was no dialogue, just a lively sound track of ornamental keyboards under the plucked strings of an angelic harp. The story line featured the four as they went about their days. The screen split into quadrants to follow the four stories.

"There's personal attention," the voice went on, as the scenes portrayed four people coming to and going from sunny facilities, engaging in pleasant interactions with uniformed people much younger than themselves.

"Full health care . . ." Each person was involved in receiving some sort of health or human service. In one quadrant an African American man was receiving an eye exam. "Therapeutic programs . . ." In another square an Asian woman went through the slow restraint of tai chi.

"Individual nutrition counseling . . ." In the third box a silver-haired woman in a chrome wheelchair was being shown a chart by an eager young man in a white suit. The people providing the various services were all dressed in uniforms of different colors—white and soft shades of pink,

green, and apricot—and they appeared wholly appropriate
to the service or mood of the cheerful place.

"Whole-health service . . . ," the voice proclaimed.

The fourth quadrant was filled with a white-smocked figure beneath a benevolent smile, a stethoscope draped
around her neck.

George thought about his experiences with the staff so
far; the tinted visors, the gloves, the automatic weapons, the
camouflage flak jackets atop the black jumpsuits, the hazmat
agents and hot zone treatment, the abject fear that filled him
with dread. But the health care professionals from the video,
in their calm, cool colors, had smiles that were more menac-
ing than automatic weapons—manufactured smiles, velvet
lips that hid a razor's edge.

"We respect your quality of life," the voice went on.

On the screen, quartered and repeated all along his line of
sight, George saw what a cheerful place this could be, and
how things could work. All you had to do was get along.

"As long as you cooperate." The narration had changed in
tone; and it made George wonder how you were supposed to
know whether you were cooperating correctly or not.

"All you have to do is do your part." Cooperation with the
authorities, the doctors, the administrators, the security,
and the staff was shown as the way to a happy and secure life
here in Cootsland. This was the point, George realized. The
Conglomerates weren't selling the system; they were directing the Coots to buy into it.

"Cooperation is key," the voice said, and George didn't
know what scared him more, the armed agents in the black
jumpsuits, or this video.

While George watched the video, his stare transfixed, Patsy, no longer looking out the window, was transfixed on George. It hit him like a blow when he realized it had come down to this. Patsy turned away from George and looked at the buckle resting against her hip. She swatted it as if it were a bug, and the belt shot open. She rose from her seat and said in a strong voice, "Who's got the remote?" She waited a second and said, "Let's turn this crap off!"

The bus, which had been quiet, became completely still as everyone looked at Patsy. Then the passengers started to laugh, a nervous laughter at first, but pretty soon even the bus driver was laughing. Soon everyone was talking and there was so much chatter that George couldn't hear the Conglomerate narrator at all anymore.

IT WAS GOOD that everybody had been able to have a laugh on their way to their new home, because once they got there, nobody felt like laughing. George had seen the glare of mid-day Arizona from the bus. Now he, Patsy, and the other passengers stepped out into it. The dry, hot air seared the lungs. The angle of the sun through the clear air made the light blinding. The change affected everyone as people shaded their eyes, gasped for breath, or just simply sat down and covered their heads with their arms. It took George a minute to realize his eyes were adjusting to the light. Not many of the passengers had brought sunglasses, and few, if any, had brought hats. There were no chairs to rest on, no benches to sit down upon. There was no water to drink, or to wipe away the dust from their lips. There was no shade from the sun, or break from the heat. The atmosphere was disorienting, and the lack of a place to sit was disheartening. Everyone shuffled around from foot to foot, to relieve the pressure in one at the expense of the other. Everyone seemed to be looking for something, toward the buildings in the semicircle before them, or off to the horizon, waiting for their luggage to arrive. George realized they were looking for the place they had seen in the video.

Patsy and George were next in line to enter the single-story administration building. George felt a cramp in his stomach. What if they figured out about Patsy? He took a deep breath and let it out slowly. "One more hurdle," he said, and Patsy looked at him, leaned over, and kissed him.

"Don't worry, babe," he said. "Stick with me and let me do the talking. This has got to be the last one of these for a while." George suspected not one word he said was true. He realized that Patsy probably knew it too, but she had the grace not to say anything. Patsy's mind was entering a stage where everything seemed both familiar and foreign at the same time. He realized that everything Patsy did seemed to her as if she were doing it for the first time, but also that she would know what she was supposed to do if she could only just remember it. It was at the back of her mind; it just needed a nudge.

George felt that in some ways it had been a benefit to Patsy to fall prey to this disease simultaneously with her being moved out West. Since everything now was new to Patsy, the move from Staten Island to Phoenix did not appear to overly affect her. She did have trouble understanding anything completely, and was living by her instincts, but

Patsy's instincts were solid gold still, and right now, forgetting things that happened to her as they happened to her wasn't such a bad idea. She didn't have time to dwell on what had befallen her and her husband, because she was too busy trying to predict what was going to happen next.

And, George realized, at this point that was his problem too.

The door to the administration building opened and a white-uniformed attendant motioned for Patsy and George to come in. They both had a wave of goose bumps as the cold of the air-conditioning enveloped them. Even though Patsy and George had the benefit of sunglasses, adjusting to the unnatural light and the shade from the sun took some time getting used to, and this added to an overall disorientation.

They were led to a desk with a pair of seats facing it. They were told to sit down. They were each given a small glass of water to drink. George thought that the water was a way of getting the interviewee to feel more at ease and to have a sense of gratitude to the interviewer. It also made the physical act of answering the questions easier. Nonetheless, George was grateful for the water, the seat, and the break from the sun.

Seated at the other side of the desk was a woman about thirty-five years of age dressed in a white pantsuit. No biohazard zoot suit but a bona fide pantsuit, but not the pastels of the health care professionals in the video. The only visor she wore was a green-tinted plastic bill that shaded her eyes from the fluorescent light overhead and was held with elastic around her head. She was facing away from Patsy and George toward the computer screen and she had the keyboard in her lap. The woman was extremely pale, especially considering she was in Arizona. The blue light coming from her computer reflected against her white skin as if her skin were a movie screen. The woman was intent upon her keyboard and monitor. She stopped to turn on a scanner and asked Patsy and George to hold out their wrists in a piece of choreography to which they had both already become accustomed. The woman barely looked at them as she asked them to state their names and Social Security numbers. George thought he'd handle it for both of them and was thinking of a way to tell this woman, at which time Patsy said, "Salter, Patricia," and she barked out her Social Security number and date of birth.

The woman stopped with her rubber-gloved fingers poised above the board, and looked toward George. He had been so nervous for Patsy that he couldn't remember his Social Security number. He stammered out, "G-George Salter. I mean, Salter, George," which the woman typed in. He couldn't think of his own Social Security number. "Isn't the number on this thing?" George asked, holding out his wristband. Patsy said, "Oh," and George thought she was expressing concern, but she continued with, "oh, six, oh," and the series of numbers that he instantly recognized as his Social Security number. *And I'm worried about Patsy screwing things up,* George thought.

"You're lucky you're with this girl," the woman said, to which George replied, "Don't I know it!" He thought he would ask about reclaiming their possessions from back East, but before he could, the woman, still looking at her screen, said, "Not to worry. You'll have everything you need waiting for you at your new accommodations."

George wanted to say that wasn't the question, but the rest of the interview went swiftly and without a problem. Most of the woman's questions seemed to confirm that the information on the bracelet matched what the person wearing the bracelet said. George found this interesting and hopeful; maybe there were a few problems in the bracelet operation? Or maybe folks had traded bracelets between the plane and here? And he thought with excitement of the nerve it must've taken to do that.

Finally they were dismissed and told to go out behind the main building and wait for a van that would pick them up and deliver them to their new home. George took Patsy by the arm as they headed out the back door.

SITTING ON A bench in the shade of a shed behind the administration building, waiting for the ride to their new accommodations, Patsy and George were alone for the first time in hours. George slumped down on the bench, his elbows on his knees, his head on his clenched fists. They hadn't passed any cul-de-sac streets, or walkways teeming with people and energy like they had seen in the video on the bus. They had passed rows and rows of what looked like storage sheds, baking beneath the afternoon sun. George was about to say something about their stuff, when Patsy reached over and placed her hand on George's shoulder. "We were walking along Victory Boulevard in front of Clove Lakes Park," she said.

There must've been a hundred days during their life together when Patsy and George had walked through Clove Lakes, but George knew exactly the day to which Patsy was referring. "The sun had just come out after what seemed like days of rain," she continued. "And the ground was covered in leaves like a carpet of colors my mother would have chosen, all yellow and orange. But you didn't notice it because I had just told you that my period was late, ten days late, and I wasn't feeling too good. God, you were so serious. As soon as I told you that I thought I was pregnant, you took my arm so that I wouldn't slip on the leaves. And I thought, well, that wasn't quite the reaction I was expecting, but it was a good one."

George turned his head just enough to look at Patsy. He took a deep breath and said, "Holy—" But before he could complete the expletive, Patsy said, "And I believe we concluded that discussion of our mutual plans while waiting for a bus."

Just then a van pulled up, the door opened, and Patsy and George got in.

THE REALITY OF the attitudes of the agents, attendants, and administrators of the retirement program did not foster care or concern for the emotional needs of the arriving "retirees," as the video on the bus had advertised. In fact, they couldn't have cared less. If anything, it was worse than that. Most who worked on the transport resented the arriving Coots, even though the Coots provided these people with a livelihood. The Coots also constituted a whimpering, slobbering, crying, pissing group of people they couldn't wait to be done with. George saw that as an advantage. And that was what he learned on his first day in Cootsland, in the age of the Conglomerates.

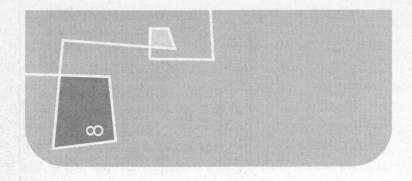

The Coots' Café

They had been in their new home in the Southwest for a while but they still hadn't gotten used to it. The change in climate between Staten Island and Arizona had them dehydrated, and even with sunglasses the light was extreme. Their living unit couldn't have been more different from their home back East. While that house would never have been called stately, it was large in comparison to the one-room unit they now called home. There was no home about this place, and Patsy certainly couldn't save it. There was no cat, no garden, no kitchen window to look out of. There were no photographs or souvenirs of the life they had shared.

But it was the time change that affected them the most.

They would wake up at five-thirty A.M., just as they had back in Staten Island—except now it was two-thirty A.M. Arizona time. Among other things, this made staying awake in the evening a problem. Come six-thirty in the evening, George could hardly keep his eyes open, or his head up. *Why not drug the Coots?* he thought. A sleeping subject was a less demanding subject.

But when George awoke each morning at five-thirty/two-thirty, he felt neither hungover nor stoned. He felt refreshed, renewed. Really, in fact, he felt kind of remarkable. It would take Conglomerate-approved funding to anesthetize the Coots, and that wasn't going to happen. Besides, the Conglomerates had the heat and the camp conditions to break the Coots' spirits and dull their will.

Not if I can help it, George thought.

A loud owl hoot was Patsy and George's wake-up call, and George often heard the owl before he opened his eyes. He wasn't sure if it was the owl that woke him or just his anticipation of it. George couldn't wait to get out of bed.

Back on their first night in Arizona the owl had sounded as if it were right outside their door, but when George bolted from their bed and opened the door, it was gone and the astronomy that greeted him was more than he'd ever seen. He took a step backward into the doorway and held his breath; he didn't even have to look up to see the night sky. The horizon was unobscured; the desert lay out in front of the open door. The heat of the day had burned the moisture from the air, making the details crisp. There was no glare from competing artificial lights. George stepped outside and stood in a blue dome.

"Hey, Patsy, get a load of this!" George called out, but Patsy didn't budge from their bed. He was looking at a sky he had seen every day of his life, but this sky was different.

"The Dippers are there, both of them, with a whole pot of Milky Way to ladle from. Entire constellations are up there." He could see the North Star, and he said, "If we followed that for a while, and then made a right, we'd be back in Staten Island."

"Home" Patsy said, and started to get out of bed as George went back inside. He ran the tips of his fingers in a circular motion on Patsy's back, and felt her pulse, fast and hard.

"It's all right." George said. "It's just nighttime. Go back to sleep and I'll wake you later. I promise, you won't miss anything." He wanted to get Patsy to lie down. *No wonder Patsy's confused,* George thought. "Get up, Patsy. Lie down, Patsy." George kept up the circular motion with his fingers, applying the slightest pressure on the middle of Patsy's back. He hoped the touch of his fingers would remind his wife of who he was.

The word "home" had broken through the disease and sparked in Patsy a desire to get there. Could this discourage the disease? But the word had also provided Patsy a charge of adrenaline, and what were the ramifications of this to a seasoned heart?

Touching Patsy had always centered George, and he still could feel that warmth.

"HOME" MADE GEORGE think of their daughter, and his thoughts turned cold. Although, the last time they had spoken, she had sounded better than she had in years. There was a new man in her life, a very successful Conglomerate, and she was moving on. George had thought right then that that might mean he and Patsy were moving on as well. He knew what was coming next. She said she had no choice; all those who had reached their age had to go. He knew she had been brainwashed, like the rest of the Conglomerates, thinking this was the right thing to do. Their daughter was calling to let them know that the papers had been signed and that he and Patsy would finally get to retire out West. George thought she was buying what the Conglomerates were marketing. When she told him about her plans to discard Ximena for her own good, George was sure she had lost her soul to the Conglomerate vision. She wouldn't listen when George attempted to argue for their granddaughter. She said she had to go, and they hadn't heard from their daughter, Judy, since. As soon as their property transferred to the state, their daughter would get her cut. "Blood money," George said. She hadn't even come to say goodbye. He wondered what they had done to her to make her so hard, but, then again, everyone became hard in the age of the Conglomerates.

George thought of his granddaughters. Christine had left home as soon as she could get away from her mother; she'd become a doctor and had done well. She had been their first grandchild and had been an unusual child. Patsy and George had been crazy about her. But her sister, Ximena, they had not really gotten to know. She was withdrawn almost from the beginning, and their daughter had never brought her around to Staten Island, the way she had Christine.

But all this also made George think about how Patsy had handled their daughter when she was an infant and toddler. Patsy had had no patience for baby talk. She had addressed their kids in a normal speaking voice. Patsy said that the children had grown accustomed to their mother's voice for nine months in the womb; she thought it confusing to change it once they were born. Unlike George, who had cooed and gawked and spoken in a high-pitched voice whenever he saw children. George would do anything to get them to smile, and usually wound up scaring them instead. Patsy had decided that the best way for children to be normal was to act normal toward them.

If Patsy's disease made her more like a child now, George resolved to treat Patsy as she would have treated a child—he would just speak to her in a manner with which Patsy herself was familiar. He decided he'd explain everything to her in detail as it happened. Why shouldn't that work? It had been successful before, and Patsy might recognize the process, and that could help her.

Just then George saw the flare of a dying star, so fleeting that to notice it was almost too late, and just like that star, his comfort passed in an instant. "What exactly am I going to be explaining, anyway?" he asked the night, which buzzed and twitched.

He knew that there were creatures in the desert he was unfamiliar with, but George jumped every time he saw a lizard. The vultures, too, gave him the creeps. It was worse out there than in the movies. *I don't know what any of this stuff is. So how am I going to describe it to Patsy?* George thought as he looked back at his wife. The shoulder of her nightshirt went up and down. He was glad she was asleep.

"ROSY UP THE mornin', hon," Patsy said a little later. Somehow she had slid over to his side of the bed, where he had fallen asleep.

"And the sun has begun to do just that!" George replied.

"I'm hungry," Patsy said as she looked at the landscape. "I could sure go for an English muffin."

"Apricot jam and coffee too, while we're at it," George said. A guy could dream. He knew they didn't have anything to eat in here; they would have to go to the communal dining room. They even had to boil their drinking water. George thought maybe Patsy would forget that she was hungry. But he was too!

He wrapped his arms around Patsy's shoulders and drew her closer to him. She came easily. They both looked toward the mountain, breathing in rhythm. George was surprised to see flecks of white in the windows of the houses across from them on the mountainside. George was surprised there were houses there at all.

THEY HEADED TO the camp's common mess hall. The Conglomerates called the place the Coots' Café, but it reminded George of the cafeteria at Susan E. Wagner High School back in Staten Island. It had the same drone of conversation and dragging feet. It even smelled the same, industrial cooking and sweat. He had tried to avoid going to the cafeteria because he thought Patsy might be found out, or that it was a breeding ground for infectious viruses. And he was afraid that Patsy and he would become separated or for some reason that she would be taken away from him, or worse. He wasn't sure why he felt this way, but that wasn't going to stop him from worrying about it. Where would they bring her? Where was she going to go? But George didn't want to think about an alternative to this place.

It wasn't as if there were doctors or attendants at the mess hall. All the work was done by other Coots. But there were cameras everywhere, and George couldn't trust the Coots who worked in the mess hall. Maybe they were offered perks for turning in other Coots to the authorities for "treatment"—if Coots argued, or if a Coot had serious health concerns—in order to make room for more paying customers.

Patsy and George worked their way through the line and got their oatmeal and water. George couldn't believe they served hot oatmeal in the hundred-degree desert, but hunger had its own demands.

They sat down at a table with like-minded souls. Some complained of the heat and the food, but George was glad for the company and it gave him a chance to compare Patsy's condition with others. She didn't seem any worse than some of the folks who shared the table, and George took comfort in that. Patsy stared at her dish, and George's comfort vanished. Feeding her would be a sure sign that she couldn't take care of herself; everyone at the table was eating their food; everyone was eating but Patsy.

George willed her to pick up the spoon, and when that didn't work, he whispered, "Like this," and showed Patsy how it was done. On George's second demonstration Patsy leaned over and stole the oatmeal from his spoon with a gulp and a smile. *This might work*, George thought, and decided to make a game of it. Patsy responded as if she were a queen worthy of such attention, and he couldn't tell what the men and women at the table thought.

One of the skinniest guys George had ever seen approached the table with a towel over his shoulder and a bucket in his hand. He even looked like a custodian from high school.

"Whatta ya think, this is a cruise?" he said. George doubted that anyone here, no matter how deep the delusions, would confuse this with a cruise. "Let's get a move on," the guy said. Yeah, George thought, it was just like high school.

EVEN THOUGH ALL of the possessions—photos and souvenirs, the tangible accumulation of Patsy and George's life—had never arrived, Patsy hadn't stopped looking for them, every day, in fact. George let her do it. He thought the review might lead Patsy to memories of their life and help keep her mind alive.

How Patsy loved those dishes, her periwinkle-blue china set. Truth was, George didn't miss them much, but he thought Patsy would enjoy seeing them.

Maybe she'd eat better on them, George thought. *And she'd probably eat better if we had a little food.*

He understood now that their lives had been stolen from

them, like so many periwinkle-blue china dishes. The contributions they had made in the world had been received without gratitude, and Patsy and George had been cast aside,
depleted goods. And there was a whole heap of such goods,
a desert full of used people, sent to turn into dust in the
Santa Ana wind. Most of them were too old or too defeated
to fight back, or even to resent it, but for George the won-
ders of this Western world kept sidetracking his anger.

George looked out the open door and listened to the desert
creatures. Patsy didn't like the sound of the owl; she thought
the coyotes sounded like lost babies, the bats like angry cats.
But it was the sound of those mourning doves that got her
goat. Their plaintive coo used to drive her cat crazy back in
Staten Island, and they still annoyed her. When they began
their song, Patsy's head would pick up. The cry seemed to cut
through her disease, and George, who used to hate them too,
now had come to enjoy the little drama between the birds and
his wife. He'd come to view it as an intellectual exercise that
worked the muscle in Patsy's failing brain.

George had decided that he was going to have to learn a lot
about his new environment if he hoped to relate it all to Patsy,
let alone help her survive. Also, George figured, he needed to
hone his intellectual capacities, what remained of them. This,
of course, presented an additional problem: Like how?

As usual, Patsy took care of that, and, as usual, in a very
unusual way.

GEORGE HAD DOZED off on the back step. He felt his shoulder
shake, and the movement brought him around. At first

George thought it was the middle of the night, and then he noticed how bright it was. He became aware that Patsy was sitting on the side of the step outside and was not in bed next to him. She had something on her lap and she was talking.

"Isn't this yours?" Patsy was repeating, and she was tugging on the sleeve of his shirt. There was a laptop computer on her lap.

George finally said, "What'd you say?"

George looked down and saw the old laptop computer. She must have thought this was his, as it was just like the one they used to have way back when. It must have been fifteen years ago, when their granddaughter Christine was a teenager and she used to e-mail her grandfather about school, or home, or just about her day. George loved those e-mails, and he would read them out loud to Patsy and she would join him in his response.

The laptop was clumsy and weighed a ton. "Where'd you find this?" George asked.

Patsy replied, "I don't know." And it looked as though she were going to cry from George's questioning. She must have felt as though she had done something wrong, from the way George was speaking to her.

"Thank you, honey," George said. "How'd you know I was looking for that?" Patsy seemed to feel better and pointed toward the kitchenette. George stood up, walked inside, put the computer on the kitchen table, and covered it with the blanket from the bed. The cabinet beneath the microwave was open, and he reached in and pulled out a tangle of two cables. One was to attach to the electrical outlet with a battery recharge box, and the other was the old modem and phone cable. George thought he could probably recharge the battery in the outlet that ran the microwave, and he would worry about the phone jack later. He wondered if whoever had left the laptop had also left instructions. George realized that they were probably on the computer. He wondered how he was going to get into the computer to read them. He was getting very excited, and then he froze. He twisted his neck as he looked all around him. Patsy flinched, startled. She wondered what George was looking for. What George was looking for was whether someone was watching. Could the security cameras have picked them up? There were no sirens, no alarms to alert the authorities. Were they busted?

"Well, what exactly could they bust us for?" George asked himself. "Let's see: For the possession of stolen property, possession of unreported personal property, possession of an unauthorized communication device? Insubordination? Treason?" George said, "For starters."

George peeled the blanket away from the laptop. It was a dinosaur but it looked to be in pretty good condition. He was going to open it, but then thought better of it. True, the Conglomerate Rangers hadn't broken down their door yet, but George decided he'd better wait until he calmed down.

"Holy . . . ," George said. "We have the phone hookup and the electric outlet right here by the cabinet." As soon as he had said this, he realized that this had been used for this purpose before. The cabinet was a communication station, a renegade outpost in the desert, and that made George nervous. "Holy" was right.

. . .

GEORGE WAITED UNTIL the middle of the next day to hook up the wire to the back of the computer. Since no one had approached them at their home or at the Coots' Café, he thought the authorities must not know about their finding the computer. His heart was racing as he pushed the plug into the wall. He jumped when the machine began to whirr. He had never been so excited at the sound of these synthetic strings before. In fact, he'd rarely heard them. Now it sounded as though he'd entered heaven.

George couldn't click through the fields fast enough. He went through all the simple steps and had all of the files scrolling in front of him, and he didn't see anything that he recognized. He went again to the beginning and started looking at the file names, line by line. Somewhere along the line Patsy got up and joined him.

"Start here," Patsy said, stabbing at the air. George ignored her. He was really starting to worry that he'd done something wrong. "Start here. Start here." Now Patsy was jabbing his side with her two index fingers.

He typed in the letters S-t-a-r, and even before he had entered the second t, a file popped up on the screen, and the file opened with a flash and a whoosh of sound of the word "welcome" as it appeared on the screen.

"If this should be found by the authorities," a voice said, startling Patsy and George, "there is little here that the authorities don't know. The point of this program is to inform the residents that life in the Conglomerate camps isn't the only way. There is an alternative to their tyrannical rule." It sounded like the voice was taking a breath. "The authorities have got to feel like prisoners too, stuck in the same conditions as the Coots." The voice paused. "There isn't enough manpower to track you down if you leave, or to care. Start to store what you need; prepare, rest up, come north, and join us. . . ." The voice trailed off.

"What're you supposed to do, talk to this thing?" George said. Then it hit George that they had become like spies awaiting instructions. There was an insurrection going on in their room. He could only imagine the penalty for treason here in the Conglomerate Wild West.

George typed in the word "next" and pressed enter, and what seemed like minutes passed before the voice resumed its narration. Patsy and George both jumped.

"Let's start at the beginning," the voice said as the screen filled with text subtitles to the audio. "You are now located in the Valley of the Sun in central Arizona." A map of the state appeared with the cursor blinking at their position. "You are in a Conglomerate-operated community of anywhere from fifteen thousand to twenty-five thousand residents. There are camps scattered throughout the state and neighboring region whose function is to warehouse the elderly." The voice took a breath, the locations turned colors on the screen, and the text waited for the next word.

"There is a segregationist approach to the makeup of these camps, but it is not a segregation based on race, creed, et cetera, but rather by ailment or disease. The authorities are responsible for deciding who suffers from what debilitation and sentencing the resident to 'the appropriate facility.'

This is a cost control mechanism to limit the medical staff needed for treatment, a mass-produced disease treated by the least amount of staff possible."

George looked over at Patsy and thought about the idea that the authorities could separate by disease. Why did the Conglomerates care?

"The Conglomerates rationale for this system of segregation is for the alleged care of the afflicted," the voice said. "They market the concept to Congress that it is better for the patient and the system to have the disease separate and centralized, to maximize the employees they have to handle the care." The voice took a breath; George didn't.

"You are currently in a holding facility, one that receives all comers prior to the determination by the authorities of where the resident belongs."

George was determined not to submit Patsy to any tests, or himself either. The two of them had avoided the authorities, so how were the authorities to know about Patsy? It was then that he seized upon the hope that this message was for him and would tell him how Patsy and he could get around this separation stuff.

"There's a guy getting out of a truck," Patsy said, and there was. George panicked, pulled the plug for the laptop out by the wire, and everything stopped. The screen went blank before it turned black. Patsy looked over at George. He grabbed the blanket and threw it over the machine and the countertop.

The guy was opening the back of a truck, pulling out a small hand truck. He dropped a large water bottle onto the hand truck, pulled out a rectangular box, placed it on top of the bottle, and started to wheel the hand truck up toward their door.

"Water," the guy yelled out as he made his way up the walk.

"He's delivering water," George said, as if he didn't believe it.

"Yeah, I am," the guy answered. Patsy looked past his wide-brimmed hat and the Conglomerate uniform, and she saw that the guy was one of them, a Coot. The guy said, "You're gonna have to help me too."

"What do you want me to do?" George said.

"Well, for one thing," the guy said, "you could get out of the way."

The man headed right toward the cabinet that the microwave was on, and when he was right next to the cabinet, he swung the hand truck around and brought it to a halt. He took a box cutter from his hip pocket and sliced the top of the box open like a surgeon. He wedged the water stand in next to the cabinet.

George began to sweat as soon as the water stand was next to the computer. At least that's how George saw it—as if the guy were headed right for the computer. *Did he know? George thought. Could he tell?*

"You all right?" the guy asked.

George nodded.

"Welcome," the guy said, "but we still got to lift this bottle up here." The guy reached over and plugged a wire from the stand into the plug below the microwave. That was where George had just had the computer plugged in. The laptop wire hung behind the cabinet. The sweat was rolling off George.

"You sure you're all right?" the guy asked George again. "Well, anyway, you're in business. Hot and cold water when you want it."

George thought this guy sounded a little like the voice on the computer. He wanted to hear more. "Why are they giving us water?" George asked. "There aren't any other amenities."

This was funny, the guy thought. There weren't many people who asked him anything. While his real mission was to network candidates up north to Dr. Dunne's medical refuge, he would look for the best and the worst—the best because Dunne needed individuals that could help, and the worst because Dunne's facility was the best for those who needed the most help.

The deliveryman said, "I didn't ask 'em why, but I'm glad they do. It keeps me employed and hydrated. If you ask me, and you did, the real reason is Congress needed a pet project as part of the Family Relief Act." The guy took a breath; he wanted to make the most out of this chance to give his opinion. "In this case it fell under elder care, health, and nutrition. The Conglomerates would provide drinking water, and as far as they were concerned that took care of both health and nutrition. Besides, somebody and their constituents have to be making out on this deal, and whoever sold them this piece of crap made out pretty well too, that's for sure." The guy tapped the top of the empty box. "Their day will come, though, when the people have their way," he said. He hoped he hadn't gone too far. Once he got started . . . "In any case, I gotta go."

"Wait a minute," George said. He wanted to find out if

there was a way he could verify the information he had just received from the file on the laptop. George was about to ask him, when he realized that no matter what this guy said, he might have been sent by the authorities to determine what their disabilities were, and how bad, and where they really belonged. George wanted him out of there. "Well, I guess you're busy," George said. "You'd better go. There's probably a lot of people waiting on their water."

"The people I work for," the guy said, "they don't hold much for marriage, family, commitment—or much else, for that matter. They'll take you away from your wife for most any reason. Erratic behavior, for instance," the guy said, looking at George not Patsy. "So, if you don't know, or remember, what it is you're talking about, the best thing is to keep your mouth shut."

"Well, I'll try," George said. "And thanks for the water. Can we expect to see you again?" He hoped to get the guy's schedule so he'd be better prepared next time.

Wife's kind of quiet, though fine-looking, the man thought, *especially for being a biddy and all. Who knows, Dunne might be able to use them.* It wouldn't kill him to keep an eye on these two, he thought as he looked at Patsy. No, it wouldn't kill him at all.

"Well," the guy said, "I expect you can be expecting me again. Thanks for the offer."

What offer? George thought. But instead he said, "Always welcome."

The guy tipped his hat toward Patsy and headed back to his truck.

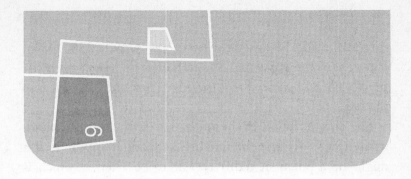

We

Christine found the envelope with her name written on it. It had been pushed under her door. Her first thought was to call the investigators and report her find, but she dismissed the idea and went into the bathroom. She reached into the cabinet beneath the sink for a plastic bag and the small doctor's bag she kept as an emergency kit. She removed a pair of rubber gloves and a surgical mask, put them on, opened the medicine cabinet, took out tweezers, and headed back to the front door. She picked up the envelope with the tweezers and dropped it into the baggie and went back into the bathroom. She held the baggie up to the light. She opened the toilet seat in case she had to dispose of whatever was inside. She used the tweezers and pulled the folded paper from the envelope. She unfolded the paper with the tip of a file and glanced at it quickly before she placed it into the bag.

She closed the lid of the toilet, sat down. It was a hand-written note. At first the line breaks made it appear as if it might be a poem. It didn't appear to be a letter, which is what Christine had hoped it would be. But the more Christine looked at it, the more she was convinced it had to have come from Gabriel. He liked to talk about poetry and writing and the books he had read. She wondered if it was a trap. But the handwriting was unique, and difficult to make out. In fact, she wasn't sure what it said. If it had been a setup by either the investigators or her boss, why would they have made it so hard to read?

Christine decided to look at it as if it were a math problem. "What's the given?" And it came to her. She focused on the letters of her name written on the envelope and transposed the letters from the envelope to the writing on the document, and between the two vowels and the handful of consonants, Christine was able to establish a key.

We

We abide among the abandoned.
A collection of the isolated,
We enrich the space reserved for the marginalized.

We make utility from others' excess, we
Equate the necessary with the beautiful, we
Excel at experience, made at a young age.

We pirate animation from rails long forgotten.
And traffic in ink and lead in
Lines connecting history to invention.

Left to learn from relics
And remains of stone,
Steel, cinder, ash,

We are a congress of kind,
Born from a common currency,
Grounded in laws: elementary, practical.

The writing ended there. No matter how many times
Christine read the note it always stopped at this point.

Christine hadn't eaten or slept since she'd found the envelope a few days ago. She hadn't left her apartment. Was it
from Gabriel, or was it that she wanted it to be from Gabriel?
She didn't care. She decided it was from him and hugged the
paper to her pounding chest.

But how had Gabriel been able to deliver this to her apartment without being caught? And if he'd come here, why
hadn't he stayed? Was Gabriel including her in "we"? Her
mind was racing. How did this fit with the chairman? Christine thought about her boss, and the board.

The poem had to be about the Dyscards, she thought.
So, Gabriel was with them. She had heard about the
Dyscards. Everyone had, but Christine knew a little bit
more about them than most, not only because she worked
at the med center, but also because the medical center was

held partly responsible for the problem. Christine had no idea where they lived after they were discarded, or how they survived. After reading this note, Christine still had no idea about the Dyscards. But now she was determined to find out.

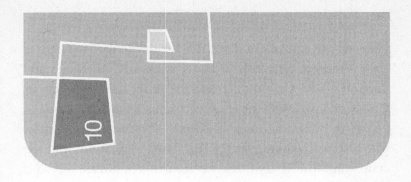

10

It's the Recovery
That's the Problem

The people around Christine pretended that nothing was different, while the truth was, nothing was the same. Gabriel wasn't there, victim of a violent crime many had watched happen. Christine felt she was a victim as well. Had Gabriel deceived her? She wasn't sure, and she wasn't sure she wanted to believe he had used her. She still missed him, and no matter how hard she tried not to, she thought of him often, daily in fact. Meanwhile, there was the bizarre note. And she had been implicated in the clandestine operation Gabriel had been conducting at the Pool, even though Christine didn't want to believe that Gabriel had been involved in that either; yet he was.

What the investigators implied was that Gabriel had not

followed the customers' directives for the genetic makeup of their children, and instead had "radicalized" the gene and tampered with the product and the profit center, which, as Christine knew, was the most egregious form of treason.

But the implications ran deeper. They wanted to know who else was working with Cruz. They were afraid that the center, and the system, had been further infiltrated. And if the Conglomerates thought this was true, Christine was afraid it might be.

And, of course, a link had been made between Gabriel and the underground resistance movement, the Dyscards.

Gabriel had achieved such access at the med center that the authorities assumed Gabriel must be part of a sleeper cell of Dyscards who were infiltrating the Conglomerate machine.

As a result, Christine had been investigated over and over, and was the subject of constant surveillance. She had been forced to forge her character into something it was not; duplicity had never been her forte. She had to be an actor, and play a part with every answer. Every move had to show that she had been transformed, redeemed. She had to remember every lie she had ever told and store it with the person and situation so as not to slip up. She was exhausted.

And if that weren't bad enough, Christine had to be in bed with the Conglomerates. It was the only way to survive and find out what happened, and where Gabriel was. She shivered for an instant. Of course it could be worse: she could really be in bed with the Conglomerates. The chairman, however, had asked her to join him in something that might be even more repulsive. She had hesitated an instant before she said, "No."

. . .

SHE LEFT THE bedroom and looked out her front door to see if there was another envelope underneath. There was not. The red message light on her phone was blinking, but she doubted that would be Gabriel. She had turned her cell off at about three o'clock A.M., thinking that might help her sleep. She flipped open her phone and crinkled her brow when she saw the number.

"Good morning," the chairman of the Conglomerate party's message began. He even paused as if he were expecting Christine to answer. "I am outside and will wait for you here."

Christine pictured the chairman sitting in the back of the town car; she thought of the silent driver. "First a shower and then a cup of coffee," she said as she considered her next move.

She knew she might be playing with her life, to string the chairman along, but she felt that at the moment she might have a slight advantage she wouldn't have for long. The chairman had gone too far with her, regarding his desire to continue his chairmanship through genetic manipulation toward youth; he could not retreat without serious consequences, but the guy had enough of the bait to salivate. Right now Christine was the best thing the chairman had going.

"There is no time like the present when your future is in doubt," Christine said, and got herself ready to go to work.

. . .

THE BLACK TOWN car was double-parked outside Christine's building. The engine was silent. When Christine approached, the door opened. A blade of white light fell onto the street, and then the door closed and the light went out.

"Ah," the chairman said. "Here you are."

"Good morning," Christine said, "What can I do for you?"

"What is the date?" the chairman replied.

"The end of June," Christine said, thinking this might allow her some time while providing him with a not-too-distant goal.

"I don't want to wait that long," the chairman said.

The truth was that she wanted time to find out where Gabriel was and then to try to get in contact with him. Christine said, "You think it's easy getting this arranged for you, without raising suspicions, but it's not. Especially after all the trouble I'm in. Certainly you know about that." Christine took a quick breath. "And your time and attention has only increased the speculation and suspicion surrounding me."

"You do this job well, and in a month," the chairman said in a monotone that pronounced each syllable, "you'll be the only one left standing. You and me, that is." To which Christine could only shiver. She realized her T-shirt was wet and cold from perspiration.

The temperature inside the car adjusted almost immediately.

"Tell me how the procedure will go," the chairman said.

"The procedure is fairly routine. It's the recovery that's the problem." Christine stopped there for a moment, to let him think about that. She had put a lot of thought into this presentation, and now it was time to follow through. She was in no hurry, and the longer the chairman had to think about it, the better.

Even though Gabriel was no longer around, he had helped Christine formulate a plan that would now be a possibility for the chairman. When Christine had learned some of the accusations against Gabriel, she had been surprised at first, then more hurt than surprised. She felt that Gabriel had not held up his end of the bargain in exchange for what Christine had brought to the relationship. She hesitated each time she got to this part—the relationship. She hadn't held anything back, but after she had dealt with the blow of his disappearance, what Gabriel was allegedly up to hadn't really surprised Christine. That he had decided to undermine the Conglomerate plan of parenting, after what he had said about his own childhood experiences, seemed only natural.

Christine thought about Gabriel's behavior in relation to her own situation with the chairman, and she thought, *Why not?* What the chairman was asking for was a new procedure that had not been perfected yet. She thought it best to act as if it were clearly in her command, and to try to figure something out, something stronger and more effective for her means.

Christine looked at the chairman; he looked impatient.

"The procedure begins with a simple swipe from the inside of your mouth," Christine said. "Then I will do my work. Initially I will extract your genome and take an inventory, determine and quarantine the defective genes, delete them and replace them with repaired genes. Then we do a

complete resequencing of your genome, all from that one
swipe on a single slide, bathed in a rejuvenating solution,"
Christine said. "Then I will confirm that the DNA accepts
the replacement as its own. As it is formed from your own
genetic base, there's no reason why it shouldn't." She took a
breath; all of this had not been fully tested yet. "We supple-
ment the gene with an enzyme that speeds up the replica-
tion of your new genetic structure. We use an IV drip and
eventually it replicates through your whole system."

She looked at him. "And then that's where your work
comes in." She waited. "We will need to sedate you during
the procedure, prior to inserting the repaired gene. The
process should be rapid, and the emotional reaction you feel
could be dangerous. We can't risk that." Christine wanted to
make the chairman feel that they were partners in this operation.

"It's dangerous," the chairman said. "How?"

"To your nervous system, for one," Christine said. "Not
to mention your heart. The change to your brain and nervous system could produce shock, which could result in car-
diac arrest. On the other hand," Christine said, "if your
brain and nervous system are not conscious of the changes
your genetic makeup is going through, you will, in effect,
sleep it off, in as little as eight to ten hours. You will wake up
a changed and more youthful man." The chairman of the
Conglomerate party stared at his reflection in the tinted
glass. They were heading through the Queens-Midtown
Tunnel as though the car knew where it was going.

"Why eight to ten hours?" he asked, still looking at his reflection.

Christine didn't say that she thought she might need that amount of time to get a head start in the run for her life. Instead, she said, "For your own good."

"How so?"

"Sleep will aid the rejuvenation process," Christine said. "And as stated before, to avoid shock. As you're an intelligent man," Christine said, "you would naturally intellectualize the changes your internal wiring would be going through, and that process might overload the circuits and burn your hard drive."

"I can handle it," he said. "I can't be out of it for that length of time."

"Do you want to risk having a breakdown? And in front of your subordinates?"

The chairman turned his head away from the window and looked at Christine.

"Okay," he said. "We'll do it your way." He paused before he said, "Do you know what that means?"

Christine knew this agreement meant that she had accepted responsibility for its outcome, and with that acceptance, the consequences. She nodded and shook the chairman's hand.

He looked directly at Christine and said, "Aren't you interested in the whereabouts of Gabriel Cruz?"

"I'm interested in the welfare of all of my employees," Christine said.

"He's alive, you know," the chairman said.

"I imagine you must have him in custody," Christine said. She hoped they had not caught him since he'd left the note.

To her surprise, he said, "Cruz got away. He was dumped.

I think the idiot agents who broke into the center got spooked, and they dumped him." The chairman turned back to look at Christine. "Have you heard from him?" he asked. It felt like a slap across the face to Christine. She was trying to apply these facts to what she knew about the break-in and Gabriel's kidnapping and not let on about her confusion, or the fact that she thought she had heard from him.

She tried not to think about the note in her pocket as she said, "Cruz would be crazy to contact me, after what he did to my department. He'd be getting off easy if I just turned him in." The chairman was staring into Christine's eyes, and she decided she had better shut up and stare back.

"It would be in your best interest to turn him in, should you hear from him," the chairman said, and looked away.

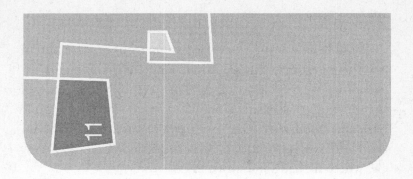

11

The Collaborator

So, it's X, is it?" X's companion asked. They were making their way south, stepping between steel columns and iron rails along the A train tracks just beneath Central Park West and the old Dakota at Seventy-second Street. In the perpetual fluorescent glare of the underground station, it could have been noon. Even hunched over, the guy towered over X as she tried to keep up with him. He had told her that he'd been on the run as long as he could remember and had found his way to the underground on his own. He was thrilled to meet other kids like himself and had no problem fitting in with the misfits. The forsaken found his resourcefulness useful.

X had been waiting since she had met this guy for him to ask this question—any question, really, but she hadn't expected it just then. She was preoccupied by the menace of the third rail that gleamed lethal on either side of her, while her companion was acting as if he were strolling down Central Park West. He said they were headed for Columbus Circle, where he had some work to do.

X had been surprised that he had a job and had asked what kind of work he did. He'd answered that it would be easier to show her than to explain. At first X thought he was being evasive, and then decided that of course he was, but it didn't bother her. What was normal down here?

In the blue-lit space between stations, the light reflected off the track rails like a laser line to guide them: X's companion was counting off his paces. The light from the Columbus Circle hub didn't seem so far away. X thought it was bad enough walking in between these tracks; she didn't want to have to contend with navigating through the confusion of Columbus Circle, where trains were going every way at once.

They were at an alcove recessed a few feet into the wall. Her friend pulled a flashlight from his jacket and lit up the area. There was a steel door with large rivets and bolts and an old-fashioned keyhole. The door called for a special tool, and X's companion handed her the flashlight before he reached inside his coat and pulled out what looked to be a knitting needle and picked the old-fashioned lock. "This way," he said.

They walked a few steps to another door, with a bell etched into the frosted glass window. It looked like it had been there forever. He reached into his jacket and pulled out a small key and opened the door. It was a room full of multicolored wires connected to tall panels and squat boxes. There was a hum like a motor. She felt the air circulate above her and saw an exhaust fan in a transom window on the other side of the room.

Her companion said, "Communications." X looked for a microphone, a receiver, a soundboard. Nothing.

"Come in," he said, and he disappeared into an aisle between the panels. X heard a scraping sound as he returned dragging a wooden bench out into the space at the end of the panels.

They sat down, and he said, "Keep the light here, please." She directed the light toward the side of one of the panels while he took out a Phillips head screwdriver and opened up the end of the panel.

He reached into his coat pocket again and pulled out what looked like a red telephone receiver complete with a coil wire that looked frayed at the end. Then he took out a small keypad with four wires sticking from the top. He matched the ends to connectors inside the panel and they heard a dial tone. He took the four wires from the keypad and attached those to the same connectors and punched a series of numbers into the pad. X heard a phone ringing.

"Hi," her companion said. "I'm at Columbus Circle."

X couldn't make out what was being said at the other end but her companion said a series of yes's and uh-huh's until he finally said, "Goodbye."

"Telephone," he said, interpreting her look.

"Well, I see that," X said. "How's it work?"

"You don't need no satellite, don't need no laser beam,"
X's companion explained. "You need one of these," he said,
holding up the red receiver, "and some of those," he said,
pointing at the open panel, "and all those ancient, unused,
forgotten phone wires in the air and under the ground. Except, we use them."

A FEW DAYS after X had been released from quarantine, she'd
walked through a connecting tunnel between subway lines.
There was steady foot traffic in both directions from the citizenry of the underworld, the huddled masses continually
moving in search of warmth, shelter, food, and something
to do.

X blended into the crowd and got lost. She straightened
up on her toes and looked ahead of her and then turned to
look behind. She heard the people pushing against her
grumble and curse. She got caught up in the crush and
started to move with the crowd in hopes she wouldn't get
knocked off her feet. She hadn't been paying attention to
where she was going, and the crowd was now pushing her
toward a platform she hadn't noticed before. It was hard to
breathe and impossible to go against the flow of the crowd.
The hum of humanity was deafening. X was surprised by the
headlights, and then the train roared to a stop with a screech
that the din couldn't deny. The train doors opened and the
people pushed in, carrying X along with them. The windows
had all been painted black and sealed. It was an air-
conditioned train, or built to be, but the air-conditioning

wasn't working, or at least it wasn't on. It was hot and there was no ventilation. Between all the bodies, the smell was making X sick.

The train started with a lurch and a groan. X had nothing to hold on to but the person next to her, and she wasn't going to do that. But she couldn't have fallen, as there were passengers tight on either side of her and it felt as if they were in her pockets. She didn't even have enough arm room to pull off her gloves or open her coat. The overhead lights blinked on and off and X's stomach turned with each plunge into darkness. The vibrations she felt through the soles of her feet rattled her knees and made her nausea worse.

It must have been an express train; she could tell by the change in sounds, the level of the racket to the rhythm and rattle. Just when she thought her stomach couldn't take much more, the train jerked to a stop and she was sent like a slingshot through the open door. She couldn't have cared less where she was; she was just glad to be out of that train. She gulped at the air and pushed ahead; she didn't want to wind up back in that cattle car. She made it to the station wall and pressed herself flat against the tile and hoped she could catch her breath, settle her stomach, and get away from people. She reached inside her shirt and took a deep breath. She still had the necklace.

The train left the station and X's head began to clear. She lifted her nose and sniffed at the air. It tasted sweet and she started to feel better. That's when X noticed she was outside and wasn't in Manhattan anymore.

"Must be Queens?" X said out loud as she watched the

steam of her words dissolve in the air. "And that must've been Roosevelt Island," X said, thinking of the train station she thought they had gone through without stopping.

The rejuvenation X felt turned to a chill. While the subway platform was far from empty, the crowd had dissipated. People had boarded the train before it had departed, and a number of people now seemed to disappear.

"This can't be good for me," X said, and watched her words puff in the cold air. "One minute I'm hot enough to pass out, and then the next minute I'm freezing." She shivered, and with her back on the tile wall she slid down and pulled her knees to her chest for warmth as she surveyed the station.

It was the eyes that first attracted X to her companion and him to her. It wasn't as if they were looking for each other, and it was hardly an attraction at first. Their gazes collided only to bounce off the other like opposite fields of a magnet; X couldn't look away fast enough. But when X looked back, the eyes and the person behind them were gone, and for some reason she found herself disappointed. So instead she looked at the city and sighed.

"I'll just go back the same way," X said with a confidence she didn't feel, because X wasn't sure how she would go about it. She pushed herself up and pulled her coat closer. She was glad to have it, along with the gloves and the hat, but it wasn't enough covering to be outside for long. Besides, as funny as it seemed to her, she couldn't get comfortable being outside and exposed to the Conglomerate world. She felt like a target. And she didn't want to think about the fact that since she'd become a Dyscard, she hadn't been back on the outside alone until now.

X walked down the platform looking for a way to the other side of the tracks and the train going back. She didn't see one. She walked to the other end and still didn't see a way across. There was a short staircase that led to the track bed. The only thing stopping her was a small fence, and she knew she could get over that. And after all she had been through, she didn't see the harm in crossing these tracks and hopping up onto the platform on the other side. She thought about it a minute and jumped the fence.

The first thing X noticed was the traction beneath her feet. Her feet crunched on the gravel and cinder of the track bed. This was different. She wasn't sure of her footing should she need to move fast. She looked both ways and held her breath. No train had been through since the one that had coughed her out into this station. X exhaled and thought about it and broke for the other side.

Something had X by the ankle; she went down. Before she could do anything, whatever it was that had her, had her by the wrist as well and was pulling her under the platform. X was a good six inches beneath the platform before she could dig in to resist, and that's when the train went by. Now it was X who was scurrying under the platform. She ripped her coat on the gravel, but she didn't care. Sparks flying from the train wheels went over her head. The train was gone in a couple of seconds, and then she felt the swirl of air left in the train's wake.

"Whew," X said, and she looked for her savior. There was

little light. She had trouble focusing on the silhouette in front of her, and then she saw the eyes.

"Thank you," X said. "I didn't see it coming."

"So, I guess you're not a cop," the voice said. "Your attempt at crossing the track demonstrated a lack of training."

"What are you doing down here?" X asked and patted the ground beneath the station.

"Getting away from you, actually."

"Because you thought I was a cop?"

"Well, yeah," he said.

Now X laughed. "Why's that?"

"You seemed out of place," he said. "Well, more lost than out of place. I thought you were on the job."

"On the job?" X asked.

"Yeah. You kept talking out loud as if you were miked, and then you patted yourself down. And if you're going to keep repeating what I'm saying, I'll have to think of better things to say."

"What're you, on the run?" X asked.

"Aren't we all?" he said.

X looked out where the train had just passed, and said, "Then, while we're at it, maybe we can run out of here?"

That had happened a few days ago, and they had been together since.

"YES, MY NAME is X," X said as they walked together. She stepped ahead of him as the passageway narrowed. "What's yours?" she said, her heart in her throat.

"Y," he said.

"Why!" X said, and stopped.

"Because I'm following X," he said. She punched him in the arm and he laughed.

"John," he said.

"John?" X said.

"That's my real name," he said. "Yeah, I know, not too fancy. Remember, I came here on my own, felt funny about taking a name. That is, until now." He stuck out his hand. "Y," he said, and smiled. "Johnnie Y."

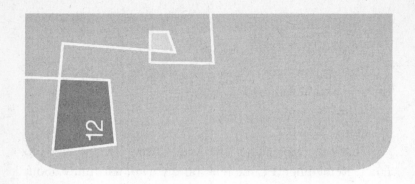

12

When It Rains . . .

Patsy's head popped up when she first heard the shower running. She thought it was raining. She stared out the open door and into the blinding light. Patsy didn't like this rain you could hear but wasn't there.

She wasn't going to take a shower if George didn't give it to her; it wasn't as if the idea of giving his wife a shower repelled him. Hardly! What bothered George was that Patsy wouldn't think of taking a shower without him giving it to her. It was as if Patsy had forgotten about cleaning herself, and that wasn't all. If George didn't escort Patsy to the bathroom, Patsy wouldn't go. She would wait all day. Patsy wouldn't eat unless George fed her, and most mornings Patsy would wake up fully dressed from the night before. George knew this wasn't right, but sometimes he gave up.

"Can't we leave well enough alone?" she would say.

Problem was that when Patsy got out of bed, she would walk over to her drawer and pull out a shirt and put it on, on top of the ones she was already wearing. It was as if Patsy had forgotten she was dressed. George thought that when Patsy woke up she knew she had to get dressed. What had been lost was the need to get undressed the night before.

Patsy's rapid debilitation had made it difficult to leave the unit. George couldn't predict what Patsy would do, or say, or where she would go. Each day was getting worse. But they did have to eat and exercise, and it wasn't as if they had a choice.

When Patsy and George went to the cafeteria, he didn't want to leave her alone for a second. Yesterday they walked up to the main door of the cafeteria and the two of them waited outside while George scouted out the crowd inside. It was busy and he looked for a break in the line. He had their two I.D. bracelets and his timing down. In this instance George was more concerned with speed than attention. Maybe he could be faster than their ability to notice him. George always forgot about the cameras.

He led Patsy around like a toddler, and he hated treating her this way, but he didn't know what else to do. He balanced two bowls of oatmeal with two bottles of water tucked beneath his arms. Patsy was holding on to his belt and they were trying to find a table, when someone took George by the arm. It was the guy who had delivered the water, who looked down at Patsy's fingers curled around George's belt loop.

"Are you all right?" he said to George.

"Am now, thanks," George said, a little quick in the reply. George placed the bowls on the table and took Patsy's hand, trying as hard as he could to look relaxed.

"My truck's not far," the deliveryman said. "Why don't I give you a ride back to your place?"

They had their food and they could get out of there and back to the unit. The offer sounded almost too good to be true.

"Not necessary," George said.

"I think I should," the man said. "It isn't a problem for me and I'm going that way, anyway." He noticed the change in Patsy. It hadn't been that long, he thought. "It'll get you out of here," he said.

Soon they were all strapped inside the deliveryman's truck, and it was a good thing too, because the guy's truck needed new shocks and every bounce was a jolt. The truck was a hybrid of solar and electric power, a vehicle that may have been ideal for the sun in this region but was not designed for the roads.

"Wooo," George said as his stomach dropped.

"Once a quarter," the deliveryman started, "citizens of these camps are designated for 'reassignment,' as the authorities call it. But when the buses roll in, they round 'em up and ship 'em out in a massive Coot drive."

"Coot drive?" George said.

"Slang term," he answered, "referring to the collecting and gathering of the Coots, and the distribution of them to an appropriate facility."

"How?" George asked.

"Usually a representative will come to your room to serve the papers."

"Is there a reason given?"

"The blanket statement is that more appropriate accommodations have become available. That the guest would not only be more comfortable but, more important, would get more appropriate care. It covers everything. The procedure is used for its pacifying effect on the patient, but the result is to place us by need, so to speak. Convenience is more like it. There is no desire to service the need."

"What criteria do they use?" George asked.

"Whatever criteria they please. Degree of nuisance, attention required, or anything else: being in the wrong place at the wrong time." That answer brought George's questions to a halt. "And that's where the buses come in," the guy said.

The guy seemed to be confirming what George had heard from the program on the bootleg laptop.

"Be on guard while you're out," the deliveryman said as they bounced along the road. "Don't be fooled by the behavior of other people. They'll all go. Lie low, and when you need to be out, be quick and careful. Let your wife walk in front of you, or figure some other way of staying together than the one you were using. Look, there is a place where you and your wife can go to get away from here, when the time is right. It is a place where your wife can receive help and respect. Just be patient, and be careful. For now, I shouldn't say anything more about this than that." And he didn't.

"But instead," he said, "let me tell you about this place and what to look out for first. The old Biltmore hotel in Phoenix serves as the Conglomerate headquarters in the Southwestern quadrant. While the Biltmore is still the elegant structure that the architect intended it to be, the fine old building is, well, old.

"The closest the board of directors of the Southwestern quadrant gets to the camps is the TV monitors that line their offices and conference rooms. The brass don't ride buses, and they certainly aren't about to go to the camps. Can you imagine watching us on TV?" He stopped for breath and their consideration. "Well, neither can they, and the only thing they monitor on the monitors is the productivity of their employees. And in most cases, they watch to make sure said employees' productivity is for the good of the party and thus the board and not for the good of the self. The board doesn't mind if an employee shakes down the patients; they just want to make sure that the results of any given investigation are returned to the board, the proper owners of all personal property. Sometimes the board can be pretty busy."

"What do people have that would be worth it?" George asked.

"You'd be surprised what some people are able to get past security to bring out here with them, or what they can get ahold of once they're here. But when it comes down to it and people feel they've got nothing left, you'd be surprised what someone will offer up to survive. Some of the agents for the Conglomerates got some pretty good deals.

"When the camp was first established, many of the workers saw these offerings as an opportunity to better their position and possessions, and they did so. It didn't take long before their bosses noticed. Management found that the evidence of some of this independent contracting wasn't detectable until the employees returned to their rooms. And that wasn't determined until management started to monitor the personal housing of the employees.

"As you might imagine, one of the results of the constant monitoring is that morale among the staff is low.

"So, if the Biltmore has seen better days, the Conglomerate employees stationed in the camps have even less than people have at headquarters. Not much of a detail, and either way, they're sentenced like the rest of us—probably worse for them. We haven't got a future and they do." The deliveryman took another breath, this one with a bit of a wheeze. "They'll be all over you if they think you've got something to hide, like cash, or drugs, and they'll separate you in a minute if they think it's to their advantage, especially if they think you have something to pay to get a loved one back. Remember, you're the enemy, and anything goes. It's nothing personal, they just hate you. They believe they're better than you.

"From the industrial revolution on, it has been the same. Every generation has reached the conclusion that their particular intelligence is singularly attained. Each generation perceives that they have grasped what others before them could not. And it is through their own unique efforts that they alone have been able to alter systems, eco and otherwise, to fit their will. Each feels that they alone have reached the prowess and the power to mold the world around them to their own unique situations. Each feels as if they alone have manipulated time to maximize productivity and the clock.

"The hubris that attends such an arrogant assertion only leaves its holder vulnerable to the counterattacks of experience and history. Since each generation has placed themselves above and beyond what has preceded them, they fall unsuspecting victims to the onslaught of time, every time."

He stopped the van and opened the door for Patsy. "Well, here we are," he said. "We'll pick this up another time." George had wanted to know about the other place, where they could take care of Patsy, but he had gotten confused around the industrial revolution, and Patsy had long been distracted by something else, and now here they were. So instead George said, "Yes, maybe another time," as the deliveryman drove away.

THAT WAS YESTERDAY. Right now George's biggest problem was the shower. He couldn't waste the water, but he had to coax Patsy out of her clothes and into the shower. George knew a bath would have been easier, but they didn't have a tub. He had tried giving her a sponge bath near the sink, but that hadn't worked either. Whenever George would get busy with something, Patsy would look out the door to see if it was raining. She said that she wanted to see what the desert looked like in the rain. Patsy was cooperative; it wasn't that.

But taking her clothes off could take time. She would wear shirt upon shirt, and sometimes she would freeze at the sight of the water spurting out from the showerhead. It was as if she had never seen it before.

George never knew how Patsy was going to react when he was able to get her under the water. By this time he usually had less than seven minutes left of water before their little tank ran out. He would have to soap her up, squirt some shampoo onto her head, rub it in, lather up her hair, and then rinse her off, all within seven minutes. He got it done.

But the shower was indicative of a larger problem. It indicated one more aspect of Patsy's decline that called for a level of care George knew might be beyond his ability. It sure was beyond his experience.

GEORGE WAS WRITING on the laptop, something he was doing more and more. But it was never easy. He got anxious every time, and that made Patsy anxious. So George had taken to using the laptop when Patsy was asleep. It was funny how their roles had reversed. Now she slept and George broke out the machine.

He hadn't been able to get back the program they had seen when they had first come across the laptop, and George still hadn't had the nerve to try to contact anyone yet. He was tempted, but afraid. Granted, they wouldn't be able to identify who was using the machine, but what if his contact were traced. George did wonder why they would bother to tap into the old phone lines. There would be a cost associated with following the activity on the phone lines, and the

Conglomerates would see that as ineffective spending, and they would be right. George might have the capability of contacting the outside world, but what would he say, and to whom? He thought about all of the e-mails he used to send to his granddaughter Christine. They both had loved that.

George wrote an account of his day-to-day experiences on the old laptop. At first he thought it would be a way for him to keep track of things for Patsy, but he soon found that it was a means of dealing with all that happened to them. George found that when he put their experience into words, he was able to sort it through and come to some conclusions or, at least, to come up with some plans. It felt better to get it all out. Besides, he figured it was a good exercise for his memory, to record the day, and the typing was a way to maintain his motor skills.

"What the hell," George said, as he thought of Christine. He filled in the subject heading with "Follow-Up." "Innocuous enough," he said as he clicked send and sent his story to Christine's old e-mail address.

GEORGE LOOKED OUT the open door just in time to see an ancient saguaros burst into flames as a bolt of lightning struck the ground. It took a full second for the crack of thunder to follow. Rain, steady and strong, pelted their roof and the dirt outside the open door.

Patsy got up from the bed and walked toward the bathroom.

"No, Patsy." George jumped up, but then he didn't know if she was kidding him or not, until Patsy started to laugh. George did too.

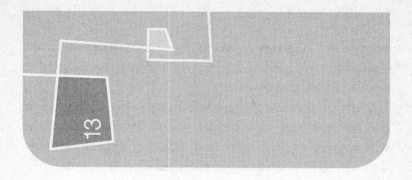

Ichabod's Train

As the need for capital had continued, the Conglomerate discontinuing procedure had trended upward. And the Dyscards, a growing populace of the rejected, had established a more and more sophisticated system to unify that which had been thrown away. Order and a rationale developed a more complete organization based on their common experience and necessity.

This development ran counter to the Conglomerate vision of the Dyscard solution. The Conglomerates projected that the Dyscards would die out of natural causes due to the hardships of being forced to live like rodents and vermin. But the Conglomerate calculations had not factored in the survivalist skills instinctive to those abandoned, and the Conglomerates underestimated how the discarded youth would survive and grow.

The Conglomerates grew more disgruntled as this result became more and more apparent, and the chairman of the Conglomerate party mandated that the authorities introduce an agent into the Dyscard populace that would do the Conglomerates' destructive work for them.

"The smallpox in a blanket scenario," the chairman had said.

As they did with most of the ideas from the chairman of the Conglomerate party, the party lackeys had jumped at the chance to please the boss. They had come to a consensus: they would release hard-core criminals into the community of the Dyscards in order to dominate and destroy the Dyscard social structure.

The first criminals were dropped into the underground one at a time, but it didn't take long for the Border Patrol to pick them up and remove them. A pattern began to emerge.

The Conglomerates had been so sure of their solution that they had failed to consider that it might not go according to plan. The Conglomerates did not consider that the criminal—and the more hardened the criminal, the more true was the case—was one who had been discarded himself. They were people who had been shunned because of personality, appearance, economics, or a tick of the brain, and they had lived outside of the Conglomerate law. But Dee had considered that. Dee knew they would be grateful for their release, and if they weren't, the Border Patrol was good at convincing drop-ins that it was in their best interests to play along. Either way, the Conglomerate counterinsurgents didn't have much choice.

OTHER ENEMIES OF the Dyscards were those who wanted to exploit an opportunity the vulnerable presented—intruders from the city who were out for a risk and a kick, who wanted "to do a freak." Once these guys were able to boast about it with their friends, they would come back in packs to exhibit their prowess at making kids scream. It was a habit encouraged by the Conglomerates, and some intruders even felt sanctioned by the chairman himself.

Word was spreading among the young citizens of the underground, and the Dyscards wanted to know what A and Dee were going to do about it.

So did they.

The combined energies of A and Dee were nearly consumed with the daily issues of an emerging culture: organization, housing, utilities, health care, security. And to have one of the leading health care and security issues come from an invasion from the people who had thrown the Dyscards away was troublesome.

While the burgeoning society of the Dyscards experienced many difficulties, it had avoided acts of aggression and violence, or more serious crimes. Sure, there had been sporadic episodes, but they had been more the expression of frustration than anything else. Most kids didn't possess much of anything in the first place, so there wasn't much to steal. Besides, the discarded were too dependent on one another. They relied on one another's skills and experience in order to obtain what they needed to survive. No one thought of destroying that. So when word got back from the Border Patrol that there was a new breed of creep working the underground, A and Dee knew they had another attack from the Conglomerates.

It was no surprise to Dee when the solution to their security problems fell into their laps. Like most problems, it took a while to know the solution was at hand.

"It's simple," Dee finally said, "we get the Border Patrol to continue to work with the convicts the Conglomerates send down here, which is going quite well, and as a reward for service, the convicts get to unleash their aggression on the creeps who want to hurt a kid. Patrol can even show them how it's done and leave the convicts to do the rest. I'm sure they'll pick it up fast."

Dee took pride in the idea that the Conglomerates were concerned enough by the growing community of Dyscards that they would launch such attacks on them. Dee liked it that the Dyscards might recruit and return this infection to the Conglomerates in kind.

THE THREE-QUARTER moon rose through the face on the Clock Tower Building and arced across the city skyline. The chairman of the Conglomerate party looked from behind the glass. He didn't focus on the moon or the light it cast across the buildings of lower Manhattan. He never did. Instead he ran through his plans as if another option might occur to him. It didn't. He had no problem with the moral decision; he'd passed that point. It was the implementation that concerned him. There was no new revenue to apply to the situation, and the rising costs were killing the Conglomerates, along with everyone else. It wasn't as if the chairman could buy his way out.

When the Conglomerates had chosen to segregate themselves from their problems, as they had done with the Coots relocation program to the West and with the Dyscards here in the East, the Conglomerates had reduced the costs associated with care for the elderly and social services for the young. They had even been able to manipulate the reproductive issue into a profit center by offering second-chance parenting. But now that revenue stream was past further exploitation. There was no choice but change.

The chairman would cut off any further spending on the elderly. They produced nothing but costs. Let them fend for themselves in what was left of the communities to which they had been shipped. The weather out there was ideal, after all. It was a good place to die. The chairman would have the people in administration out there stay behind as well. He would instruct the employees of the Conglomerate party that they would have to pay their own moving and transportations costs to return to the East. They could afford it, as the workers in these posts had been ripping off the party for years. They had stolen from the Coots and gotten rich on the black market.

The chairman's plans for the Dyscards would be even harder to implement. They had been remarkable survivors and they had spread out, splintered into factions from Detroit to San Antonio. It would be hard to affect them as a whole entity, but he could attack their power base, the home to the largest population of Dyscards: the New York City subways.

The idea of obliterating the Dyscards appealed to him. He couldn't flood them out without damaging the infrastructure further, nor could he burn them out, though he liked the idea. It would have to be something drastic to disarm the Dyscards. Intelligence hadn't worked. Neither had infiltration or terrorist tactics. The Dyscards had proved resistant to those measures and had, in fact, deflected such attacks back at the Conglomerates.

The Dyscards existed as parasites on the society that had gotten rid of them in the first place; this gave the chairman the idea for his method of attack. He would cut off their power. He would order a power failure, a blackout that would encompass the urban sprawl from Boston to D.C. and cause mass panic and further distress to the nation's economy. But he would have to risk it to gain victory over the Dyscards and retain control over the party by saving the nation. The chairman felt that the greater the threat, the greater the glory.

It was true that there were auxiliary generators in the subway system, but it was only to keep the third rail live. It was not sufficient to maintain lights and ventilation. If he could cut off those two elements, the panic in the dark with an active third rail would result in death and injury beyond their limited means to respond. Such a tactic, the chairman reasoned, would deliver a crippling blow to the Dyscards and overwhelm their ability to treat the wounded and still care for the increased population. Yes, there would be some collateral damage among the Conglomerate citizens who were using the system at the time and also among those working there. Such losses were minimal in light of the Dyscard problem, and were necessary. The Conglomerates would have to go public and acknowledge the problem, and in so doing they would transfer blame to the Dyscards. The chairman would report that the crisis for the citizens of the city was due to the Dyscards' continued theft of energy, which had caused the system to overload and had resulted in a shutdown that had brought down the power for the entire East Coast.

He would have to be careful that his new doctor did not know about the plans for the Dyscards. The chairman saw through Salter's disregard for Gabriel Cruz. Maybe there was a way to use Cruz as a bargaining chip, the chairman thought. That could be useful. The chairman did what was good for the party, and what was good for the party was good for the nation. The rest took care of itself.

The chairman needed Salter's loyalty, and the last thing he wanted to think about was what her retribution could be and to what lengths she could carry it out. It was these thoughts that occupied the chairman, not how he was going to inform the administration of his decision. The administration did what he told them to do.

AT FIRST, X had protested when her companion had wrapped the strap across her lap, but now she was glad he had. He extended it to include himself and clipped it at his hip. Their thighs pressed against each other. That is, when they weren't bouncing on their butts as the I train barreled down the Lexington Avenue line. X knew it couldn't be, but it seemed that everything got out of this train's way, because they were flying down the tracks and taking the turns as if they couldn't flip over. X and her companion could have been in space as they shot through the dark and watched the blue, red, and white lights recede behind them like stars.

The I train was black, and in between stations the train looked like a shadow sneaking between tunnels. X's companion was speaking to her, but she couldn't hear him even though he was shouting. Between the squeal of the train wheels that echoed throughout the system and the back draft, X's ears where ringing. It was a good thing she hadn't heard him, because if she had, she may not have believed him, and if she had believed him, she would have been even more scared than she was now.

Her companion was telling X that the I stood for Ichabod, as in Ichabod Crane from Washington Irving's *The Legend of Sleepy Hollow,* which, of course, also employed the headless horseman. As no one in the current generation had read the book, the details were fuzzy and the characters confused, and the train with no driver had become the headless horseman named Ichabod Train, which became the I train with the ghost driver, Ichabod.

Since the I train made no use of its interior lights, or the exterior headlights and taillights, there was no visible tip-off that the I train was coming. The I had steel-edged wheel rims and side grating. The train was one car made of stainless steel painted flat black with black gloss appointing and black tinted windows. No one had seen the driver, nor even a shadow or silhouette of the motormen. It was a train that appealed to the imagination.

THE DRIVER HAD been an engineer in the heyday of the MTA and he, like many others, had been forced to retire. Later, when the Family Relief Act was instituted, he, like many others, was ordered to relocate out West. But unlike the many others who did relocate, the driver of the I train refused to make the move. The engineer had other options. He knew the subways better than the police did, and he submerged himself back into his old work world years before the banishment of the Dyscards.

The engineer prepared by setting up supplies—gathering tools and paint in an abandoned toolshed and workshop at the hub of an obsolete network of tunnels—before he made his ultimate move. He had been collecting maps of the subway system since he was a kid, and he had made a hobby of studying them and memorizing lines and routes long forgotten.

The engineer found a work yard and two abandoned subway cars. He moved his tools to the work yard. The engineer's new home was spacious and utilitarian, with huge hoists and pulleys above the section of track. The yard was outfitted with a welding area complete with equipment and tanks of propane gas, which to his surprise were full and ready to go. Welding had been a job he had earlier had time to develop.

The I train took shape. The driver lined the exterior with a four-inch catwalk to which he attached a wrought iron railing welded onto the outside of the train. He knew the train width was not enough to breech the tunnels or the steel support columns. He used razor wire around the steps and the undercarriage. He lined the windows with chicken wire prior to applying the black tint. And then he sanded the stainless steel by hand so the flat black paint would adhere to the car; he proceeded to give the car coat after coat to make sure. He had the time. He couldn't help it and painted the razor wrap and the railing in high-gloss black.

It was about that time that the accident happened. He was getting careless with the torch. He had a steady hand, and he had used the torch so often on his moveable fortress that he felt he could deal with any problem, because he had so far. That is, until the hose leaked. The high-pitched hiss of the leak caught the welder's attention, and he hoped the stream of propane was not headed toward the nozzle. His focus switched to the flame as the stream of gas encountered the nozzle, causing a flare of magnesium right before his eyes. And before he realized he was looking at the flame, that flare fused his optic nerve, producing an instantaneous white-blindness. He kept his eyes closed and counted to thirty and prayed the blindness was temporary. His experience told him to stay still, and he held the torch exactly where he had it, away from his body. He didn't want to lose track of that. He was sure his vision would return—he hoped so—but if he were to burn his hands, or his legs, he would be in even more serious trouble.

He opened his eyes, but his sight had not returned. Instead the flare inside his head grew in intensity, as did the pain behind his eyes. He would have doubled over if it were not for the lit welding torch in his hand. With his free hand he followed the hose to the propane tank. He touched the top of the tank until he found the valve. He twisted the valve to close and felt the pressure in the hose diminish. He ran his fingers back along the hose toward the torch, careful not to touch the nozzle. Only then did he put the extinguished torch down; only then did he put his hands to either side of his head and scream.

He remembered thinking that while he felt completely different, outside of him nothing had changed. He thought of the locations of his workbench, tools, and supplies, and he called them out loud again and again, sure that that would help fix them in his mind.

The engineer wasn't exactly sure just how he was able to drive this one-car train, but the method he was using matched the vibration of the wheels on the rails beneath him with the visualization of the system map that was impressed into his memory. It was funny. Without having to be distracted by watching what he was doing, he was able to picture the position of his train in relation to the map in his mind. After all, he had driven every kind of train over every inch of track, so that he could have driven the system with his eyes closed.

"WELL, NOW I get my chance," the driver said aloud, but he didn't think about that for long, because just then he heard a change in the tone of the hum of the wheels and it felt almost as if the train were digging into the turn. He knew no one would believe him, but he could feel the wheels on the tracks anticipate the switch. He leaned to his right as he swung the helm with his weight and his customized train followed the command.

X hadn't heard a word that her companion had said about the train driver's story. Wasn't that just the way with this guy, X thought. It seemed that either he was talking to her when she couldn't hear or she was talking to him, only to find he wasn't there. X was beginning to have her doubts, except that he kept taking such good care of her.

"Why do you keep doing that?" X asked her companion. But of course he couldn't hear *her* either. He wasn't about to let go of his grip on the back of the bouncing I train, so he just shrugged his shoulders and smiled.

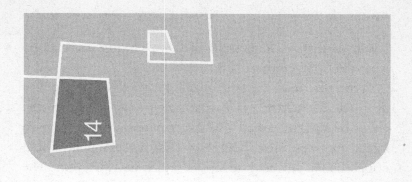

14

Change

The chairman of the Conglomerate party stood in the center of his office as the light dissolved and the skyline across the Brooklyn Bridge disappeared behind a curtain of rain. A jolt of thunder sent its vibration through the Clock Tower Building.

He reviewed the details of his plan. He had reaffirmed his decision to implement the attack. He would move up the date for his procedure with Salter. The attack on the Dyscards would occur during his recovery. The idea had come to him in a dream, though the chairman of the Conglomerate party never really slept. He had nodded off in the back of the town car as it twisted through the streets of lower Manhattan. Something had awoken him. He realized what the timing of his plans should be.

If the chairman was unavailable for direction and policy decisions during the crisis, that absence would add to the chaos he had unleashed. His party puppets would have to figure out what they should do. That process alone would cripple them. It would be like an attack on two fronts. The administration would have to deal with the effects of the power hit to the financial districts of New York City, Boston, and D.C., all in the midst of a question of leadership. The chairman saw himself suddenly appear in the midst of this mayhem, recovered from the genetic procedure, a more youthful and decisive person in the face of disaster. He would restore confidence in the party while he restored the power grid and, more important, restored control and management to deal with the catastrophe and response. Then the chairman would apply his skill at crafting the information. He would admit to the Dyscard crisis, in order to direct the blame. He would use the disaster for the party's advantage and convince consumers that the Dyscard squatters had poached the power, causing the system to overload and shut down. This would sway public opinion even further, allowing the party to gain points on political polls and boosting the people's confidence in the Conglomerate party leadership. The chairman's value would be apparent and his colleagues' inadequacies just as visible, and his position as chairman would go unchallenged.

True, the chairman had work to do, but it was a strong concept, the implementation of which would be a formality. He would have to manipulate the management of a few

and Dee's administration, and enough of a reason for Walters as well. Gabriel hated to think that he and Christine
might be part of the reason for the babies' being there.

There were about a dozen incubators crowded into the
end of the med tent. It wasn't the most they had ever dealt
with, but it was more than the med tent's pediatric ward was
equipped to handle.

Gabriel heard a noise—weak, but in the hum of the pediatric ward the little sound made Gabriel's heart pound. He
knew it could mean only one thing. He looked up, trying to
take in the whole space at once. There was a baby in distress,
turning blue inside the white blanket. The baby looked as if
it was trying to spit something out. Gabriel flipped the baby
over as carefully as he could without disturbing the tubes
that ran from the baby to the bags on the pole next to the
bassinet. Gabriel massaged the baby's belly until he found
the spot he was looking for and exerted a gentle push of
pressure, which caused the infant to exhale through the
mouth, and a lump of mucus shot out of the baby's mouth
like a cork. The baby's face changed from blue to red as the
gasping turned into a full-throated wail. Gabriel smiled and
wiped the baby's chin, and then Gabriel gave the baby a little hug, along with a soft grunt before he flipped the baby
back, not wanting to disturb the little one anymore.

"Sleep tight, sweetheart," Gabriel said, and he kissed the
air above the baby's head.

"Go sweetheart yourself, why don't you?" Dr. Walters said.
Once Gabriel's feet were back on the ground and his heart re-
turned to his chest, he turned around. Walters came toward
Gabriel from out of the dark.

"Nicely done," Dr. Walters said. "With a good bedside manner, you might have a future yet."

"I'm not going to have a future if you do that again," Gabriel said with his hand over his chest.

"Thank you for being here," the doctor said, changing her tone. "I don't know why you were here alone, and I'll find out, but I am glad you were. You saved that baby's life."

"For now," Gabriel said.

"Yes, for now. But that is the idea, no?" Walters answered. "We don't know what will happen to any of these kids." She waved her hand across the row of incubators and pointed at Gabriel and herself. "We don't know what the future will be, but we're here to protect them now. This is our job," she said. "At least that's how I see it." Dr. Walters spun around to face him.

"I have an additional job for you, Gabriel Cruz," she said, and paused again. Gabriel wasn't sure how to respond. The baby that Gabriel had helped now stopped crying, and the babies around that one settled down too.

"You have done well," Walters said, "but they were simple tasks. We would be entrusting you with some vital information and, potentially, some very valuable cargo." Dr. Walters waved her arm across the nursery again and paused over the baby that Gabriel had just saved.

"We would like you to meet a friend of ours who will take you to an old train driver, who may be conducting a very special transit to transport these kids for us. We have to move them to better conditions, and the driver has the equipment we need to make the trip. If he'll do it," Walters said. "You're to find out," she said. Then she added, "Or maybe you can convince him?"

"Thank you," Gabriel said. "I think. Can't you contact him yourself?"

"No," Walters said, and laughed. "This guy doesn't take calls, or e-mail."

Now it was Gabriel's turn to change tone. "I mean, I am grateful for the work and responsibility you have given me, especially considering how I arrived here and from where I came. That said, I have some reservations. Can't one of your guys do it? You don't sound convinced that I'm your man."

"If we are being honest," Walters replied, "then I too have a few reservations. They do in fact go back to how you got here and from where you came. You were brought here as if you had been captured, a prisoner of war. And if rumor be truth, and I know that it never is, you were at the heart of the problem. But then there are conflicts, like the condition you were in when you arrived, and then there has been your work here, exemplified by your actions just now. I ask myself how such a gift could have been corrupted, co-opted into the Conglomerate mind-set. I find that hard to reconcile with the person who just saved this baby's life." She paused a second. "Even if it is only for now.

"And no, I am not convinced that you're my man," she continued, and sighed. "What makes you think I am looking for such a thing?" Gabriel had to smile at that.

"The driver might trust you," Walters continued. "You're not one of us. As for details, why would I withhold them?

You'll get what we can give and we'll take what you've got when you get back."

"Let me get this straight," Gabriel interjected. "You're not sure you can trust me to go out and risk my neck to meet a couple of people you don't know and see if they will do something for you, or not, and bring you back information?"

"That sounds about right," Walters replied.

"And why should I do it?" Gabriel asked.

"Let's see," she responded, "we could run through your options, but what would be the point?"

Gabriel had to admit the doctor had a point there.

"When do I start?" Gabriel asked.

"I was hoping you'd say that," Walters said. She disappeared behind the room divider between the pediatric ward and the rest of the med tent. When she came back toward Gabriel, she was followed by two of the Border Patrol.

"Oh, no you don't." Gabriel stepped back.

"Oh, no I don't what?" It took Walters a second to realize why Gabriel had reacted as he had. "Don't worry; we're not going to interrogate you," Walters said, "At least not in the pediatric ward. We need to go over a few things with you, and give you a message to deliver to the driver. Or, if that's not possible, to our friend in the field."

CHRISTINE'S BACK WAS against the wall. She had been in this apartment for years and she hadn't changed the layout of the furniture since she had moved in, and never once had she assumed this position before—sleeping, or trying to, with her back propped up against the wall. That is, until she had started working for the chairman. Not even after her run-in with the law and management at the med center after the Cruz affair had she felt the need to watch the door. Now she did. She wanted to be ready when they came for her, the way they had come for Gabriel.

Christine hadn't slept well in days. She looked out the window and knew she wouldn't have to wait much longer for morning.

Her stomach rumbled but she wasn't hungry. She couldn't recall the last time she had eaten a good meal. She pressed her fingertips into her abdomen to relieve the cramps, and took a long pull from her water. She didn't take her eyes off the door. She had to stay hydrated, but it was the water in her empty stomach that made her stomach rumble.

Christine sat up as if the wall had given her a shock.

"I haven't packed," she said. She hopped out of the bed and flipped on the light. She went over to the window, pulled the shades down to the sill, and then walked the few steps to the closet. She had a backpack in there, but that would be too obvious.

Christine decided on her gym bag. She hadn't been to the gym in a while and she had to rifle through her stuff to find it. She saw the handle of the bag poking out behind the bright pink dress bag. Christine gave the gym bag a good tug, which knocked her off balance and pulled her old laptop from the pile of clothes and sent it sliding across the floor. Christine couldn't get over how big and awkward it looked.

Her grandfather had given her the laptop computer when

she was a kid. He'd given it to Christine to use in school, and in hopes that she would stay in touch with him. Christine had, and so had her grandfather with her. Some of the e-mails she had received from him had helped her get through her teenage years, and some of the e-mails she had sent him were full of ideas, dreams, and broken hearts. It made her feel better just to think back on them.

She wondered where her grandfather was now. He had to be older than eighty, so Christine had a good idea where he was. Was her grandma with him? Christine hoped so. She felt like e-mailing him. She could use him now. When no one else had been there for her—not her mother, who had been occupied with showing off the designer sister, and not her father, who had had one foot out the door—her grandfather had always been there. He'd asked her about her life and listened to her, and they had done it through e-mails on this machine.

When she had moved out of her mother's house, she hadn't wanted her mother, or her sister, to find them, and she sure didn't want to delete them or throw the machine away. She swore she would reread her grandfather's messages, and she had, but not in a long time, long enough to forget the machine was there. And now it was in the middle of the floor.

Christine felt as if security had found a bomb among her things. She looked over at her covered windows. Her eyes scanned the room. She got up off the floor, reached into her closet, grabbed a sweatshirt, and tossed it on top of the laptop before she kick-slid it toward the bathroom door. She wiped the sweat from above her lip. She was too nervous to do anything with the computer, so she did what she had intended to do: she carefully packed her essentials and headed into the bathroom, dragging her sweatshirt-covered laptop with her. She wasn't ready to pick it up yet. She retrieved what she needed and finished packing. She walked into her bedroom and threw the gym bag onto the bed. She looked from the bed to the bathroom door.

She thought about Gabriel's poem. She was sure that there was nothing in it about laptops, but the poem wasn't direct either. She was going to find out. And to do that she was going to find the battery pack and the electrical and phone cables. Christine was glad to have something to do.

She went back into the bathroom. She was going to have to do this sooner or later, and the longer Christine waited, the more things could go wrong.

There was a plug for the old phone lines in the bedroom wall near the bathroom door, and there was an electrical outlet next to the medicine cabinet in the bathroom. Christine plugged her computer in there and stretched the phone cable out and around the open bathroom door. It barely made it. Christine pushed the on button and jumped back as if the old laptop were rigged, startled by the whir of the fan and the sequence of lights. She looked up into the mirror in the medicine chest. Her eyes were red and her face was breaking out.

By this time the old laptop was purring like a cat. A window on the screen asked for the user name and password.

Christine sighed again, her heart stopped, and the file scan began. When the computer requested a confirmation of the date and time, Christine realized she didn't have much time before the town car would come to pick her up. She was too busy to be frightened. The column of icons appeared one by one.

"Okay," she said to her reflection in the medicine chest. She double-clicked on the mail icon; the old phone number appeared in the setup box. "What the hell," Christine said out loud, and double-clicked to continue. The dial-up connection started, and Christine almost went through the ceiling. She looked around her apartment again; surely somebody must have heard this?

It took ten seconds for the dial-up to connect, but it felt like ten minutes, and Christine hadn't breathed until she gasped. The static evened out and the connection was made. She wondered just what it had connected to. The machine hummed, and now all Christine had to do was click again and she would be in her mailbox.

She thought of the millions of times she must have done this without thinking. She expected her click to activate an onslaught, and it did. Along with endless offers that had piled up in her old mailbox, there was a message from a number next to the name southwestbell.com. When Christine glanced over to the subject, "Follow-Up," she was intrigued. After all, she was waiting for follow-up from Gabriel. She opened it and saw "Christine, it's your grandpa George." She felt like she had seen a ghost. She had thought of him, needed him, and here he was.

In that moment, all issues ceased for Christine: Gabriel, her job, the attack and investigation—even the chairman of the Conglomerate party slipped from her consciousness. And in their place the image of her grandfather grew. If she pictured her grandfather George, then her grandmother Patsy must be close by. They were always together. She pictured the house in Staten Island. The muscles in Christine's shoulders loosened and her shoulders dropped. She let out the breath she was holding, and the knot in her gut came undone. That is, until the first note from her cell phone erupted.

Christine checked the time in the bottom right-hand corner of the laptop, but she knew it was the chairman calling from the town car. She looked back at the message heading from her grandfather. She had no idea what this could mean, but she didn't have time to figure it out now. The cell phone rang again. Christine looked at her apartment. All the lights were on. The chairman could be looking at the same thing.

Could this e-mail be a setup from the chairman? Christine wondered. How would he have found out about her grandfather? Easy enough, Christine reasoned. But why would the chairman send a message. That was another matter, and Christine couldn't come up with the solution. Even if there might be a reason, the chairman wouldn't need to do something like that, would he?

The phone continued to ring.

She turned on the shower and picked up the phone, said, "Five minutes," and slapped the phone shut. She clicked on her grandfather's message and her screen filled with text. She hit the page down button and the screen was full. Again, the same. She wasn't going to be able to read this now. She closed her grandfather's message, popped out the memory card from her cell phone, slid that into the back of the laptop, and downloaded the laptop's hard drive onto the card. She figured this old machine couldn't hold that much and wouldn't crash her phone. Anyway, that was what she hoped when she popped the card back into the phone.

Then it occurred to her: What if someone found the laptop? *That would not be good,* she thought.

The cell phone was ringing again: it hadn't crashed. She opened the phone and said, "Right there," and snapped the phone shut.

She looked in the medicine chest and pulled out the same nail file she had used on Gabriel's poem. She popped open the back of the laptop and unscrewed the hard drive from inside the computer. She closed the computer without it and put the laptop's hard drive into her gym bag.

She still had her bathrobe on over her pants. She dropped the robe; grabbed a shirt, socks, and shoes; and dressed as fast as she could. She had to get Gabriel's poem. She went back to the closet, jammed the computer onto a shelf, retrieved the poem and the gym bag, and was out the door.

When Christine closed the door of the town car, she was assaulted by an arctic burst from the car's air conditioner. She shivered from the cold hitting the sweat on her back, and her hair was still dripping onto her shirt. Christine looked down and saw that in her haste to take care of all she had to do before she came down to meet the chairman, she had put on her shirt without putting on a bra. As she noticed this, so too did the chairman of the Conglomerate party.

Great, Christine almost said out loud, except that she noticed a small triangle of white paper was peeking from her hip pocket. She looked back at the chairman and at his driver, both of whom were still fixated but not on her pants. She tucked her fingers into her pocket and pushed the paper in along with them.

"Sorry to have kept you waiting," Christine said as she crossed her arms, "but such is the cost of research. Successful research."

That caught the chairman's attention. He raised his eyebrows along with his gaze.

"I've made some significant findings that could impact your recovery time considerably," Christine said. "Nutrition," she said.

"Nutrition?" the chairman said. "How am I supposed to eat when you've got me sedated?"

"Nutritional supplements," she said. "We'll mix a vitamin and herbal rejuvenating agent into your sedative drip. This will enrich both your blood and oxygen count, replenish cellular structure and suppleness, revitalizing brain function not only faster but to a greater depth. When you awaken, you will be a radiant light of leadership atop the imperial republic."

Where'd that come from? Christine thought. She had better knock it off. But the chairman looked captivated by what Christine had said, and his eyes flickered with her vision that lit up like the city on the hill. The idea unleashed a heat from his central nervous system outward, relaxing the muscles and tendons along the way. He wasn't thinking of the process, or of the immediate future. "A light of leadership atop the imperial republic." *Why, I will have to use that with the board,* the chairman thought. Maybe Salter was worth more than he had contracted her for.

". . . , Mr. Chairman." The chairman heard Salter's voice as if from a distance.

"Yes, yes." The chairman came around. "Excuse me. I was busy planning ahead. Which nutritional supplements should I be taking now?" She had never been a nutritionist. Fruits and vegetables seemed to Christine a safe way to go.

"Vitamin A, D, the B group. C is important and E will aid molecular recovery," Christine said. She knew she was tired, because she wanted to laugh out loud that she had used the first five letters of the alphabet.

X, ALONG WITH her friend John, and Ichabod the driver of the I train, followed the arc of their flashlights into the workshop. X was taken at the sound—or, rather, the lack of it. The smells of oil and other lubricants were strong enough so that she could feel it in the back of her throat.

X moved the flashlight. She had never seen so many tools. Some of them she recognized: drills and hammers, and C-clamps of every size. But there were more that X had never seen before. She brought the light down to the foreground; there were work stations equipped with large battery packs in measured intervals across the floor. As X's flashlight swept the area, she saw racks of wheels and racks of axles, and sections of track that held completed wheel assemblies. Above her there were huge hooks and hoists with thick chains, and there were pneumatic drills and power lines suspended from the beams that crisscrossed the ceiling. There were no lights other than the flashlights. All things to be amazed by, but what got to X was the quiet. X had never seen tools at rest, a work area without workers, a space that spoke of labor, like this place, and yet there wasn't a sound.

The flat black I train revolved on a platform designed for this purpose. The train driver was showing off his train. X would have thought that the process of turning a train around would be deafening, but like almost everything else in the workshop, the procedure was nearly silent, except for the muted clicks of the well-oiled chain that pulled the huge wheel that turned the section of track that held the train. If it weren't for the fact that it was impossible and that he had dark glasses on, X would have sworn she saw a sparkle in the blind man's eye.

They boarded the train and pulled out of the workshop. The train evened out to a steady sway and made its way across town. It wasn't long before the driver slowed the train down and brought it to a stop, and the doors of the I train opened into the darkness. The train driver came out of the cab and headed for the void.

X knew her companion was surprised. He fumbled with the flashlight when he passed it to her. She realized they must have been pretty far underground because the temperature was cool against her skin. The light trailed along what was a subway station, and X saw that the station was elaborately decorated. The design featured acorns, bushels of them; inlaid ceramic tiles with an acorn cast, stenciled acorns along the borders, and acorns carved into the giant wood beams that arched across the vaulted ceiling.

"It was one of the Vanderbilts' personal subway stops below Times Square," the train driver said. "Back in the early 1900s, when the subway was built, Astor and the like wanted their own, exclusive subway cars. The Vanderbilt clan did them one better and built secret subway stops just for their family's use. This way they didn't have to mix with the masses and they still could get around town. They had a few stops like this one at Times Square, one at Wall Street, and, of course, their own berth beneath Grand Central Terminal. They were kind enough to reserve it for us," he said. "It's not like this is on any map, so I don't think anyone knows we're here.

"We'll take the elevator up," Ichabod went on. "Follow me." The three of them walked into the dark. The beam of light was bouncing all over the place and there were details wherever the light fell, until it was stopped in front of them by what looked like two massive oak doors complete with brass knockers shaped like acorns.

"What's with the acorns?" X asked, but Ichabod didn't hear, because he was concentrating. His hand reached out beyond the beam of X's flashlight and returned as the two doors swung open to reveal the elevator before them. He stepped inside, and X and John went in behind him. The driver reached between them and pulled the outer elevator doors closed. The elevator looked like a small dining room, complete with a small crystal chandelier. The driver pulled out a battery pack that looked like a portable game player, flipped it open, and ran a wire from the unit to the control panel. He punched in a command on the keyboard and the elevator car's inner door slid closed and the elevator ascended. The ride was smooth.

"They had better materials then," Ichabod said. "If you happened to be a Vanderbilt, that is. The craftsmen were artists and they used only the best materials, shipped in from wherever needed."

It was only a few seconds before they reached their floor.

"Here we are," the driver announced.

It didn't look like anything to X, just more of the same blackness, but she could tell the difference in the smell immediately. This place smelled of dust, mold, and wet insulation.

"Careful," Ichabod said. "There are pipes running overhead. There is a wall covered in wires about ten inches from the opening. We'll have to shuffle off to the left for a few feet, where it will widen into a passageway. Try not to bump into anything." And he paused for a second while X and John tried to get in the middle of this small opening. X had to hold the light straight down at their feet, as there wasn't enough room to bend her arm. "The wiring is ancient and the walls are even more so and we don't want to do anything that might cause damage, or cause the walls to come tumbling down on top of us." X and John squeezed closer.

They made it to the wider hallway, and X was able to move her arm and flashlight more freely. It looked like the junction of a million wires and wrapped cables. It was. This place appeared much different from the room where X had seen John first use the telephone. That room had been a stream of primary colors, while this place was completely gray, bone-dust gray.

"Why would a Vanderbilt, or anyone, for that matter, want to come here?" X asked.

John nodded his head.

"This wasn't always like what you see now. The elevator

came up to a hallway off the lobby of the Knickerbocker Hotel, which was also in the Vanderbilt family's holdings. That way they could avoid the crowded Times Square station if they wished, and it also afforded them a quick exit off the street, should a quick exit be what they needed. They could duck into the hotel and out through the elevator and into their waiting train, should such an action be necessary. And it was. They had their little getaways all over town."

THE BORDER PATROL didn't want anyone following Gabriel, so they sent him on an elaborate route to Grand Central. They wanted him at a place they knew would be impossible for Conglomerate electronic eavesdroppers to reach.

Gabriel climbed up from between the levels beneath Grand Central Terminal. He made his way up to the track area. From there he went over to the crosstown shuttle tunnels. He was to meet Walters's contact at a certain subway entrance.

JOHN SAID, "WE'RE supposed to meet our contact at the door of the Knickerbocker Hotel in Times Square at two fifteen A.M. Would you know where the door to the Knickerbocker Hotel is?"

"Right here," Ichabod said, pointing his thumb to the back of the door.

"What time is it?" X asked.

There was a knock on the door in response.

X jumped, followed by Y.

"Sounds like it's two fifteen," Ichabod said. He turned toward John. After all, it was his mission. The driver could feel the tension coming from the two of them. "Well, I doubt that it could be anyone other than our man," the driver said, and he walked over to the door of the Knickerbocker Hotel, put a key in the lock, and pulled the door open. X shined the flashlight toward the door and the light shone in Gabriel's face.

"Gabriel Cruz?" X said.

"What're you doing here?" Gabriel said.

"How do you know him?" John asked.

"It's a long story," X said.

"Follow me," Ichabod interrupted, and they all fell in behind him. "Shine your light this way," he said, and then they saw that in front of them was a huge hand-carved oak bar with a massive liquor case enclosed in glass behind it. There were brass spittoons beside leather-topped stools that spun atop white tiled pedestals attached to the floor. Behind the bar was an empty brass pit about a foot deep and six feet wide. X couldn't imagine what that was for, so she asked.

"Oysters," the old man said. "Served on a bed of crushed ice."

They were so busy taking in the place that they were startled when Ichabod cleared his throat and said, "Gabriel, what do you want with me?"

"I'm supposed to give you this," Gabriel said. "A letter for you from Dr. Walters of Ward's Island."

"Maybe you could read it to me?" Ichabod said.

X took the envelope, opened it, and read the letter out loud.

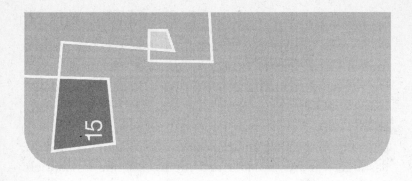

15

The Conglomerate Rangers

Patsy and George saw the buses emerge from the clouds of dust. One by one they burst through the swirls like football players coming onto the field. There had to be three dozen of them, traveling at high speeds. George walked over and slammed the door to their unit shut. He couldn't decide if it was better to run away or to stay where they were.

"C'mon," George said, trying to sound calm, "let's grab a few things and go out for a while."

Patsy's back was rigid. She had seen the buses. George said, "I don't think it would be a good idea for us to be here."

That was all George needed to say. Patsy moved to the door while George filled a water bottle and grabbed a flashlight and a few other things. He wasn't sure where they should go, but staying in camp didn't feel like the right option either.

IT WAS DARK and they were lost. George had led them north, or at least that's what he hoped. Both the computer and the water guy had said there was an alternative to their camp up north. But without the sun, George wasn't sure which way they were going. When the clouds cleared for a minute, George could make out the shapes of housing units up ahead. Had they walked in one big circle? Then George noticed the silhouettes of two people who must have heard Patsy and George approach.

"Who's there?" a man's voice called out, sounding too young to be a Coot.

"Just Coots," George said.

"Where are you going?"

George thought that a curious question. "We're returning to our unit," he said.

"You can't do that," the voice said.

George flipped on the flashlight, thinking to show themselves and that they were not a threat. "Turn that off," the voice said.

"And who do you think you are?" another voice spat out.

George heard the crunching of gravel, and then suddenly Patsy and George were illuminated in a floodlight.

"Why are you going back to your unit?"

"My wife left something," George said.

He saw the camouflage flak jacket of a Conglomerate

Ranger and knew that if they were returning for anything of value, these Rangers would be all over them. All personal property was liable to be seized.

"What's so important that you would ignore an evacuation order?" the Ranger asked. He looked at George's wrist. "No I.D. tag, no residency. In any event, the evacuation order has been issued." George realized he was not wearing his bracelet; it was back in the unit.

"What's she doing here in the first place?" the other Ranger asked as he scanned Patsy's wristband.

"Never mind," the hostile Ranger said. "We're taking her. She's in the system." He looked at George. "Are you running drugs? This lady's prescriptions? Cash? What? Tell me."

"Nothing," George said.

The Ranger spat on the ground. "I don't trust you," he said. "I don't want you in my van. You're lucky we're busy, or I'd arrest you right now."

It was taking George a minute to comprehend what was going on.

"Wait a minute. We can't be separated," George said. "She's my wife."

"Who the hell are you to tell me what to do?" the Ranger said, and swung George around so his wrist was behind him. He swept his foot behind George's legs and dropped George to the ground.

"Easy," the less hostile voice said.

"She is my wife," George said.

George started to show him his wedding ring, but the partner said, "C'mon, why bother? We were ordered to evacuate the camp and I'm evacuating the camp. He's not part of this camp. She is."

"What if he really is her husband?" his partner asked.

"What if," the other Ranger said, "we've got enough of our own Coots to deal with, before we start adding? Without a bracelet he's unaccounted for. Let's leave him here."

Patsy's eyes went wide.

The Ranger said to Patsy, "Let's you and me go. I'll take care of you." George feared she would panic and might make things worse.

"It's all right," George said in his gentle voice. "You go along and I will clear this up with the man and join you in a second."

Though Patsy didn't like it, she walked off with the Conglomerate Ranger. George tried to go after her, but the hostile Ranger knocked him back down.

George heard the van start up and a voice say, "Let's go." It was the worst thing George had ever heard.

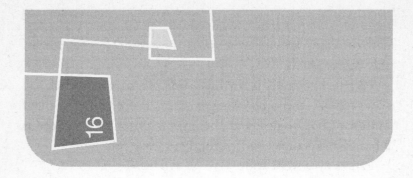

16

Gone

George, disoriented, went back to their unit. The area looked deserted. Patsy was gone. He had always been afraid of losing Patsy, but he had thought that he would be the first to go; husbands often were. But this was worse. Patsy was gone and he didn't know where, or why, or how to get her back.

He sat on the edge of the bed and ran his thumb along the edge of his wedding band. What else did he have left? His wife had been taken from him, twice—first by the disease he didn't know how to combat and then by the authorities he was too old to fight. George felt so alone, he just stared at the door, waiting. Then he began to think.

He couldn't stay here. Patsy wasn't coming back here. He would have to find her. He would do it, even if it killed him.

He noticed a hum coming from the little refrigerator against the wall. The power was still on. Maybe there was something in there to eat. He remembered the old laptop he had in the cabinet. What was the point of taking precautions now? He pulled it out of the cabinet. If the Rangers busted in now, he didn't care. He brought the computer into the bathroom, wrapped it in a towel, placed it inside a camp-issued shirt, and put all of this into a canvas bag. He put in some underwear too, and as many water bottles as would fit. Patsy had a habit of collecting things, and the kitchen drawer was full of stuff. He stuffed some things that looked useful into the bag, and then he left.

It took George almost an hour to make it to the top of the grove. He knew he would be harder to identify in the dark, but he was tired, and he lay down on the ground. He saw a half dozen flak-jacketed Conglomerate Rangers headed in his direction, but they didn't see him and the Rangers kept going.

He didn't know how long he hid there. He was high enough to see the lights in the valley below, and he wrapped his arms around himself and hoped it would be light soon. All he wanted was to find Patsy.

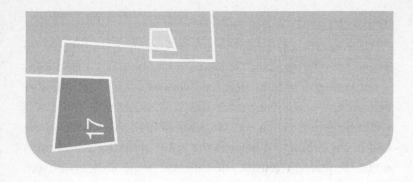

17

The Break-In

Why don't we just launch a grenade at the Clock Tower Building right now?" Dee said.

"We don't have a grenade," A said, "and we don't have a launcher. And, I may want that office someday."

They were suspended inside a maintenance car on cables beneath the roadway on the Brooklyn Bridge. The gondola car was used by painters and made of meshed metal speckled with a million little dots of beige and gray paint. When it was too dark to paint a bridge, the unused gondola served as a secure conference room for the two Dyscard leaders. Here they could talk about their troubles without the other Dyscards around to hear.

Now was the time to move, before it became difficult to do so. They rappelled down the stones and dropped down on the Manhattan side of the Brooklyn Bridge. By the time they reached Canal Street, the night's starless sky had turned slate-gray. They walked single file, hunched down into their jackets with their collars up, headed for Ward's Island. It was too hot to be wearing coats but all the Dyscards did. They needed a place to keep their stuff as they moved around.

IT HAD BEEN about fourteen hours since the chairman's driver had dropped Christine off at the med center. Besides a dozen cups of coffee, Christine hadn't had anything to eat or drink all day. It was a humid evening and she walked home from her train stop too tired to be anything but oblivious. When she was near her building, she saw a red light flashing in front of her, and a half dozen blue and white NYPD squad cars were parked in a herringbone pattern. She took a deep breath and walked on.

When she reached her stoop, a cop stopped her to say this was a crime scene. When he realized who Christine was, he called ahead, took Christine by the elbow, and led her into the building. His grip made sure she wasn't going anywhere but with him.

There were cops on every floor, and there were a few standing outside the door to her apartment, which was open. Almost all of the cops were talking above the squawk of their radios, but everything got quiet once they saw Christine.

The place had been ransacked, things scattered every-where, her possessions in shambles.

"Who did this?" Christine said.

"I was about to ask you the same thing," a familiar voice said. It was the investigator she had faced in the Cruz affair, and she immediately knew who had ransacked her home. It hadn't been a robbery; it had been a search.

She put her hands on her hips and felt the messages inside the pockets of her pants. She straightened herself up and said, "I have nothing here anyone would want to rob, and as I look around, it does not appear that I have been robbed." She looked directly into the eyes of the investigator and pointed to the computer and the TV screen. She wondered if she should contact the chairman. It was possible that he was involved.

The investigator paused a moment before he said, "We'll have a few questions for you."

The so-called questioning lasted several hours. In between rounds of questions, Christine took a visual inventory of her apartment and possessions. Everything had been turned over and tossed around. They must have made a racket. Christine wondered what type of threat it had taken to keep her neighbors uninvolved.

She was glad she had the hard drive in her bag tucked beneath her arm. She would have to inspect the place to see if they had installed any cameras.

When the cops finally left, the only thing Christine wanted to do was collapse. The bed had been stripped and the mattress flipped. There was nothing to sit on that hadn't been broken. It looked to Christine as if the cops had gotten so frustrated at not finding anything that they had taken it out on what little she had.

She checked through the mess and straightened up what she could. She didn't come across any cameras or bugs. She walked into the bathroom and closed and locked the door. She ripped a piece of toilet paper from the dispenser and closed the toilet lid. "Men," Christine said as she stood on the lid. She ran her fingers along the molding and inside the light fixture. She checked the bulb and then stepped down and ran her hands along the tile. No sign of any device. She sighed as she looked into the mirror. "What a wreck," she said. She opened the medicine cabinet. Nothing was left; it had all been knocked to the floor.

When Christine was finished in the bathroom, she looked for her old laptop and found it where the cops had thrown it, a useless-looking item.

She opened her phone and called the chairman's car. She had never done this before but she wanted to see his reaction to the break-in. She didn't know yet if she should blame him for it.

"I need to see you," Christine said, and closed her phone.

Only then did she realize that whoever had broken into her apartment hadn't broken in at all. They must have had a key, because it looked as if they had walked right into the place. She went downstairs and out the service entrance. The chairman's town car was waiting. She wondered if he had been waiting there all along. As soon as she got in, she said, "My apartment was broken into and ransacked. But I was not robbed. The only thing missing was the hard drive from my old laptop. I found the police in my apartment when I got home." The driver had gotten out of the car to hold the door for her. She stopped now because the driver was back in the car, and while he was not able to speak, she didn't want him to hear this. Instead she looked into the chairman's eyes, waiting for his reaction. And his reaction surprised her. His expression did not change, nor did his mannerisms. He just returned Christine's stare. Then he picked up his phone and said, "Attorney general."

He waited a second but kept his eyes on Christine. The attorney general herself must have answered the phone, because the chairman said, "I need to know about a current investigation in Manhattan." There was no sense of a question in the tone of his voice; this was a demand. "Salter, Christine, doctor. I want to know who authorized this investigation, if the DA is involved, on down to the resident precinct." He hung up.

"You think I am behind this," he said, looking at Christine. "Why would I terrorize my doctor before I put myself into her hands?"

The phone rang and interrupted them.

"What did they find?" the chairman said. Then, "Good," and he hung up.

"The break-in was an NYPD operation. Seems they were following up on an open case. My question is, why are they still investigating you over Gabriel Cruz?" He raised his eyebrows as he waited for her reply. Christine hadn't said anything yet when he asked, "Has Cruz been in contact with you?"

Christine had to assume that the chairman and the NYPD knew that Gabriel had been in contact with her. Perhaps Gabriel had been being followed when he went to her apartment; the cops would have reported his movements.

She panicked at the thought that the chairman knew that she had been in touch with an enemy of the state. His eyes did not waver, or blink.

"Yes," Christine replied. "Regardless of his subversive activity, Cruz was the best geneticist in the leading genetic facility in the country. He was my top technician, and the genetic grafting procedure was his strength. I wanted to review my notes with him, on your behalf, and with your identity protected, of course. In return I offered him immunity from prosecution, as bait. But instead of contacting me, he came to my apartment when I was not at home. Too bad," she said. "We could have caught him. Shame the police didn't."

The chairman's hand reached for the phone again. "Attorney general," he said.

This is it, she thought. They got me. She looked out the window. They were heading across town, and she wondered where they were going to bring her. The chairman said, "Tell the district attorney to close the Salter investigation. Here is what you will do. Inform the district attorney that the investigation has been transferred to the Feds. Do that, and then close the case. Work it up, get it done, and close it down. Today." He hung up, looked at Christine, and then signaled to the driver to take Christine back home.

"There will be no more attempts at contacting Cruz?" he said.

CHRISTINE SAT BY the window with the e-mail from her grandfather in her hand. She felt that she should be crying and she felt too tired to cry. Her emotions had moved past sadness. "Maybe I'm next," Christine said to the mess that made up what was left of her apartment.

She retrieved the laptop, installed the memory card from her phone, and watched as little lights on the laptop blinked in a syncopated rhythm and the screen lit up.

She stared at the mail icon. She wasn't sure if she wanted to see any more messages. There weren't any.

"WELL, I DIDN'T see that coming." Ichabod was referring to a request that he deliver twelve babies from the Lexington Avenue station to Van Cortlandt Park in the Bronx. They were back at Ichabod's workshop.

"So, what're we going to do?" John asked.

"Make room for the babies," he said, "and a place for supplies."

"WHAT DOES THAT mean?" the chairman of the Conglomerate party asked himself out loud from his desk inside the Clock Tower Building. He was alluding to the fact that a rogue investigation into Salter and Cruz had proceeded, without his office being informed. Who was behind it and why? He could think of several candidates who would like his seat as chair of the Conglomerates. "I have a war on many fronts," he said. "All the more reason to seek the energy of youth."

Then there was the missing hard drive from Salter's old laptop. It was missing when the cops got there. Somebody had gotten there before the cops. Why? And how could he not know about it? Not one but two break-ins at Salter's apartment and he wouldn't have known about them if Salter had not told him. What else was going on that he did not know about?

The chairman was a detail-oriented leader, and that was how he had been effective and successful. He needed for this genetic procedure to proceed, and soon. He wanted his power back and he felt he was running out of time.

When Salter had summoned the chairman, it had angered him at first, but when she had told him what had happened to her apartment, delivering that message to the chairman himself, he had been impressed. Her behavior showed loyalty, intelligence.

The chairman stared at the back of the glass clock face.

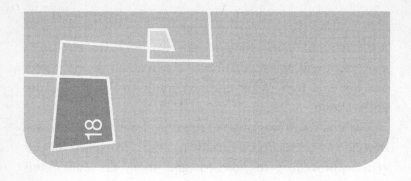

Angelo

I t was three days since he'd lost Patsy and two days since he'd left camp, and George was dehydrated and delirious and he knew it.

He had headed north and he was sure of it this time. He had met people along the way. Some were looking for lost loved ones, as he was, and other people were just lost themselves. George feared Patsy was among such a group. He had come across some situations where the stronger were taking care of the weaker. He had gotten his hopes up at every group he saw, but no Patsy. He was beat, and after all the years of sleeping with Patsy, George found sleeping without her was impossible.

What he had heard from the program on the computer and from the deliveryman was confirmed on the road to find Patsy. There was a place where the Coots who had become unmanageable, or economically tapped out, were deposited. The camp was said to hold a large population of the broken-down. If it was the largest such community in the area, it would be the largest in the nation. Everyone was frightened of succumbing to a debilitating disease, and everyone feared being alone among strangers. He was afraid that this was where Patsy had been taken.

"I'll find her," George said.

GEORGE SAW A group of people trudging along ahead of him. When he caught up to them, he saw that some of them were far along in their problems. George saw that he could probably be of some assistance, and this group might get him closer to Patsy.

"Can I come with you?" George asked.

"Sure," one of the men said. "I could use some help. Follow us. I'll lead and you bring up the rear. I'm Angelo," the man said, shaking George's hand.

A pair in the group started bickering. Angelo heard the disturbance and went back, motioning for George to take the lead. *Funny place for the guy bringing up the rear,* he thought.

"Where are we going?" George said.

"Straight ahead," Angelo said.

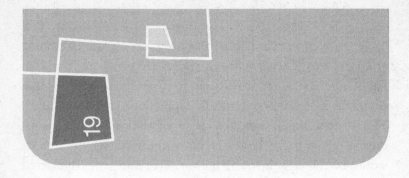

Heat

It was too hot to think; something was wrong with the air-conditioning. Christine wanted to contact Gabriel, but how was she going to do that? She let her phone ring twice before she answered.

"Yes."

"What do you know about air-conditioning?" the chairman asked.

"What do I know about air-conditioning?" Christine repeated in disbelief. "I know I wish I had some."

"You too," the chairman said.

"Con Ed must be cutting back."

"This is one more reason why we need to move our procedure ahead."

Christine's heart stopped. "I will have to make arrangements."

"I want to do it tomorrow," the chairman said. He had already terminated all services to the Coots; he had cut them loose. He had ordered power brownouts in the East in preparation for the shutting down of the power grid. He would still have the element of surprise in his favor, but he also wanted to ensure that he would not be surprised.

"I will need forty-eight hours," Christine said, "to blend the vitamin and herbal supplements with the sedative for maximum results. I want you at your best when you come back. I'd prefer to have that amount of time to assure potency."

"Forty-eight hours it is, no longer," the chairman of the Conglomerate party said, and hung up.

He pulled out the drawer of his desk and removed a pad and pen. He printed the word "Coots" across the pad and drew a line down the page diagonally through the word. He put the pen down and folded his hands.

He felt he had effectively dealt with the elder problem. He was the architect of the Family Relief Act and had guided the legislation that had assumed all of the Coot assets and transferred them to the Conglomerate coffers. The chairman picked up the paper and tore it in half.

"Let the strong survive," the chairman said, "or not."

He imagined himself remade. He ran his hands through his sweaty hair and wondered what Christine Salter would think of him when he came back from the operation. He pictured Salter, wet and cold and on the backseat of his town car.

CHRISTINE WINCED. "FORTY-EIGHT hours," she said. She looked down at the pad where she had written "48 hours," as if she'd needed to be reminded of it.

"Forty-eight hours," Christine repeated. "And if I keep saying it, it'll be gone in no time. Why didn't I ask for more time?"

She wondered if she could set the chairman up for treatment and then just slip away while he was under sedation. No one knew about the procedure except the chairman's driver, and it wasn't as if he were going to tell anyone.

"Forty-eight hours," Christine said, though she knew that wasn't true any longer. It was less.

THE CHAIRMAN WROTE "Dyscards" on his pad and drew a line on an opposite angle from the one he had drawn across "Coots."

He had officially authorized power conservation during peak periods, and his intention was to begin his campaign against the Dyscards by causing a power crisis to the city's populace and blaming it on the Dyscards. This would make it easier to direct emotion against them. The chairman was glad he had not contacted Con Ed about his decision to shut down the electrical system: he would give the northeast corridor no warning.

He picked up his pen and wrote "Imminent Threat" on the pad. Then, "Operation Lockdown." He looked up and out at the backward clock face.

"Forty-four hours," the chairman said. That would be when the chairman of the Conglomerate party would inform the administration of the imminent threat posed by the Dyscard insurgency, and of his decision to assume control of the nation's utilities and services, and to cut off the energy to the northeast corridor.

True, they were attacking the Dyscards only on one front, New York City, but that would allow him to raise the alert status to red, which would legally unleash the Conglomerate Rangers into known Dyscard population centers throughout the country. Once they were in, they were free to interrogate the local leadership to determine their role in the insurrection, or their level of cooperation in the fight against the threat. The chairman would prohibit media coverage in order to control what citizens could see of his reaction to the domestic terrorism and to allow his plans to proceed unimpeded by the public's attention.

He closed his eyes and pictured the Dyscard crisis beneath him. He envisioned the casualties caused by the loss of power and the live third rail. He checked the word "Dyscard" off his list. "Done," he said.

The chairman focused on the dust particles riding the heat currents around the room. He closed his eyes, which stung from the sweat, and he smiled at the discomfort, and the discomfort about to befall the Dyscards. The chairman knew he could not eliminate them, they were an emerging social class. But he could damage the foundation. The chairman leaned his head back and let the sweat roll down his face.

CHRISTINE WAS LOOKING for Gabriel. She was using her old laptop and she was placing a great deal of trust in her hope that the old phone company landlines had been ignored by the Conglomerates.

She connected to the med center server under her old assistant's user name. She figured it might set off a red flag if she used her own name, or that of Cruz. When the server called for the password, Christine remembered her assistant's wedding day and tried that. And as simple as that, she was into the med center system, and this gave her confidence to try something riskier. The med center was part of the municipal bureaucracy, and as such Christine was able to enter into the NYPD information system. She entered Cruz's name. She hoped that an inquiry originating from NYPD regarding an open investigation would not seem out of the ordinary.

Gabriel's case file appeared. She typed in "last known location" and clicked the go button. Her apartment address came up. "Great," she said, and typed "previous." Another address. Christine clicked to begin an advanced search. The screen ran a series of numbers until they reached their numeric destination; then the screen migrated to a schematic rendering of a map that peeled away to reveal a subterranean level. The cursor blinked with a red light, indicating the geographic position of the sighting. Christine studied it, and then stood up.

"Well, now I know where he was," she said.

What she needed to do was get to that place, somehow, and hope that Gabriel was still there. She still had to get the vitamins as well as the sedatives. She grabbed the gym bag, found her portable lab kit in her closet, added that to the bag, and headed out.

THE CHAIRMAN OF the Conglomerate party was dreaming, and in his dream he sat in a high-backed chair of blood-red velvet, with gold leaf on the arms and feet. He was wearing a wine-colored robe made of crushed velvet emblazoned with gold-embroidered collar and cuffs. The garment was soaked with perspiration, which made the velvet heavier and harder to move. He was overlooking the pandemonium he had unleashed.

Beneath him he saw people grabbing at one another, trying to save themselves as the other would-be survivors kicked and screamed. There were raw patches of flesh where hair used to be. Everyone was running, trying to get free.

In the dream a clay urn of water was at the chairman's side. He offered none to the victims, the hordes. Instead he dipped his hands into the water and let the water drip onto his face. Occasionally he would lean his head back and laugh, and his mouth would fill and he would spit the water at their feet.

IT WASN'T MUCH cooler out on the street than it was in her apartment, but Christine was glad to be outside. She was too excited at finding Gabriel's location to stay home. She made herself walk until she was sure she wasn't being followed. She had in mind Gabriel's location, and had determined it was a spot on the number seven subway line.

Christine bought a MetroCard and entered the subway system. She walked down the stairs and headed toward the number seven train. She felt as if she were playing a children's game and was getting warmer. There were doorways set in the wall in a few locations within the passageway, and she wondered if those could be the spot. Since there was plenty of passenger traffic going from one point to another, and there were surveillance cameras everywhere, Christine thought it was unlikely that she could gain entry into one of them. She took mental note of what she saw and kept on toward the seven train.

A seven train screeched into the Grand Central Station stop, and Christine got on board. She studied the tunnel as they passed through it but hadn't seen anything that might be the spot. She got off at the next stop, at Vernon Boulevard in Queens. She walked up the stairs, crossed over to the Manhattan-bound platform, and got on the seven going back to the city. She stood near the door on the return trip, looking out the window, staring at her internal debate. An announcement about congestion ahead came over the speaker system, and the train slowed. Christine was trying to figure out how she could get into those rooms along the passage to the seven without being seen. She saw the recess in the wall along the catwalk inside the tunnel, and she saw a metal door set within the recess. She knew that was the door and the spot on the map.

Her heart began to pound. At Grand Central she made her exit slowly. She scanned for cameras, waited while the stragglers left the platform.

She backed her way toward the end of the platform, reached the end of it. She sprinted past the sign that read DO NOT ENTER OR CROSS THE TRACKS, went down the ladder onto the track bed, across the tracks, and up the metal stairs that led to the catwalk. She was up and out of the sight line of the platform in no time. She gagged at the smell of urine. Why would Gabriel be here?

The snake eyes of an oncoming train appeared in the tunnel ahead. She would have to make it to the recess before the motorman spotted her. She pressed up against the shadows and held her breath until the train passed her by.

It was dark in the doorway, but there was a lightbulb in the fixture. She reached up and gave the bulb a twist, and then jumped when the light came on. As she turned the doorknob to pull the door open, the door swung in, pulling her with it. She thought for sure she would see Gabriel standing there, but instead she saw two kids, a boy and a girl. They looked as surprised as Christine was. It wasn't as if the girl looked familiar to Christine; it was more like she felt familiar.

"Ximena?" Christine said.

"Ximena?" John said. His eyes went from one woman to the other. "Who's Ximena?"

"Christine?" X said.

"You two aren't sisters, are you?" John asked.

.   .   .

IT HAD BEEN years since they had seen each other. Things between the sisters had always been difficult. Christine had been twelve years old when her mother had brought home "the new sister," Ximena, and Christine had been confused because her mother hadn't been pregnant and then her mother had come home with a baby girl. From then on, all Christine seemed to hear about was Ximena. One was compared to the other and both always seemed to come up short. One was trained to be superior, and the other was designed to be. But their parents expected more. Christine had left home as soon as she could. She never looked back, but then again, she realized, she had never had real relationships, or trusted other people either. Instead, she put herself through medical school and went out on her own.

When she had thought of her sister in the years since, it had been with regret, and then she'd moved on.

And here Ximena was, in front of her and, despite the difficult circumstances, looking like a strong and attractive young woman. She clearly was shocked to see Christine too. She was the sister that Xemina was supposed to be better than, and Christine was the sister that X had never lived up to: a doctor, a powerful member of the Conglomerate party. They still looked like sisters, with a genetic similarity that a laser couldn't cut.

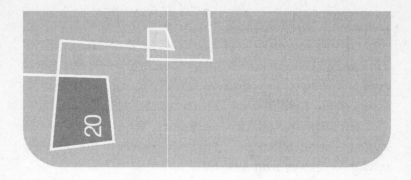

20

Time

The chairman opened his eyes with his mind still in the pandemonium and his head on the tabletop. He hadn't known he was sleeping until he'd felt the wood pressed against his face; he wasn't where he thought he would be. He picked up his head and winced as a sharp pain pierced a point above his right eye. He touched his forehead and his fingers came away red. There was blood on the tabletop. Had he passed out?

But there was that dream, the chairman thought as he rubbed his face.

· · ·

"SALTER," THE CHAIRMAN said from the back of his town car. They were headed across the Brooklyn Bridge. He had showered and dressed the cut above his eye, but it still hurt. He was going to have to leave her a message. Again.

The chairman said into his phone, "Where are you? You should be available to me." He saw his driver in the rearview mirror look away from him.

"I'm here." Christine's voice was on the speaker phone. Even though the chairman had called her, he was startled.

CHRISTINE WAS SITTING at the kitchen table, but in her mind she was back with her sister. After the shock of seeing each other in the subway, X, as she was now called, told Christine about her time as a Dyscard. She told her about what happened after Christine left home, the changes in their lives. She told her about their grandparents, that their mom had a new life, was a new wife with a baby on the way, which left no room for X at home, and with the new husband, who was a big-time Conglomerate. X hesitated, remembering her sister's job.

Christine decided she only had time enough to be honest and told X why she was there—she wanted to find Gabriel Cruz.

But while X was curious about her sister, she was reluctant to tell her what she knew, or didn't know. After all, when she came down to it, even though they were sisters, Christine couldn't be further removed from the culture to which X belonged. X was a Dyscard and Christine a Conglomerate. There was no getting around that. It didn't matter anyway; she didn't know where Cruz was now. Christine seemed hurt by her sister's silence and X felt bad but her situation told her to hold back.

Even though it was years since they had seen each other, and they had never really been close, Christine wanted to ask her sister if she was all right. She wanted to get her alone, put her arm around her, and make sure she was safe. She wanted to tell her the past was behind them, that they were on the same side. But Christine saw her sister's dilemma and decided not to press. She would have to earn her trust.

"WHERE HAVE YOU been?" the chairman demanded. "We're coming to pick you up." Christine put her head down on the table in front of her. She could not turn off her thoughts.

"I'm on my way down," she said.

In the town car, the air-conditioning was on and it was a relief.

"Is the compound ready?" the chairman asked.

Compound? she thought. *Oh, right.* "Yes," she said.

"We'll proceed tomorrow," he said.

"Tomorrow," she agreed.

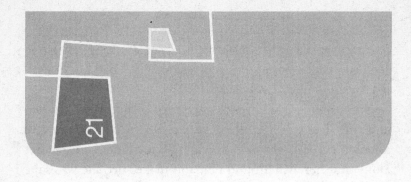

21

Tomorrow

Dr. Walters worked her way around the rows of cots that lined the floor of the clinic on Ward's Island. There were patients asking her questions, and there were patients in pain. Walters was so busy she didn't notice Gabriel Cruz enter the emergency room.

They'd convened with the Dyscard leaders and reviewed what Gabriel had learned. A looked toward Dr. Walters, and said, "When can you be ready to go?"

Walters looked toward Gabriel.

"Tomorrow," Gabriel said.

"We'll be ready," Walters said.

Some of Walters's people had already broken into groups, organized themselves, and prepared to be directed. As Walters reached her workers, she said, "We must be sure the equipment we're taking is sterile, or as close as the underground will allow." To Gabriel, Dr. Walters said, "Please confirm with transportation that our cargo will be ready to go tomorrow. I'll be going with them and I will need accommodations too."

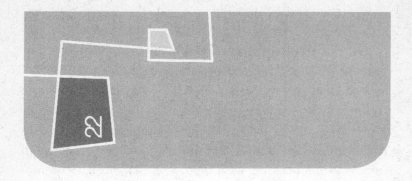

22

To Do

W hen she entered the New York Medical Center, Christine said her name out loud as she walked past the security checkpoint into the elevator and rode up into the Pool.

There were no patients waiting to see Christine these days, no meetings. She closed her office door behind her.

She knew the place was bugged, tapped, videotaped, but there was also a certain privacy in the isolation. She logged on to her computer and opened to her most recent departmental results. The Pool had more than made budget and as usual was carrying the med center. Christine thought that if they were going to be watching her, they would have to look at what was at stake if she were gone.

She still had the piece of paper with her "to do" list. She had located her sister, a bonus, but she needed to find Gabriel and warn him. She looked down at the list and realized she had a plan. She wasn't going to get it accomplished in her office. When she thought about it, what did she have to lose? She removed her I.D. badge, placed it in the desk, and left the Pool.

GABRIEL STOOD ON the south side of Forty-second Street and looked over at Grand Central Terminal. The fog had cleared and the sun shone off the statue of Mercury, who looked out over Gabriel as he crossed the street and went inside. Gabriel could hear the hum of thousands of in-a-hurry commuters. He would be hard to pick out in a crowd, should anyone be looking for him. Gabriel was glad he had detailed instructions.

He walked across the grand concourse beneath the sky-blue dome, past the information booth with the four-faced brass clock, and up the marble staircase. He wanted a vantage point that would let him see the big picture. He turned around, and then he saw her. She was cutting through the crowd toward the number seven train. There had to be fifty yards and several hundred people between him and Christine, who was moving like she had a force field clearing the crowd. He followed her to the number seven train. As she reached the turnstiles, he put a hand on her arm.

She spun around and he put his arms around her; he couldn't help it. "Christine," he said. Then he started walking toward the train. "I've been trying to find you," she said, and felt a rush of relief that Gabriel was okay. She was excited to have his arm around her and she loved the way this felt—except . . . "I don't know where to start," she said. "Are you all right? Where have you been? What happened? What were you really doing at the med center?" It all came out in a stream.

He wanted to tell her that all he did was miss her; he wanted to ask her if she'd found his note, if she was okay. He wanted to tell her he was sorry. But instead Gabriel stopped a second, turned, and looked at her. "I didn't use you," he said. "I used my job." Christine slid her arm through his and they started to walk as he continued to explain. "It's funny. My business at the center and my business now . . ." He paused a moment. "I am trying to save as many babies as I can, then and now. Let me take that in order," he finally said. "I am okay. I have been working for a Dyscard doctor who deals with everything from addiction to pediatrics. At the center I did the best job I could for you and for the families we worked on, by leaving their kids alone, leaving them to what nature planned.

"And, as for you," he said, and smiled, "I wasn't trying to make you look bad, or hurt you. I was falling in love with you. I hadn't intended on that. As for what I am doing now, you're not going to believe this, but I have a bunch of babies to save." Then Gabriel told her about the meeting he had planned.

Christine thought about the vitamins, the procedure ahead, the chairman, her sister. She looked at Gabriel. She had one third of her "to do" list right here.

CHRISTINE COULD SEE why they called this terminal grand. Even the back staircases and freight elevators were well designed. The banisters were brass and the stairs were black wrought iron with marble steps. The doorways were discreet, fireproof, heavy. Then it was too dark to discern design. They dropped down onto a work track deep beneath Grand Central.

"It can't be much farther," Gabriel said. Then he knocked on the door and it opened. The two sisters found themselves facing each other again.

"Ximena," Christine said.

"Christine," X said, as if it were old times.

Gabriel said to Christine, "You can explain this to me later, please." He turned to the group and said, "But now we don't have much time. We need to get the babies out of Ward's Island and up to Van Cortlandt Park, where Dr. Walters has a place she feels will be safe."

"Excuse me," Christine said, "but I have some information that may change all of that." And then she told them about the plans of the chairman, and her hunch that he wanted his operation now because he was planning an attack on the Dyscards.

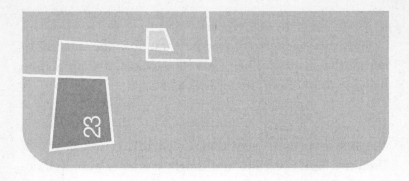

23

Paradise

It was like a negative eclipse; the sun filled the black mouth of the tunnel of trees as George and the group he had joined reached the ridge. The direct sun blinded them, but when George's vision adjusted, he saw that one side of the landscape was barren and rust-colored, and the other side was green, a display of thick vegetation. There were rows of trees surrounding wide, green clearings. He had never seen a strip mine before but he knew this brown side must be one. There were terraces connected by roadways wide enough for a truck, and it was all dug several stories down into the ground.

On the green side—Well, George was familiar with golf

courses, but he had never seen one quite like this. A mine on one side and a golf course on the other and they were joined by a roadway, a zipper that connected one to the other.

George looked at the golf course, putting greens, the sand traps and water hazards. There were figures moving across the greens, and for some reason the water traps were pretty busy too.

When George looked back at the strip mine, he saw lots of activity around it. There were no trucks rolling in or out of the abandoned mine, no brown industrial haze, no cargo cars or anything else associated with mining. There were people filing in and out along the truck routes. There was a group of people on the road ahead, approaching them.

Soon this group was leading George's group to a dining area. One of the most diminutive people George had ever seen walked toward them.

"I'm Maureen Dunne," the woman said. "Dr. Maureen Dunne." She pulled out her chair and sat down.

Her face, which reached to just above the tabletop, was lined, but her eyes were clear, magnified behind thick glasses. She did not exhibit the disabilities associated with the elderly, and she conveyed a sense of authority that left no doubt who was in charge here. George noticed there was an empty chair.

Dr. Dunne sipped at her water and observed the group.

"Tell me a little bit about yourself," she said to George.

"I'm looking for my wife, Patsy," George said. When it came down to it, this was all that mattered right now about himself. While he didn't know anything about Maureen

Dunne, he did sense that this might be an opportunity to get help in finding Patsy.

Once he started to talk about Patsy, he wasn't able to stop. Finally, Dr. Dunne pushed her chair back. She liked this guy; he hadn't mentioned himself once in this self-description. His definition was in the other. "Let's look for her," she said, "while there's still time and light." In an instant the entire group was on their feet.

"Where're we going?" George asked.

"You and I are going to the fairway. The rest of you, please stay and rest," Dr. Dunne said. "Don't worry; we're not going there to play golf."

"I THINK PATSY would like it here," George found himself saying. There were no golf carts buzzing around, no balls sailing overhead, just a meadow and trees, but the place was very active. George and the doctor walked past the course's largest water trap, where a group of people were filling bottles, buckets, and canteens.

"This provides a freshwater source, with the plumbing for intake and drainage," the doctor explained as they walked by. "If you look out beyond the water, you will see a series of irrigation ditches that we have extended well into the rough. We were able to establish a series of mini-reservoirs here that provide water for our animals and for an irrigation system."

He was so captivated by the utilitarian use of this resort that, for a moment, he lost track of what the doctor was saying. Then he realized that Dr. Dunne was talking about something called the Arbor Ward.

"There are corridors of small trees planted in rows around the fairway." She pointed: tents and blankets were scattered across a field, with small groups of people around each. There were larger tents in different colors where people came and went. From the sixteenth tee, George had a clear view of what Dunne was talking about. It was a fairway that had been transformed into a campground.

"Along the outside of the fairway, beyond that row of trees, is a passageway of indigenous bushes, palm, and other small trees. That is where we have our ward for the more serious cases. We can look for your wife on this fairway and make our way back through the ward before dark. Maybe we'll get lucky and find her." She set off with a quick step. George was right behind her.

"As you have seen," the doctor said over her shoulder, "each golf course is equipped with a clubhouse, locker room, showers, restrooms, water fountains. The patients and the workforce have a number of places to go to use the facilities and get fresh water."

"Each golf course?" George said. "You've got more than one?"

"Oh yes," Dr. Dunne said with a laugh. "There are a dozen in this area of the state." George's heart sank a little at the thought of trying to find Patsy.

"Who would have thought that golf courses would provide such a community resource for housing, utilities, goods, and services?" Dr. Dunne said.

"Do you live here?" George asked.

The doctor said, "It is my responsibility to move within the larger community. I travel a lot, taking care of patients with severe needs, and providing aid to the dying, here and elsewhere."

Dr. Dunne stopped when they reached a large white tent. "I'll check in here; you look around," she said.

There were about a dozen men and women seated outside the tent. George knew immediately that Patsy wasn't among them, but he looked around anyway.

"No luck," the doctor said when she returned. "New people every day, but none named Patsy, or at least none that I was able to identify. It is only the first tent, though. Let's keep going."

They had checked into a dozen tents by the time they reached the end of the fairway, on the sixteenth green. They stood on the green and looked back at the long stretch of grass. The sun was no longer on the tee, and the sky was pink.

"C'mon. We'll go back down here," the doctor said, and turned into the Arbor Ward.

"The Arbor Ward consists of a series of rooms that are constructed with screens and tarps hung from lines between the trees." They walked into the first space, a semi-shaded quadrangle that provided space for a bed or a sleeping bag, and a place for an attendant.

"The layered vegetation provides shade, and insulation, and the air flow can keep the ward up to ten to fifteen degrees cooler in late day." As if on cue a breeze blew through.

"But all this doesn't help us find your wife." She went to check with some of the helpers.

The people in the ward were in bad shape. George walked into one of the rooms and saw a woman on her side stretching toward something. He walked over to the bed and asked if he could help her. The woman rolled her eyes toward the table next to her. He saw a bottle of water. He tucked the sheet in around her and brought the bottle of water to her lips. He couldn't help but hope that Patsy wasn't in this ward, and that if she was, there would be someone to take care of her.

"Is that your wife?" the doctor asked.

"No, but she could have been, I guess," George said.

"Look," Dunne said to George, "it's going to be too dark to look any further tonight. Come with me."

IT WAS DARK by the time Dunne and George reached the abandoned mine. While there wasn't much moon, the wide night sky was filled with bright stars and the air was clear. George and the doctor walked the truck roads that crisscrossed along the terraced surface, the gravel road crunching beneath their feet.

"There are hundreds of abandoned mines in this state," Dunne said. "Not many as preserved as this one, but there are a few."

"Not many next to a golf course," George said. He was getting the feeling that Dunne was selling him on the place, as if George had money to contribute to any cause.

The road was wide enough for two 18-wheelers to pass each other, and it was steep enough that George could almost hear the truck gears grind.

"We appropriated this mine, renovated the grinders, smelters, blowers, and refiners until we had ourselves a working mine. But we aren't using it to pillage the earth; we use it to power the place.

"The mining company's base was here too. That's why the golf course and the palatial homes."

By this time George and Dr. Dunne had gotten to the end of the truck road and to the bottom of the pit. It was almost too dark to see, but there were boulders and rocks scattered about the site and massive pieces of equipment. There was a railroad track with a mounted rotary drill the size of a locomotive, used to bore through to the ore. The railroad track disappeared into the side of the mine. It was cold at the base of the pit, and George began to shiver.

"We'll be warmer soon, don't worry," Dr. Dunne said. George followed her into a hole and he could feel the heat as soon as he crossed the threshold. This was the cave where the railroad tracks were, and as George walked farther into the cave and followed the tracks, he came to an elevator shaft. The doctor motioned to George, who climbed up and into the elevator.

The light grew brighter as the car evened out and came to a stop. There were six white-coated attendants waiting for them.

"Doctor," one of them said, and George could have sworn he noticed the rest of them bow slightly to her. The one that had spoken held out a hand to Dr. Dunne.

"This is George Salter," Dr. Dunne said. Behind the six attendants was what looked to be a vault door. The opening was big enough to drive a train through, and the train tracks ran right through the center of the opening.

"What kind of mine is this?" he asked.

"It is our command center. We took the technology we found here and adapted it to our needs. From here we can control and direct the energy to run everything from the sprinklers on the golf course to the lights in the mine. We run the irrigation systems for our agricultural needs and sewerage."

She took George's arm, and together they entered the control room.

Inside there was the hum of machines and ventilation fans and there was the hum of energy from the people working there. George shouldn't have been, but he was surprised that all of the workers and attendants were as old as he was, if not older.

"I'm sorry that our equipment and data aren't enough for us to locate your wife," Dr. Dunne said. "We can manage the physical place pretty well, but the population is beyond our control. People being our reason for being in the first place. We had to find a means and a method to house and care for as many people as we could. Especially now, since the Conglomerates have killed what little elder funding there was for the Coots—even though the funding came from the money they stole from us—and they fired all the workers. More people come here every day. We have not found an effective way of staying on top of the identities and backgrounds of the individuals in our community. It calls for more resources than we have available to us. We commit our resources to care.

"However, that is general. You have described Patsy and her symptoms. She may very well have lost track of her name, or perhaps become concerned about giving any information to a stranger." The doctor stopped.

George was busy picturing Patsy in the camp. He thought of the woman he had helped, the others he had seen. "Well, it does look like you could use a hand here," George said. "I mean, it looks like you have everything in hand here. I couldn't for the life of me see how I could contribute unless there's a broom near by. But I could help out up top," George said.

"Good. We could use you," the doctor said.

"You keep saying we," George said. "There was an extra place next to you at dinner. Maybe you're not alone in all of this."

"Meet my partner," Dr. Dunne said.

George turned around and saw coming toward them one of the biggest human beings he had ever seen.

"This is Mary. We call her Aunty Mayhem," Dr. Dunne said. "Meet George Salter."

"Is it Mary or Aunty?" George asked.

"Aunty's fine," she said.

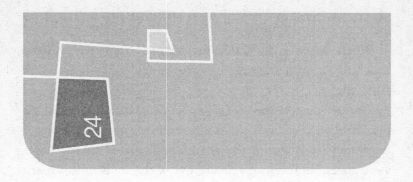

24

An Order of Mercy

George awoke in the same position he had been in when he had fallen asleep, the bag with the computer cradled in front of him. He was stiff and sore. He stretched and saw the water bottle on the table next to the bed. It hadn't been there the night before. He reached for the bottle, noticed a basin, a pitcher of water, and a towel folded beside it. He saw an envelope with his name written on it in a neat, crisp script. Someone had been there while he slept. He looked down at the computer tucked into the bed and opened the envelope.

"Good morning. When you are finished, find us. Maureen Dunne."

When he was finished, he opened the door. "Good morning," a woman standing outside said. "You're to come with me."

George slipped the strap of the computer bag over his head and went outside to find himself in a vast, open space, excavated from within the abandoned copper mine. There were dozens of dwellings carved out of the walls in this man-made cavern. The Coots had moved into these caves. George reminded himself that they were hundreds of feet below the ground.

They took the elevator up to the ground level.

"Ah," the doctor said, "George Salter. We are going to meet up with Aunty."

AUNTY LOOKED LIKE a monument. George could see her from a distance. She was working in a camp at the foot of the mountain, and the fact that she was dressed in medical white among a population of beige- and gray-clothed patients made her appearance even more pronounced. George watched her move from place to place with steady resolve.

Dr. Dunne was recording notes into her headset. She seemed to have forgotten that George was with her, and this gave George a kind of freedom. He looked around, looking for Patsy. The more he thought about it the more he was convinced that his wife was up ahead.

"HOLD THIS," AUNTY said later, handing George an IV drip. "I'm glad you're here," she said to Dr. Dunne. And just as quickly she went back to work. "Glucose solution," she said. George looked out over the rows and columns of cots and he realized they were all occupied by Coots in bad shape, some with attendants with them. A lucky few had a spouse, a family member, a friend to hold their hand.

"Most of the patients here have been here for a while," the doctor said, as if she knew what George was thinking. George had to admit that the doctor and her partner had constructed a good place to spend one's last days. A kind of reverse nursery, where a comfortable end of life could take place. The Conglomerates might try to strip the elderly of their dignity, but dignity was a quality that had eluded the Conglomerates and hindered their ability to control the souls of the dignified.

"As we approach evening," Aunty began, "and through the night, those who can no longer hold on give up. And if they make it to the morning, the will outlasts death, at least for a little while, anyway."

Aunty continued, "We have a crew who administers what comfort they can: reading, singing, speaking. In most cases it's just holding the hands of these folks."

"And then there's the practical matters that have to be attended to," Dr. Dunne said. George knew both the practical and the spiritual were necessary, and neither one was easy to do. *And,* George thought, *that's why there are two of them.*

ONCE THE DOCTOR and Aunty were sure the hospice was secure and attended to, they moved on, in a golf cart with Aunty driving and George in the back. They drove at a pretty good pace but people stopped to wave anyway as Aunty's golf cart drove past.

The customized golf cart circled a field that stretched straight up the mountainside. The entire surface of the field appeared to be covered in a series of mirrors, rectangles that glinted in the sun. George tapped on Dr. Dunne's shoulder and pointed at the field of reflected light.

"Solar panels," Dr. Dunne said. "We have thousands of them throughout the desert, and in prime sun spots such as this. That's one of the ways we power the place."

They drove into the black light of a tunnel, and skidded to a stop. Aunty and the doctor jumped out, ready to be briefed by a team of attendants. The place was full of busy people, and as in the other places, these workers were older folks, in good physical condition and engaged in their labor.

"What do all these people do?" George asked.

"There are more than a quarter of a million people living with us," Aunty said. "All of them had been left to die. We are here to take care of them."

"And, frankly, that's why you're here," Dr. Dunne said.

George thought they had been looking for his wife, but Aunty went on, "We need able-bodied people here, people who can help others," Aunty said. "And you, George Salter, are one of those." The lilt in her speech pattern, the rhythm of the hums and taps of her consonants and vowels, rolled over George, and he felt himself being lulled into submission. "We, the able, are outnumbered here by the helpless and the lost, thousands of people who are here through no fault of their own. So it is up to us to be their order of mercy," she said.

George admired them but he wanted to find Patsy.

"Mo has told me about your wife," Aunty said. "We wouldn't ask you to give up on her, but you might just kill yourself trying to find her. And what good would that do? Or you can stay here and we can assist you in trying to locate her."

"What can I do?" George said, knowing how ridiculous a question it was.

"Anything you do is needed and appreciated," Aunty Mayhem said. "You've been a big help already, and you can do more right now."

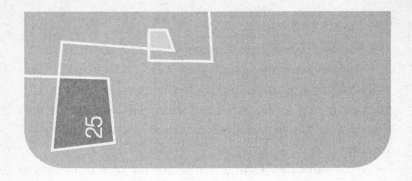

25

Canal Street Cocktail

The chairman of the Conglomerate party sat at the long oval table in his office and watched the wall of monitors. He was listening to the chatter on the teleconference call. The video was a one-way feed, so the board of directors could not see the chairman, but he could see them. While most members of the board were careful in what they said, they were under the impression that they were waiting for the chairman to arrive. It was assumed that if the chairman were present, he would not waste his time and would address them right away, and because they could neither see nor hear him, they took advantage of the moment with casual conversations that revealed a great deal about their personalities and intents. The chairman listened and waited.

Finally he said, "Thank you," and they all fell silent.

"We are in the opening stages of a significant attack on our freedom by armed insurgent forces of Dyscard rebels," he began.

"All branches of the armed and uniformed services are to be on active duty. We will seal off all transportation in, out, and around New York City and the metropolitan area, from Boston through D.C. I want every subway stop covered; no one is permitted to enter or leave. Same holds for all ports, piers, the railroad and air, all down." He paused, and then continued, "We will contain the Dyscards. Panic may ensue. Expect it.

"The nation is under a red alert. Every domestic and international transportation hub is to be limited to essential travel only. Every known Dyscard enclave will be addressed, from here in the Northeast all the way to the Northwest."

The chairman waited for his orders to be acknowledged. He watched them, screen by screen. The first to agree was the NSC; the second yes came from the Joint Chiefs of Staff, the third from the attorney general's office. The chairman noticed that the head of Health and Human Services— Christine's boss, the rogue behind the unauthorized investigation of Christine Salter—sat impassive.

"A complete curfew will be imposed," the chairman continued. "No one will be allowed to leave their homes, offices, or other locations. That order will go into effect in two hours.

"The president has decided that it is in the nation's best interest to shut down the power grid into and covering the northeast corridor. Energy, how long before you could pull the plug?"

"A shutdown?" the energy director asked, startled.

"Correct."

"The jurisdiction—" someone from the attorney general's staff interjected.

"Members of the board," the chairman said, "perhaps I did not make myself clear. We are under attack. Under the provision of the Wartime Act, the president has exercised his power as commander in chief. These are your orders."

He paused, and then barked, "Media."

"Ready," the press secretary answered.

That's more like it, the chairman thought. "There will be a complete media blackout until further notice. Any violation of this blackout will be considered an act of treason under the provisions defined in the Wartime Act. Punishment will be substantial and severe to all concerned—the reporter, the news organization, and the parent company."

The chairman checked his list. "Transportation."

"Sir?" the director of transportation said.

"Leave all emergency generators and power in place during this time."

"That would leave the third rail live during the blackout, Mr. Chairman. That could be a disaster."

"Precisely," the chairman said.

"What of the collateral damage to customers and employees?" the director asked.

"The price of freedom," the chairman said.

"Health and Human Services," the chairman barked, and he was glad that the director of the HHSC wasn't able to see him. He watched her. "You will be out of service. No emergency services, no responses, no treatment for the wounded. We will let them fall over their dead," the chairman said. "All Conglomerate workers are to be sent home, as we will shut down all federal facilities prior to the curfew."

Then the chairman asked, "Any questions?"

There weren't any.

"Good," the chairman said. "In summary: we are under attack. We have our orders. Failure to follow these orders will be considered an act of complicity with the enemy, and will be treated accordingly." The chairman paused for a moment. "It is understood that we will all abide by the provisions dictated by the Wartime Act."

The head of the HHSC sat like a stone, staring into the camera. The chairman went screen to screen and made each member agree to the terms outlined. He started with the Health and Human Services Corporation. Christine's boss nodded.

He watched as the board of directors, one by one, from screen to screen, reacted as the Conglomerate Rangers in their camouflage flak jackets, and with their automatic weapons, moved into their offices.

"Ladies and gentlemen," the chairman said, "you too are under house arrest until further notice." Some of the board members rose as if to protest and were returned to their seats by the Rangers. "Please understand," the chairman continued. "The president is thinking only of your safety. He has thoughtfully provided personal security for you until this conflict is resolved." Then the chairman terminated the call and the screens went black.

After the chairman had informed the president and the Cabinet of the imminent threat and of "Operation Lockdown," the chairman's actions to counter the threat, he'd informed the president that things surely could get ugly, as it was going to take drastic measures to eradicate the insurgency problem. The president ordered his Cabinet to the bunker at Camp David and assumed his place on Air Force One.

There was nothing more the chairman had to do. He looked out across the city and envisioned the tunnels and stations that veined beneath the city's streets. He smiled as he ran his bath. Once the tub was full, he removed his clothes and slipped into the steaming water, smiling as his skin turned pink.

CHRISTINE COULDN'T WAIT to get home and take a shower. She was elated at having found Gabriel, thrilled to have been with him again, and to be setting things in motion. Now she had to get on with the rest of the plan on her "to do" list.

She heard a siren, and then a second one. Gradually she realized she wasn't able to go home. She couldn't risk getting any closer to her apartment. She did a 180 and started walking back toward the subway. Then she realized she couldn't go back there either; she didn't have the time. There were police officers and police cars everywhere.

Before they had all parted, X's friend John had taken them down to Canal Street, where Christine had used the cash the chairman had given her to deal with an herbalist who not only had the vitamins she needed but also a relaxation formula of kava roots and Saint-John's-wort, all in liquid form. From there they had gone to a Dyscard druggist who specialized in appropriated pharmaceuticals and who recommended a blend of barbiturates, Demerol and Dramamine, which they mixed with the herbs in the druggist's shop. They bought an IV bag, a drip tube, a needle, and a vial of morphine.

She checked the time on her cell and called the chairman.

"Where are you?" the chairman said, sounding, to her surprise, more worried than angry. "There's a general curfew in effect. You have to get off the streets. I'll pick you up."

It took only a second or two for Christine to realize she didn't have any choice.

"THINGS COULD BE worse," John said. It took X a second to understand what her sister had been telling them, and then she was surprised that she could experience vertigo so far belowground. And as though it hadn't been bad enough to run into her estranged sister after ten years and conspire in a scheme of the Dyscards, then she'd found out that the unexpected was about to happen again.

Ichabod sat in a wooden chair with the back resting against the wall, the chair's two front legs sticking up in the air. It looked as if he were waiting for trouble when X and her companion arrived.

"There have been some developments," John said, not knowing exactly where to start. "All hell's about to break loose." Together they filled him in on the meeting with Gabriel and X's sister. "We've got to be ready to move."

Ichabod said, "All I have to do is get the babies."

"And you need a place to bring them," X said. "Now that the place is under attack, I mean. But, then again, maybe you two already have a place." They didn't. It couldn't be underground, as an underground battlefield is no place for babies.

"Okay," John said. "Ward's Island needs to know of the change in the operation. We need to brief A and Dee and decide to activate our plans or not. All at once, I might add."

"Ward's Island must know already," Ichabod said. "Look, we know what we've got to do. Let's do it."

And that was all they needed.

CHRISTINE SAW THE chairman's driver check her out in the rearview mirror. She sank a little lower in her seat. The sun was going down, but that was on the other side of town, and Christine wished she were there instead of heading down FDR Drive to meet the chairman. She took a slow breath and sank down even lower in the seat. She had to get ready for what she had to do next. She closed her eyes.

She had told Gabriel, her sister, and John what had happened, and that she was on their side. She couldn't wait to see Gabriel again, but that would have to wait.

She looked into the rearview mirror; the driver was staring straight ahead.

She recalled her sister's expression when Christine had finally gotten to what she knew of the chairman's plans. It had been John who had come to her defense when X had begun to ask her questions. Christine thought they hadn't believed her, especially her sister, who had listened to her with her arms folded and her eyebrows raised. But there was too much detail not to believe her.

Christine opened her eyes to the driver's eyes in the rearview mirror. She figured the driver was a plant: What better bug than someone who makes believe he can't hear or speak? Well, at least Christine knew, or thought she knew, that the only time this guy had observed her was in the presence of the chairman. In a few hours, one way or another, this entire episode would be resolved.

The driver turned the town car onto Front Street alongside the anchorage for the Brooklyn Bridge and approached the rear of the old Clock Tower Building. He walked around the black town car to open the door for Christine.

So it begins, Christine thought as she entered the building.

ALL ALONG THEIR trip through Manhattan, X and John saw the build-up of cops and security. It didn't take long for them to decide that the underground might not be the safest place for them to be. They decided to use the Vanderbilt escape hatch into the lobby of the Knickerbocker Hotel, from which they made their exit into the streets. The change in direction meant that they would have to take the long way back to Ward's Island.

They saw firsthand the lockdown of the subway, even Grand Central, as the cops stopped people at all the exits. They agreed they might be better off in Queens. When they got to Second Avenue, they saw that the Conglomerate Rangers were using the Fifty-ninth Street Bridge as a checkpoint, so they crossed over to the entrance to the Roosevelt Island tram, climbed the stairs, and kept going up a ladder that led to a platform. John hopped atop the cable car, took X's hand, and pulled her up next to him, to rock on the roof as they crossed the East River.

By the time they dropped into Ward's Island from the Triborough, A and others had assembled. Dee was there, and so were the Border Patrol, and Gabriel Cruz. The only person missing was the one who had brought them all together in the first place, Christine Salter, her sister whose unsettling speculation about the chairman had proven correct. The air crackled with tension and panic as everyone talked at once.

"Folks," A finally said, bringing the meeting to order. "What was a suspicion is now an all-out attack."

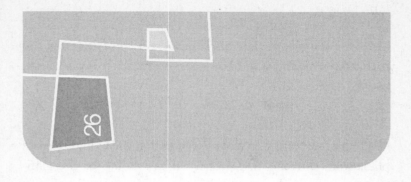

26

The Baby Brigade

At the chairman's office, Christine patted her bag and said, "I was able to prepare for the procedure. I just need to wash up and get ready."

In the bathroom Christine assumed that the room was on video camera and that the chairman had it on the monitor in his office.

She locked the door and looked around to determine just where the camera might be. She saw it in the ceiling set inside the smoke detector. Her eye measured the angles that would take in both the shower and the toilet, and she swallowed hard. She made sure it was only the hot water running, for the steam. She also turned on the faucet for the bathroom sink and started to undress and wash as fast as she could.

REPORTS WERE COMING in from the field that the Conglomerate plans were extreme. Sadism served as a bond for the Conglomerates, and their lust for Dyscard blood had become a common ground. A and Dee knew this also meant that they had to be on the move and direct Dyscard strategy, which, at this point, was to save as many children as possible.

THE MAIN MEETING tent was filling up with men and women all in black. Gabriel had gone to the nursery with Walters.

The Border Patrol was marching out of the nursery like a column of tanks, to deliver the babies to the I train, cradled in their muscled mass. The Dyscard babies were swaddled in black blankets. The babies were quiet.

The group went across Ward's Island in a hurry. A lead patrol cleared the way, minutes ahead of the main patrol, hitting the cops before they could regroup. The plan was to meet the I train at the number six stop on One Hundred Third and Lexington. They had to get from FDR Drive to the Lexington Avenue station without getting killed, or caught.

When the troop of Dyscards came within range of their destination, they discerned there were only a handful of cops occupying the station. Some of them had their hands on their guns and some had their hands by their sides, but they all were looking down the station stairs expecting the action to come from below. The Border Patrol stormed the station from behind them, and cleared the way for the baby brigade.

CHRISTINE DRESSED QUICKLY. It felt good to be clean again. A conference room had been transformed into a hospital room, with a bed, an IV pole, special lighting, and monitors to track the chairman's vital signs. There was no sign of the chairman, but she saw the blue computer light beneath a door and went into that room. The chairman's face went white when he saw Christine. He reached toward his desk and Christine saw the foggy image of the bathroom on the screen.

"Shall we begin the procedure?" she asked.

"Good," the chairman said.

"You'll need to strip down," Christine said, and she was glad when he left the room to change. She wanted to make sure it would be difficult for the chairman to leave quickly, should it come to that. While the chairman was out of the room, Christine emptied her equipment from her bag and set up her portable lab. He walked back into the room wearing a red velvet robe with gold embroidery on the collar and cuffs. Christine had never seen anything like it, but she was glad he had it on.

Along with the hospital equipment, the chairman had installed a generator in his Clock Tower office, and shades to cover the windows. The bed was beneath the clock, facing his power base, even though the shades were drawn. He sat down on the bed, lay back, and undid his robe. Christine busied herself unpacking her supplies from her gym bag. She set up the IV bag on the pole and put on latex gloves. She turned and said, "Your arm." She inserted the IV needle, taped the needle to him, and then taped the heart monitor onto his chest. It would hurt to move—enough, she hoped, to keep him still. She opened the valve and started the drip.

"Now for the swab," Christine said, and she came back with a cotton ball soaked in Novocain and clover extract. The chairman shut his eyes as Christine rubbed the inside of his mouth. She figured if his lips turned numb it would be a convincing effect. She scraped her scalpel along the inside of his mouth and placed the scalpel blade on a glass dish. She walked over to the conference table, where she had set up her lab. She looked at the sample through the handheld lens from her kit, zooming in and out on the piece of tissue. She took a vial of water from her bag and added several drops to the dish.

"Now we wait ten minutes to let it oxidize," she said. He would surely be unconscious by then. "You should start feeling drowsy," Christine said, and when he did not respond, she turned around. He was out.

She checked his pulse, poked his hand with the tip of her knife. No reaction. The chairman was out cold.

She went to his computer and placed the memory card from her own phone into it. She decided to operate it under the belief that if there was one secure computer in this world it would belong to the chairman of the Conglomerate party. She logged on to her old e-mail account.

. . :

A AND DEE were in the subway tunnel south of Spring Street and they had covered the IRT, the IND, and the BMT. It was all pretty much the same; carnage everywhere. The Dyscards were being decimated.

No one could locate the chairman, and that had increased the panic among the Conglomerates. Rumors were rampant. There was rioting at some sites where the citizens had been contained, and there were fights and fires and skirmishes all over town. Although the media was shut down, the word had spread and those sympathetic to the Dyscard cause, as well as those opposed to the Conglomerate regime, were fighting where they could.

The plan was to send the babies to Van Cortlandt Park, or further up the Metro-North line, to where the Dyscards had established a few facilities. But the Conglomerates were busting up those camps as well.

THE NEW YORK City skyline was a series of shadows in the foreground of the night. Pockets of flames flared up from the darkened streets on either side of the bridge. Helicopters hovered overhead, with spotlights on Battery Park and the PATH train entrance. They were chasing down the damned.

Dee sent a text message to Christine: "Please call this number," and he gave a number. Dee entered a code that activated Christine's phone and sent her the message. A moment later her call came in.

"Who is this?" Christine said.

"It is Dee, madam. How is the chairman?" Dee asked.

"He's under sedation and responding to treatment." She had heard about these two from her sister's friend, but still.

"We may need you to keep him that way. We're getting killed out here. We need to find a place for the babies. Everyone is under attack."

Christine looked down at the chairman's body. "I have an idea," Christine said.

AFTER BEING UNDERGROUND for as long as she had, sleeping in stations and tunnels and moving through the dark, nothing had prepared X for the moment when she entered the station at One Hundred Third and Lexington. Nothing could have prepared her.

The I train was waiting for them. The third rail emergency generator was up and running. The I train idled in the station with a steady hum. There were countless voices and cries coming through the tunnels on either side of the subway station. To X it sounded like one lone wail.

John put his arm around her and said, "There is something we can do for those babies, and there's something we can do for us." The doors of the I train opened and light spilled out, providing a path to follow, and the crowd of people did.

John stood with one foot on the platform and the other foot holding open one of the doors. The Border Patrol carrying the babies were the first to enter, and Ichabod led them to the designated space. The babies weren't so quiet now, as many were fussing and adding to the noise.

Ichabod bumped into bodies as he made his way over to John, who stood at the doorway directing people. X was holding a spot for Dr. Walters.

"It's going to be rough getting where we're going," Ichabod said. "Where are we going, by the way?"

"We're awaiting Walters's instructions," John said. One thing was clear, the babies couldn't stay here.

X was having difficulty holding the space for Walters, when into the train came the Lucky Brothers, followed by Walters and Gabriel, who was the last to enter the car. John took X by the hand and pulled her toward him while he stepped inside the train and the doors closed behind him. From the I train's cab, the driver said, "Where are we going, by the way?" Everyone looked at Dr. Walters.

"Can you get us to Newark?" Dr. Walters asked. "The airport."

The driver sounded the horn and pulled out into the panic.

FIRST CHRISTINE THOUGHT she had killed the chairman with an overdose, and now she thought he looked as if he were coming around.

"I'm a geneticist," Christine said for the hundredth time. "Not an anesthesiologist."

She had been back and forth between the chairman's conference room and his personal office a dozen times. She had sent to Gabriel the phone number that Dee had given her. She was trying to reach her grandfather, and had sent him the number as well. No response. Yet.

. . .

THE FIGHTING HAD spread from D.C. to Boston. From their position under the Brooklyn Bridge, A and Dee were trying to manage the Dyscard efforts, and their retreat. They had dozens of decisions to make, and one was a destination for the babies.

CHRISTINE WALKED BACK into the conference room and looked at the chairman. She decided that restraints were the way to go. She ripped off some tape, causing the chairman to stir. She froze, and held her breath as she reached for the scissors on the table and cut the tape. She placed the tape across the chairman's mouth, poked a hole through the tape so he could breathe, and then went back to her portable lab. She dumped the rest of her gym bag out onto the conference room table, picked out the small vial of morphine, and headed back to her patient.

She closed the valve on the chairman's IV drip and emptied the rest of the medicines from the Canal Street pharmacologist into the IV bag. She reached back to the table and got what vitamins she had left, and put them into the bag as well. She reattached the IV bag, opened the valve, and resumed the chairman's treatment. He would not be coming around anytime soon.

She checked her e-mail one more time before she shut the machine down and pulled out the memory card from the back of the computer. She cleaned off the conference table and repacked her lab kit; she took a last look at the city and imagined her route. She would walk across the Brooklyn Bridge, head to Grand Central, and take it from there. After all, it had worked before. She went over and took the tape from the chairman's mouth.

She unlocked the door and pulled it open. The chairman's driver was standing there.

She tried to block his view, but the driver laughed before he said, "Back inside, please."

I knew it, Christine thought, but that didn't make much difference now.

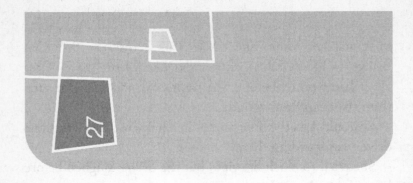

27

The Connection

George opened his computer. There were several e-mails from his granddaughter Christine, all of which had come in the last few hours.

The e-mails were short, but he read them over and over. Then he jumped up; he had to find Dr. Dunne. While the messages were extreme, so were the Conglomerates. Dr. Dunne thought about what George reported. She wouldn't put anything past the Conglomerates. Besides, she noticed there was a perverse symmetry here: they had abandoned the Coot camps, sending this part of the population into chaos. Perhaps they were going to eliminate the Dyscards.

Dunne looked at George and said, "Okay. But I have news

for you, George Salter. There is a woman fitting your wife's name and description in the Arbor Ward. We'll take care of the message from your granddaughter and you check the ward and see if it's her."

George started to leave. In fact, he couldn't leave fast enough. That was, until he thought of Christine. She was in trouble. If Patsy was in the Arbor Ward, then that was for the best. Christine needed him now. He might be able to help. Patsy would want him to take care of their grand-daughter first. He was sure of that. George turned back to the doctor. "Let me help you take care of this first."

"WE'VE GOT TO figure something out," Dee said.

Neither Dee nor A believed they could.

A call came through.

"Hello?" Dee said.

Dr. Dunne said, "To whom am I speaking?"

The two Dyscards looked at each other.

"Leaders of the Dyscard nation," Dee said. They were still precocious kids.

"My name is Maureen Dunne, and we received a message that you were having problems back East."

"Back East?" A said, his hopes rising. "Where are you calling from?"

"We're from a camp in Arizona, and we might be able to help you, if you can be able to move when we tell you to."

"I think we're ready now," Dee said. "So, that shouldn't be a problem."

.   .   .

THE CAPTAIN OF the Galaxy heard the squawk of the radio in the cockpit of the old C-5 transport. The Conglomerates had taken the Galaxy and the captain out of service, putting the Galaxy in storage along with a number of commercial aircraft that were also victims of the times. The captain had no job, no housing, and he had seen the camps out West. He had followed the plane and taken up residency in the abandoned transport. He knew the airport better than the people who ran it, and he moved with impunity in and out of his old plane. He had foraged through the neighboring planes and stripped them of batteries, blankets, flashlights, pillows, water, booze, and, of course, fuel.

It wasn't as if the captain could go anywhere. This big bird was too much to fly alone. He was accumulating all he could for the winter, as he knew how cold this plane could get. And if it got too cold, he could always give flying the Galaxy solo a try. The great beyond had to be better than this.

There it was again. It sounded like a kid playing make-believe.

"Do you read me?" a young voice said.

"Who is this?" the captain of the Galaxy asked, but as it had been a while since he had engaged another human being in conversation, his voice was out of practice and it sounded more like static.

"No use," he heard another voice say.

"Hello," he said, lifting the mike from its position on the control panel. He pressed the button and repeated, "Hello."

Dee almost jumped at the captain's response. The two

Dyscards were back on track after talking with Dr. Dunne. They were determined to see a future—for the babies.

CHRISTINE DIDN'T SEE that she had a choice but to do what the chairman's driver said. It wasn't as if she could get around him. She stepped back into the chairman's office, and the driver followed her and locked the door behind him. Christine used the opportunity to break for the chairman's private office down the hall, but the driver grabbed her by the wrist.

"I knew you were a fake," Christine said, as if that would hurt him. "You paid attention too closely to not be keeping track."

"The chairman didn't know it, never even questioned it. I had come with Conglomerate papers and that was all the fool needed. I'm on your side, by the way."

He picked up Christine's bag. She struggled to reach it, as the driver started to look inside.

"If you were really on my side, you would give me back my bag," Christine said.

"How do I know you don't have a gun in here?" the driver asked.

"If I had a gun, you would have known about it already," Christine said. "And how come you don't seem surprised to see your boss sprawled out on a cot, hooked up to an IV bag in his office, with only one other person in the room?" Christine asked.

"Why should I be?" the driver answered. "I've been watching the whole time on the monitor in the chairman's car. Nice trick with the shower, though. You really outsmarted him."

The driver stood back up and looked at Christine.

"Now what are you going to do?" Christine said.

"Drive you to the airport," he said.

ICHABOD HAD HIS hand on the I train's air horn. It was blaring through the tunnels with an ear-piercing sound. People were panicked and some were reluctant to get out of the way of the six-ton subway car; some people even pushed toward the moving train, desperate to get on board.

He regretted the violence inherent in his train's design, the wheels and deadly front end. He had envisioned these additions slicing through the Conglomerate forces. Who could have foreseen what tactic the Conglomerates would use?

X and John stood against the door, other bodies pressed up against them. No one wanted to admit they were scared. X and John squeezed their way through the crowd of the Border Patrol and refugees to the cab. The view from the driver's seat was spectacular and frightening. It was plain to see the depth of the devastation.

"I am not sure we can do this," Ichabod said.

"Don't you have any secret passageways tucked up your sleeve?" X asked.

"We could change tracks if I could change tracks," he answered.

"Stop the train. Cut the lights and the horn," John said.

The driver did.

The people pulled back.

"Have you got a way of projecting light behind us?" X's companion asked.

"Sure," the driver said. He powered two spotlights and pointed them behind the train.

The driver flipped the switch and the spotlight sent a strong beam out behind them.

The light was met with a gasp from the crowd, before a few folks realized the idea: use the light to lead them down the illuminated tunnel that the I train had cleared. It took a moment or two for the idea to grow within the collective. Soon the crowd in front of the train ran from the dark to where the light might bring them.

It was maybe a minute before the driver asked, "How's it look?"

"All clear ahead," John said.

"I HOPE THEY send someone who can fly a C-5," the captain of the Galaxy said out loud. He doubted it, of course, but what the hell. He opened up a packaged banana muffin, afraid to check the expiration date. Then he got busy making a checklist so he would know just what he had to check off. He could be ready in an hour—he hoped. He would have to be, because that was when his cargo would arrive. "I can do this," he said.

CHRISTINE WAS IN the backseat of the chairman's town car and they were speeding toward the Brooklyn Bridge. She was disoriented just to be in Brooklyn, let alone after the events of the past few hours, but she didn't think this was the way to the Newark airport. "I thought we were going to the airport," Christine said.

"We have to make a stop first," the driver said.

Christine didn't like the sound of that. Maybe it was because the guy was a spy, but Christine didn't trust him. Every time he said he was on her side, she got the creeps.

"Where?" Christine asked, and hoped she didn't sound scared.

The driver stamped on the brakes, unlocked the doors, and Dee got into the backseat next to Christine.

"It's good to finally meet you," Dee said with a slight bow. Christine looked to see if anyone else was coming.

"A will not be joining us," Dee said, without revealing how hard that was to say.

"What's that supposed to mean?" Christine asked. The driver was looking in the mirror, but this time he was all eyes on the Dyscard.

"A will not be coming with us to Arizona," Dee said. "We feel one of us should stay here. We owe it to those left behind."

"Arizona!" Christine yelled. "You mean it worked? Grandpa called you?"

"Yes, it worked," Dee answered. "We couldn't believe it either! We thought we had run out of options. As soon as we knew that moving the babies to Van Cortlandt Park was out, we sent word through the Dyscard network, contacted all of our outposts and safe havens from here to the West Coast, and they were all under siege. The damage and injury were extensive, as were the rumors of what was to come. They couldn't help themselves, let alone a dozen babies. Then your grandfather got in touch with a Dr. Dunne, who . . ." And Dee ran through the details to date.

"Well, we haven't gotten anywhere yet," Dee said, pointing out the town car's back window. Christine followed his hand and saw a police car close behind them. The driver saw it too and punched a few buttons on his dashboard.

"New York City police commissioner," the driver said.

Christine blanched, as he sounded so much like the chairman. For a second Christine believed the chairman was there.

"Yes," they heard a voice say.

"I thought all manpower was on the Dyscards," the driver said, sounding like the chairman barking at the NYPD commissioner.

"It is, sir," the voice responded.

"Then you've got an AWOL on my ass. Get rid of him," the driver said, and he even dropped his chin just like the chairman had.

"Yes sir," the voice said.

Dee had kept his focus out the back window, and reported that the cop car had dropped back and then away.

DR. DUNNE, GEORGE, and the rest of the office staff were not at their usual posts. They were gossiping in small groups, and one or two of them had even started to decorate the office inside the abandoned coal mine, when Aunty entered the room.

"Got to love you," Dr. Dunne said as a way of greeting. She gave Aunty a hug, which demonstrated their difference in body type.

Aunty had never seen her partner like this. She was usually a reserved scientist whose belief system ended with the periodic table. Aunty was not sure she had ever seen the girl in this woman before, and it was adorable.

"Thank you. I love you too," Aunty said. "Who are we expecting?" she asked.

"A stork from the East," Dr. Dunne said, and laughed. And Aunty laughed too.

George cleared his throat and said, "Excuse me. Perhaps I can be of service?"

"Ah," Aunty said, "please do."

And so George explained what was happening.

"Where do you think they should land?" Aunty asked. "It sounds like a mighty big stork."

She looked at her friend and felt sorry that George's explanation and her questions had brought back the old Dr. Dunne. But the arriving guests were going to need the doctor even more.

Aunty said, "We'll have to prepare a triage unit with special neonatal care."

"I'll take care of the unit," Dr. Dunne said, "and you take care of building an airport."

"Ha!" said Aunty, looking forward to seeing the girl in Dunne again when the babies came around.

ONCE THE SEA of oppressed people from the front end of the I train dispersed, the train driver was able to go faster. He had followed the number one line tracks down to Thirty-third Street, where the driver used a Vanderbilt passage from beneath Penn Station up to the Amtrak line. Cornelius

Vanderbilt had demanded access to all rail lines, and so did this driver.

"As I see it," the train driver said to X and her companion, "we've got ourselves one little problem. We're going to run out of track." He went on to explain that there was a transfer point from the train to the monorail.

X let go of John's hand just long enough to go and get the unit leader of the Border Patrol.

THE CAPTAIN'S INSPECTION of the exterior of the C-5 was almost complete. Everything looked okay, considering the aircraft's advanced age, but the captain was doing this inspection in the predawn, and there wasn't much he could do about the tires. It wasn't as if he could jack the big bird up and change them. Taking off wasn't going to be a problem; landing on the other end was. He checked his watch: it was time to move inside the plane for the instrument check and whatever he could do to prepare the cabin for the cargo and crew. He hoped there would be a crew. "I must be delusional," he said to the plane.

THE CHAIRMAN'S TOWN car was the only vehicle on the top level of the Verrazano-Narrows Bridge headed to Newark Liberty International Airport. The blacked-out city was off to their right while to their left a slice of moon hung above the horizon. The driver, Dee, and Christine were glad for the tinted windows when they rolled through the toll plaza and the security cameras checked the car's I.D. and tags.

There were plenty of trucks on the Staten Island Express-way. Neither war nor blackouts stopped commerce. But the driver took the HOV lanes directly into the Goethals Bridge. The town car had to be doing about ninety miles per hour when it turned into the airport exit.

GEORGE WAS TO gather as much water and as many volunteers as he could, and meet Aunty out by the field of solar collectors just at the edge of the golf resort. Using Aunty's authority, George commandeered a water tanker with the deliveryman at the wheel. He recruited Angelo and his old group from the trip into the camp. There were about twenty people who might be able both to concentrate and to do some work, and he had them follow the truck. By the time they reached Aunty, about a dozen more had joined the group.

"This is the flattest surface in the area and it might be our best location to have them land," Aunty said. George had to agree that this was a flat surface, but he didn't see how they could use it. There were solar panels planted every thirty feet. But George had learned over the years that sometimes it was best to wait and let someone make his or her point.

"We have a few hours until the sun comes up, when it will be too hot to do this," Aunty said. "But if we remove some of the center panels, we can create a runway using the panels we leave as demarcation and guidance. And after it is clear we can wet our runway down to soften the earth beneath." She took a deep breath. "Might be the best we can do."

It took about three hours, two tankers of water, and all

the energy a geriatric workforce could manage, but they had a runway and a rising sun to reflect off the remaining panels to serve as a guide into a safe haven. Now all they needed was a plane.

IT WAS LIKE a game played by giants in a hurtling subway car, but X and John were able to rearrange the train passengers for their next move, and that had to be soon because there would be no way to pull off this maneuver in daylight.

The I train came to a stop about five hundred feet from the platform for the AirTrain monorail for the airport terminals and gates. Dr. Walters told the babies that they would eat soon, and as if they understood her, they all settled into the huge arms that held them.

In between the I train and the monorail was a circular ticket booth filled with cops. The Dyscards would need the dark for what they had to do, and because of the blackout, the platform was empty, the train at rest. The only sound the I train made was a gentle sigh as the doors parted and the Border Patrol spilled out. The guards stormed the ticket booth in much the same manner they had the subway station back at One Hundred Third Street. As before, the baby brigade of the Border Patrol followed and boarded the monorail car. Once the precious cargo was stored and accounted for, the remaining refugees followed. X and John and the train driver all held hands as John led them to the front of the AirTrain.

"Ever drive one of these?" X asked as the driver settled into the seat.

"If it has an accelerator, steering, and brakes, we'll be okay," the driver answered. X and John believed him.

THE CAPTAIN OF the Galaxy had lined the cabin of the C-5 transport with as many blankets as he could. He wanted to insulate the cabin from the air temperature outside and to cushion the cargo plane for its special passengers. The captain had lowered the emergency exit stairs in the rear, as it would have taken too long to operate the nose doorway of the plane. He had nothing left to do but turn on the engine. He thought it might be a waste of fuel to do this, with no one there, but he decided he would just follow the instructions even if they did come from a kid. He checked his watch one more time.

"Where are they?" he said as he flipped the ignition switch on the main console. Nothing happened, and the captain was glad that there was no one there to see. He stood up and cursed at the battery pack beneath his seat. He sat back down, cursed again, and retried the ignition switch.

The propeller coughed and belched a gray cloud of exhaust.

"I know how you feel," the captain said to his old friend.

The air cleared as the propeller spun and the engine settled into a steady hum.

THE BLACK TOWN car with the tinted windows cut its lights as it pulled into the parking area just in time to see the Dyscard Border Patrol storm the ticket booth and assault the AirTrain. Christine was cheering in the backseat while

Dee was busy calculating time and distance. The chairman's driver was just trying to catch the train as it approached the terminals. The town car ripped through the hurricane fence between the parking lot and the monorail.

X saw them and tugged on the hand she was holding until John saw the chairman's town car too. She could see the old transport at the end of the runway. X hoped she wouldn't cry.

"Look, it's your sister," her friend said, and X looked back at the chairman's town car with her sister waving out of the back window until someone pulled her in. The AirTrain made it to the terminal, the car stopped beneath the monorail, and the C-5 transport still had to be two hundred yards away.

There was no way the town car could help with that many people. The Border Patrol started to rappel from the train with the babies swaddled inside their coats. They were followed by the remaining guards and refugees, with X leading Ichabod and John at the rear. Everyone was running toward the runway and the old plane.

THE CAPTAIN PICKED up the binoculars he kept in the cockpit and watched the debarking operation at the AirTrain. He saw the black town car idling nearby. And then he saw the flashing lights and the convoy of cop cars turning toward the airport exit.

THE DRIVER OF the town car backed into the opening at the fence.

"Get out," the driver yelled at Christine and Dee. He had seen the cops' flashing lights too. Christine and Dee froze; he yelled at them again. Dee opened the door, stepped outside. "Go," the driver said to Christine. She still didn't know whether she could trust him or not.

"What are you going to do?" Christine asked.

Dee was calling her name.

"Somebody's got to take care of the chairman," the driver said into the rearview mirror. He winked. "Go ahead," he said. And she did.

THE CAPTAIN WAS having trouble hauling in the emergency stairs by himself and he didn't have much time. It would have to do, for now. As soon as he got back to the cockpit, he released the emergency brake and put the C-5 into gear. The Galaxy started to roll for the first time in months. He hoped the tires would hold out and pointed the plane toward the approaching crowd. He would need a slow approach because of the tires, and he didn't want to suck anybody into the draft created by the huge rotating propellers. He was holding the throttle back, and the fuselage shook in complaint.

SOMEHOW THE BORDER Patrol wrapped around the baby brigade kept their tight formation as they ran toward the approaching plane, because even these badass soldiers were petrified as the C-5 transport aircraft bore down on them. The band of Dyscards had almost reached the plane when the cop cars turned into the opening in the fence. It slowed them down to go through the downed fence and then around the chairman's car, but no one was about to tell the chairman to move.

THE CAPTAIN KNEW he would have to turn the big C-5 around to provide better access for his cargo and to position the plane to make it for the runway. He made the turn as quickly as the wheels would allow and cursed because he would have to set the brake to run back and drop the stairs. The light on the console indicated the stairs were down.

"They must have dropped when we made the turn," the captain said out loud. He hadn't secured them properly and he hoped the staircase was still there. The captain opened the intercom and heard voices shouting, "Go, Go, Go."

"Would the kid in charge report to the cockpit, please," the captain said into the intercom. "And anybody back there who knows how to secure the emergency stairs and close the hatch, do it. The rest of you may want to hold on to one another. Enjoy the flight."

Dee knocked on the cockpit door. "Descartes de Kant," Dee said. "Just make it Dee." And Dee all but saluted the captain.

"Good," the captain said. "Ever copilot a plane? Never mind. Have a seat."

"I am a fast learner," Dee said.

And then the Galaxy lurched into gear.

"Rear hatch secure," John said. X patted her chest. She still had the pendant, secure, through all of this; she still had her X wrapped in the band of gold, protecting her heart. Through all of this she remained X. She took John's hand. She had come through this with him too. She put his hand to her chest on the other side of the pendant, and welcomed him to her heart.

"Medical personnel on board," Walters said, and tapped Gabriel on the top of the hand that rested on her shoulder.

"Me too," Christine said as she moved up next to Gabriel and Dr. Walters. She linked her arm through Gabriel's and said, "You know . . ."

Gabriel did.

There was something about this girl that reminded the captain of someone. He couldn't place who, and didn't have the time to think about it. He smiled anyway.

The cops were trying to overtake the transport and block access to the runway but the C-5 Galaxy was picking up speed and drawing the air along with it.

THE DRIVER OF the chairman's black town car watched it all from the front seat behind the tinted glass. The police cars had all raced around as if they knew that the party boss was watching. The driver leaned over to the hands-free mike and said in his best chairman's voice, "Terminate the chase. Repeat: terminate the chase. They're not worth the risk to our men or equipment. Let them go. Let them go."

No one wanted to argue with the chairman, or the approaching C-5 transport. The cops pulled back, and the Galaxy lifted off the runway, the plane a silhouette in front of the morning sun.

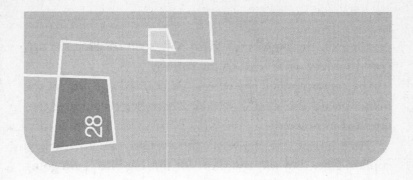

28

Landing

Even though Aunty and Dr. Dunne knew it might be dangerous, practically everyone who could make it from the camp gathered around the makeshift runway. The community had come to a compromise and given the airfield plenty of room. George couldn't wait to find Patsy, but it shouldn't be much longer. He planned on taking Christine with him. They would all be together soon, he thought.

A collective buzz sounded when the plane finally appeared in the cloudless sky, but everyone fell silent as the big plane made its descent. The captain of the Galaxy was depending on the big plane's giant wingspan to glide the air-craft to safety, or at least to the runway.

The captain pulled the wheel and pointed the nose of the plane toward the strip. It was clearly indicated and the captain was impressed.

"Nice job on the runway," the captain said to his new copilot, Dee, "but way too short for this big bird. I am going to need your help."

Together the captain and Dee cut the steering hard to the left once the wheels were on the ground. The captain knew the tires wouldn't withstand this, and they didn't. He just hoped the rest of the Galaxy would.

The big plane did a 360-degree turn, sending solar panels flying, before it came to a complete stop. The captain opened the cockpit window and gave a thumbs-up sign, even though he felt like taking a bow. The crowd that had gathered answered in spontaneous applause, so the captain got up from his seat and took his bow.

Dr. Dunne motioned George and the rest of the rescue and recovery crew ahead of the crowd. George was glad for the direction, as there were too many possibilities for him to know what he was supposed to do. He didn't want to think that his granddaughter might be hurt, or that his wife was close by and needed him.

George wondered if it was because he was thinking of Patsy that he thought he saw her walk through the open door and descend the stairs of the big plane. He realized it was Christine and she looked to be all right, but what had struck him was that she looked just like Patsy had at that age. It was her motions as well as her looks, the way she shaded her eyes as she surveyed the crowd.

When Dr. Dunne reached the plane, the Border Patrol came out and down in the same determined formation the patrol had when they had left Ward's Island. They were ready to hand over their special delivery and close their end of this transfer. Everyone's attention was focused on the babies' safe passage. At the end of this line of Dyscards was another girl who looked like Christine. Even with the short cropped black hair, it could have been Patsy at just about the age when George and Patsy met. "Ximena," George said. For the moment George wasn't sure where he was, and then, seeing his granddaughters, it was as if he were watching the story of his wife before him at different stages of her life, all at the same time. He couldn't wait to tell all this to the real thing.

That was when Christine saw her grandfather. She waved like she had when she was a little girl. She had recognized him right away and she went to her sister and pointed out their grandfather. X put her arm around Christine and started waving and walking toward him. George noticed two young men with them, following behind. He had to laugh, as that looked like Patsy too, except he had been that young man. They all came toward him.

There was almost too much to tell them, too many questions to ask, for George to know what to say. He held out his arms to his granddaughters, one for each. They pressed their cheeks against his chest.

George stepped back and took a good look at them. "Now

all we need to do is find your grandmother," George finally said. But the girls were looking over his shoulder.

"Grandma?" his granddaughters said.

George turned around and there at Dr. Dunne's side was Patsy.

"George Salter," Patsy said. "It's about time."

Acknowledgments

While writing is a solitary act, it takes a collaborative effort to produce a book. I have been most fortunate to have had the help and support of many terrific people in publishing *The Age of the Conglomerates*. These are a few:

I'll start where everything begins: to Debbie and to Aimee, Lisa, and Sarah. Thank you for sharing your life with me.

To my two brothers, Pete and Bob Nevins. And to Jim Fay, thanks for being a friend.

To Terry and Tom Magluilo, my other mom and dad, thank you!

To Random House: I am honored to have a part in the house that Bennett Cerf and Donald Klopfer built.

To Kate Medina: for her time, talent, and encouragement, and for giving me the opportunity to fulfill a dream. I will always be grateful.

To Gina Centrello: for her support, her kindness, her vision and leadership, and for the outstanding team she has assembled, some of whom worked with me to produce this story. I would like to thank the following: Dennis Ambrose, Debbie Aroff, Camille Dewing-Vallejo, Sanyu Dillon, Debbie Glasserman, Kim Hovey, Bara MacNeill, Shauna Masi, Kathleen McAuliffe, Elizabeth McGuire, Brian McLendon, Gene Mydlowski, Jack Perry, Abigail Plesser, Robin Rolewicz, Kelle Ruden, Jennifer Smith, Thomas Beck Stvan, Jane von Mehren, and the members of the Random House sales department.

ABOUT THE AUTHOR

THOMAS NEVINS has been involved in the book business for most of his life, and is currently employed as a sales representative for Random House. He lives with his family in Brooklyn, New York.

▲

NOW THAT THEY ARE IN POWER,
THERE ARE NO MORE CHECKS AND BALANCES.
THE CONGLOMERATES, AND THEIR MYSTERIOUS PARTY CHAIRMAN,
HAVE TAKEN OVER EVERYTHING AND EVERYONE.
THERE IS NO ONE LEFT TO STOP THEM.

Forty years in the future, in a world where Big Brother runs amok, a powerful political party known as the Conglomerates has emerged, vowing to enforce economic martial law at any cost. Dr. Christine Salter, director of genetic development at a New York medical center, is in charge of "genetic contouring," the much-in-demand science of producing the ideal child. But Christine is increasingly troubled by odd events, including the strange disappearance of Gabriel Cruz, a co-worker for whom she has a developing affection, and the fact that her latest assignment—making the Conglomerate chairman more youthful through genetic engineering—is an especially dangerous task.

As mandated by the Family Relief Act, Christine's grandparents are relocated to a government-designed community in the American Southwest, along with other Coots (the official term given to the elderly) who are considered an economic and social burden to family and society. But even in this cold, cruel age, the Conglomerates can control only so much.

In his enthralling debut, Thomas Nevins thrillingly chronicles a "brave new world" where one family struggles to survive by keeping alive feelings of mercy, loyalty, and love.

U.S.A. $14.00 CANADA $16.50

ISBN 978-0-375-50391-7

SCIENCE
FICTION

51400

EAN

9 780375 503917

www.ballantinebooks.com

Cover design: Thomas Beck Stvan

A BALLANTINE BOOKS
TRADE PAPERBACK ORIGINAL